THE MAGELLAN PROJECT XX

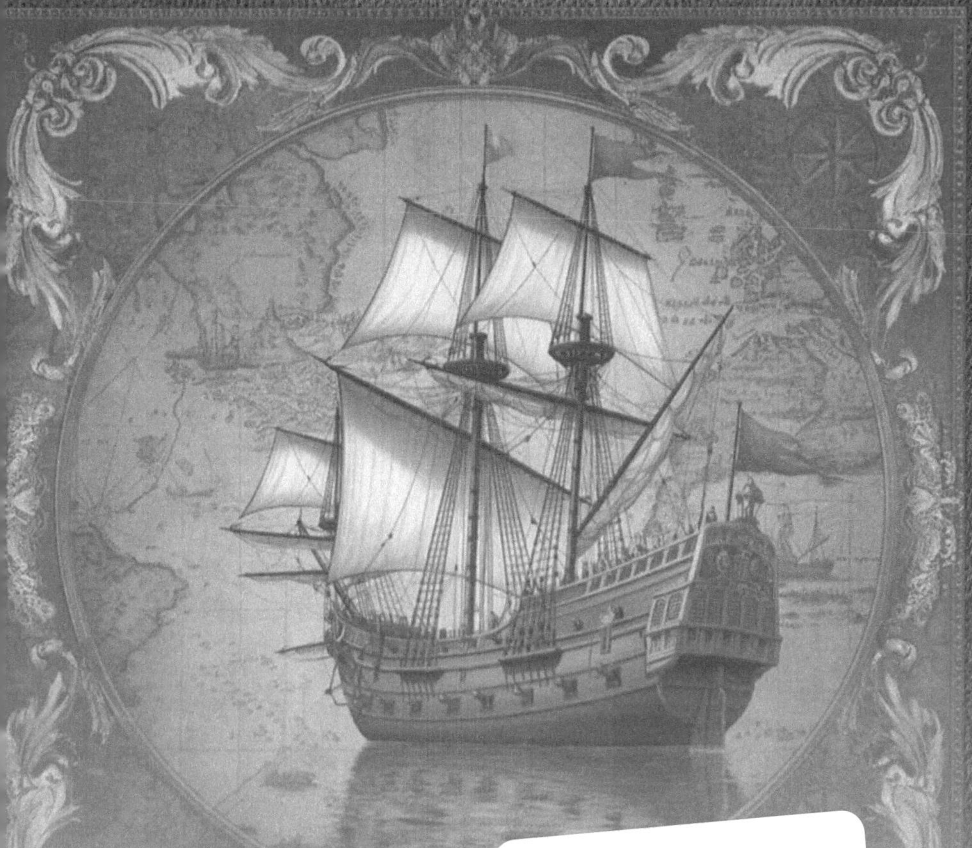

TERRY CODY

Kravitz and Sons LLC
204 E Arlington Blvd. Suite B
Greenville, NC 27834

Published by Kravitz and Sons LLC.

ISBN: 979-8-89639-504-1 (sc)
ISBN: 979-8-89639-505-8 (e)

Library of Congress Control Number: 2025918592

Table of Contents

Chapter 1

The Calm Before the Storm

Maximus graduated from the University of Illinois with a degree in Computer Science. He was a top student, known for his innovative projects and leadership in various tech clubs. His education laid a strong foundation for his successful career.

Maximus was resourceful and resilient, traits honed through years of problem-solving as a software engineer. His analytical mind and attention to detail made him adept at deciphering complex data. Despite his hardships, Maximus remained compassionate and empathetic, always willing to help others.

His determination and optimism fueled his relentless pursuit of a better future. Maximus possessed exceptional survival skills, honed through his experiences. His keen intuition and physical endurance enabled him to navigate perilous situations effectively.

Maximus had always been an adventurer at heart, with a passion for pushing his physical and mental limits. His rock climbing experience began in college, where he joined the university's climbing club. He quickly mastered the basics and soon tackled more challenging routes. Maximus's favorite climbing spot was the rugged cliffs of Devil's Lake, Wisconsin, where he spent countless weekends scaling sheer rock faces. His ability to remain calm under pressure and his keen problem-solving skills made him an exceptional climber, capable of navigating even the most treacherous ascents.

In addition to rock climbing, Maximus was a dedicated martial artist. He began training in Brazilian Jiu-Jitsu and Muay Thai in his early twenties, seeking both physical fitness and mental discipline. Over the years, he earned a black belt in Jiu-Jitsu and competed in numerous tournaments, honing his skills in grappling and striking.

His martial arts training instilled in him a sense of perseverance, respect, and inner strength, qualities that proved invaluable in his later struggles.

Maximus's love for adventure also led him to the depths of the earth. He became an avid spelunker, exploring caves across the Midwest. Equipped with a headlamp, ropes, and a sense of curiosity, he ventured into dark, narrow passages, discovering hidden chambers and underground rivers.

His spelunking expeditions required not only physical agility but also meticulous planning and teamwork. Maximus's ability to navigate complex cave systems and his unwavering determination made him a respected figure in the spelunking community.

These experiences in rock climbing, martial arts, and spelunking shaped Maximus into a resilient, resourceful, and fearless individual, ready to face any challenge that came his Way. Maximus's family was the cornerstone of his life.

His wife, Emily, was a compassionate and dedicated nurse at Springfield General Hospital. With a background in pediatric care, Emily was known for her gentle touch and unwavering commitment to her patients.

She had a natural ability to connect with children, making her a beloved figure in the hospital. Emily's nurturing nature extended to her family, where she was the glue that held them together.

Their daughter, Sarah, was a bright and curious twelve-year-old with a passion for science. She excelled in school and often spent her free time conducting experiments in her makeshift home laboratory.

Sarah's inquisitive mind and determination to understand the world around her made Sarah a budding young scientist.

Michael, their eight-year-old son, was an energetic and imaginative child. He loved reading adventure stories and often dreamed of becoming an explorer. Michael's boundless energy and vivid imagination brought a sense of wonder and excitement to the family.

He was always eager to embark on new adventures, whether it was building forts in the backyard or exploring the local park.

The family's loyal Golden Retriever, Max, was more than just a pet; he was a beloved member of the family. Max's playful and affectionate nature brought joy and laughter to their home.

He was always by their side, providing comfort and companionship, especially during challenging times. Max's unwavering loyalty and boundless energy made him the perfect companion.

Maximus, dedicated his days to his software partnership and honing his skills. He spent mornings planning diagrams and coding for the project. Afternoons were reserved for self-improvement; he enrolled in online courses to stay updated with the latest advancements in software engineering.

Maximus also found solace in rock climbing, often visiting the local climbing gym to clear his mind and maintain his physical fitness. His evenings were spent with Max, their Golden Retriever, exploring new trails and enjoying the tranquility of nature.

Emily's month was a whirlwind of activity at Springfield General Hospital. As a pediatric nurse, her days were filled with caring for young patients. She started her shifts early, often before sunrise, ensuring she was prepared for the day ahead.

Emily's compassionate nature shone through as she comforted anxious children and their worried parents. She was known for her ability to make even the most frightened child smiles. Despite the long hours and emotional toll, Emily found her work is deeply rewarding.

On her days off, she volunteered at a local shelter, providing medical care for those in need. Her evenings were spent unwinding with a good book or enjoying a quiet dinner with Maximus and the kids.

Sarah's month was marked by her insatiable curiosity and love for science. She excelled in her school projects, often staying after class to work on experiments with her science teacher.

Sarah's latest project involved studying the effects of different fertilizers on plant growth, and she meticulously documented her findings in a detailed journal. Weekends were spent at the local library, where she devoured books on biology and chemistry.

Sarah also participated in a science club, where she collaborated with like-minded peers on various projects. Her evenings were filled with animated discussions with Maximus about her latest discoveries, and she often enlisted his help in setting up experiments at home.

Michael's month was a whirlwind of imagination and exploration. He spent his school days eagerly participating in class, his favorite subjects being history and literature. Michael's afternoons were filled with adventure; he and his friends would embark on imaginative quests in the neighborhood, transforming the local park into a battleground for knights and dragons.

He also joined a local book club, where he discovered new stories that fueled his imagination. Michael's evenings were spent reading adventure novels or building elaborate forts in the living room, often with Max by his side, providing a sense of companionship and security.

Max, the family's Golden Retriever, played a vital role in each family member's life. He accompanied Maximus on his nightly walks, providing comfort and companionship. During Emily's long shifts, Max was a source of joy and relaxation for the kids. He would patiently sit by Sarah's side as she conducted her experiments, and he was always ready to join Michael on his imaginative adventures.

Max's playful and affectionate nature brought a sense of stability and happiness to the family, even during challenging times.

Throughout the month, the Magellan family faced their individual challenges and triumphs, but their love and support for each other remained unwavering. Their separate endeavors enriched their lives, creating a dynamic and resilient family unit.

As the month drew to a close, the Magellan family gathered for a cozy evening, sharing stories and laughter. Their bond, strengthened by individual pursuits and shared moments, brought a sense of unity and warmth, reaffirming their love and resilience.

Sarah, the eldest child, embraced her role as the family's budding scientist and responsible sibling. Her weekdays were filled with school and extracurricular activities, where she excelled academically.

At home, Sarah took on the responsibility of helping with household chores and assisting Michael with his homework. She often shared her scientific discoveries with the family, sparking interesting dinner table conversations. Sarah's inquisitive nature and leadership qualities made her a role model for her younger brother.

Michael, with his boundless energy and imagination, brought a sense of adventure and joy to the family. His weekdays were spent at school, where he eagerly participated in class and extracurricular activities. At home, Michael's role was to infuse fun and creativity into the family's routine.

He often organized imaginative games and adventures, involving both Maximus and Sarah. Michael's enthusiasm and playful spirit provided a much-needed balance to the family's busy lives, reminding them to enjoy the simple pleasures.

Maximus, as the head of the family, took on the role of provider and protector. He remained the pillar of strength for his family. His mornings were dedicated to his project and professional development, ensuring he stayed competitive in the job market.

Afternoons were spent maintaining the household, from fixing minor repairs to managing finances. Maximus also made time for his children, helping Sarah with her science projects and joining Michael in his imaginative play.

His evenings were reserved for family dinners, where he encouraged open communication and shared laughter. Emily's role as a caregiver extended beyond her professional life.

As a nurse she spent her weekdays providing compassionate care to her patients, often working long shifts. Despite her demanding job, Sarah ensured she was present for her family.

She managed the household's health and well-being, from preparing nutritious meals to organize family activities.

Sarah's nurturing nature provided emotional support to Maximus and the children, especially during challenging times. Her weekends were dedicated to family bonding, whether through outdoor activities or cozy movie nights.

On Tuesday afternoon, Emily was in the middle of her shift at Springfield General Hospital when she received a call from the clinic's front desk.

The receptionist informed her that one of her regular patients, a young boy named Tommy, would need a ride home on the following Thursday due to his parents needing to attend a special meeting at the school for Tommy's little brother being disciplined for unruliness.

Emily agreed readily due to her gratuitous nature and her magnanimous character.

Meanwhile, Maximus's week took a dramatic and catastrophic turn. On Wednesday, he was working on a critical project at his lab, a cutting-edge software designed to revolutionize data encryption.

The project was in its final stages, and Maximus was confident it would secure him a new position in leadership on the next project.

However, disaster struck when a sudden power surge caused a massive system failure. The lab's servers crashed, and the backup systems failed to activate.

Maximus and his team scrambled to contain the damage, but it was too late. The power surge had corrupted the project's core files, rendering months of work useless. The lab was thrown into chaos as technicians and engineers worked frantically to salvage what they could.

Maximus felt a sinking feeling in his chest as he realized the full extent of the damage. His project, which he had poured his heart and soul into, was now indefinitely disrupted.

The aftermath was devastating. Maximus's team faced the daunting task of rebuilding the project from scratch, a process that would take months, if not longer. The financial implications were severe, and the company's future was uncertain.

Maximus felt a profound sense of loss and frustration, knowing that his hard work had been undone in an instant.

Maximus sat in the conference room, his heart pounding as the CEO delivered the devastating news. The power surge had not only corrupted the core files but had also damaged the hardware beyond repair.

The project, which had been months in the making, was completely destroyed. The CEO's voice was heavy with regret as he explained that the company would need to secure additional funding to relaunch the project, a process that could take months, if not longer.

To make matters worse, the financial strain on the company meant that Maximus's vested stock, which he had counted on for future security, was now worthless.

Maximus felt a wave of despair wash over him. All his hard work, late nights, and sacrifices seemed to vanish in an instant.

As he drove home, Maximus's mind raced with thoughts of how to break the news to his family. He felt a deep sense of failure and frustration. When he walked through the door, Emily immediately sensed something was wrong. She gently asked him what had happened, her eyes filled with concern.

Maximus took a deep breath and gathered his family in the living room. With a heavy heart, he explained the catastrophic event at the lab, the indefinite disruption of his project, and the loss of his vested stock.

His voice trembled as he spoke, and he could see the worry in Emily's eyes and the confusion on Sarah and Michael's faces. Emily reached out and held his hand, offering silent support. Sarah, always the problem-solver, asked if there was anything they could do to help. Michael, sensing the gravity of the situation, hugged Maximus tightly.

Despite the overwhelming sadness, Maximus felt a glimmer of hope in his family's unwavering support. They would face this challenge together, as they always had.

Thursday as Emily got Tommy into the car and buckled him in, there was an uneasy feeling hanging in the air that she was unable to pinpoint. She slid behind the wheel starting the car and eased onto the road to drive Tommy home.

The sun had just dipped below the horizon, casting long shadows across the winding country road as it had just started pouring rain. Emily gripped the steering wheel tightly, her knuckles white with tension. Beside her, Tommy, a bright-eyed seven-year-old, chattered excitedly about his day at school. The air was filled with the scent of freshly cut grass and the distant hum of cicadas.

As they rounded a bend, the headlights of an oncoming car suddenly blinded Emily. She squinted, trying to make out the road ahead, but the glare from the slick road was too intense. In a split second, the car swerved into their lane, heading straight for them.

Emily's heart pounded in her chest as she yanked the wheel to the right, trying to avoid the collision.

The car skidded off the road, tires screeching against the gravel. Time seemed to slow as they careened towards a large oak tree. Emily's mind raced with thoughts of Tommy, his innocent face flashing before her eyes.

She reached out instinctively, trying to shield him from the impending impact. The crash was deafening.

Metal crunched and glass shattered, the force of the collision throwing them both violently forward. The airbags deployed with a loud pop, cushioning the blow but leaving them dazed and disoriented.

Emily's head slammed against the side window, and she felt a sharp pain shoot through her skull. Blood trickled down her forehead, mingling with the tears that streamed down her face. Tommy's cries pierced the air, a heart-wrenching sound that cut through the chaos.

Emily struggled to turn towards him, her vision blurred and her body aching. She saw him slumped in his seat, his small frame trembling with fear and pain. His leg was twisted at an unnatural angle, and blood seeped from a deep gash on his forehead.

"Tommy, hold on," Emily gasped, her voice barely a whisper. She reached out to touch his hand, her fingers trembling. "I'm here, sweetheart. I'm here." The minutes that followed felt like an eternity.

Emily's mind was a whirlwind of panic and guilt. She had been responsible for Tommy, and now he was hurt because of her. She could hear the distant wail of sirens, growing louder with each passing second. Help was on the way, but it felt like it would never arrive.

When the paramedics finally reached them, they worked quickly to free Emily and Tommy from the wreckage. Emily was loaded onto a stretcher, her body wracked with pain. She watched helplessly as they tended to Tommy, his cries growing weaker. The sight of his pale, bloodied face was almost too much to bear.

At the hospital, the atmosphere was tense and somber. Doctors and nurses moved with practiced urgency, their faces grim. Sarah was wheeled into the emergency room, her injuries assessed and treated. She drifted in and out of consciousness, her thoughts consumed by Tommy.

Hours later, Emily awoke in a sterile hospital room. The pain was a dull throb, and her body felt heavy and numb. She turned her head slowly, her eyes searching for any sign of Tommy. A nurse entered the room, her expression kind but serious.

"How is he?" Emily croaked, her voice barely audible. The nurse hesitated, her eyes filled with sympathy. "He's in critical condition," she said softly. "The doctors are doing everything they Can."

Emily's heart sank. The weight of her guilt was almost unbearable. She had promised Tommy's parents that she would take care of him, and now he was fighting for his life. She closed her eyes, tears streaming down her cheeks.

The next few days were a blur of pain and sorrow. Tommy's parents arrived at the hospital, their faces etched with worry and grief. They stood by his bedside, holding his hand and whispering words of comfort. Sarah watched from a distance, feeling like an intruder in their private moment of anguish.

Tommy's mother, Sara, approached Emily one evening, her eyes red and swollen from crying. "How could this happen?" she demanded, her voice trembling with emotion.

"You were supposed to keep him safe!" Emily's heart ached at the accusation. "I'm so sorry," she whispered, her voice choking with tears. "I tried to avoid the car, but it all happened so fast."

Sara's anger gave way to despair, and she sank into a chair, burying her face in her hands. "I just want my baby to be okay," she sobbed. The days turned into weeks, and Tommy's condition remained critical.

The doctors did everything they could, but the injuries were severe. Emily was discharged from the hospital, her body healing but her heart still heavy with guilt. She visited Tommy every day, sitting by his bedside and praying for a miracle.

The community rallied around Tommy's family, offering support and comfort. Fundraisers were held to cover medical expenses, and neighbors brought meals and offered words of encouragement.

But the shadow of the accident loomed large, a constant reminder of the fragility of life.

As the weeks turned into months, Tommy began to show signs of improvement. His strength slowly returned, and he started to respond to his parents' voices. The road to recovery was long and arduous, but there was hope.

Emily too, began to heal, both physically and emotionally. She attended therapy sessions to cope with the trauma and guilt, finding solace in the support of friends and family. She knew that the scars of that terrible night would never fully fade, but she was determined to make amends and move forward.

In the following week Emily began getting dizzy spells and nausea, the stress and guilt were taking its toll.

The night air was thick with tension as Maximus, Sarah, and Michael hurriedly escorted Emily into the emergency room. The sterile smell of antiseptic and the faint, lingering scent of bleach filled their nostrils, mingling with the metallic tang of fear that seemed to permeate the air. The fluorescent lights overhead cast a harsh, unforgiving glow on the scene, highlighting the worry etched into their faces.

Emily, pale and trembling, clung to Maximus's arm, her steps unsteady. Her head throbbed with a relentless pain, and waves of dizziness and nausea washed over her, making it difficult to focus. She could taste the bitterness of bile at the back of her throat, a constant reminder of the trauma she had endured in the car accident.

"Hang in there, Emily," Maximus murmured, his voice strained with worry. He tightened his grip on her arm, trying to offer some semblance of stability. Sarah walked on Emily's other side, her eyes wide with fear, while Michael trailed behind, his face a mask of concern.

The emergency room was a cacophony of sounds: the beeping of monitors, the hurried footsteps of nurses, and the low murmur of conversations. The air was heavy with the scent of disinfectant and the faint, acrid smell of medical supplies. As they approached the reception desk, a nurse looked up, her expression professional but compassionate.

"What's the emergency?" she asked, her eyes flicking to Emily's pale face.

"She was in a car accident," Maximus explained, his voice tight. "She's been feeling dizzy and nauseous ever since."

The nurse nodded, quickly jotting down notes. "We'll get her seen right away. Please, follow me."

They were led to a small examination room, the walls painted a soothing shade of blue that did little to calm their nerves. Emily was helped onto the examination table, the paper cover crinkling beneath her. She closed her eyes, trying to steady her breathing, but the room seemed to spin around her.

A doctor entered, his white coat rustling softly. He introduced himself as Dr. Patel, his voice calm and reassuring. "Emily, I'm going to ask you a few questions and run some tests to see what's going on, okay?"

Emily nodded weakly, her eyes fluttering open. Dr. Patel began his examination, his hands gentle but efficient. He checked her pupils, tested her reflexes, and asked her to describe her symptoms in detail. As she spoke, her voice trembled, and tears welled up in her eyes.

"I just feel so dizzy," she whispered. "And my head hurts so much. I can't seem to focus on anything."

Dr. Patel listened intently, his brow furrowed in concentration. "It sounds like you may have a concussion," he said finally. "We'll need to keep you here for observation to make sure there are no complications."

Maximus, Sarah, and Michael exchanged worried glances. The thought of Emily being hospitalized was frightening, but they knew it was necessary. Dr. Patel ordered a series of tests, including a CT scan, to get a clearer picture of her condition.

As they waited for the results, the minutes seemed to stretch into hours. The sterile smell of the hospital was overwhelming, and the taste of anxiety lingered in their mouths. Maximus paced the small room, his hands clenched into fists. Sarah sat beside Emily, holding her hand and whispering words of comfort. Michael stood by the window, staring out into the dark night, his mind racing with worry.

Finally, Dr. Patel returned, his expression serious. "The CT scan shows some swelling in your brain, Emily," he said gently. "We'll need to monitor you closely. If the swelling increases, it could lead to more severe complications."

Emily's heart sank. The thought of something being wrong with her brain was terrifying. She nodded, trying to stay calm, but the fear was almost overwhelming. Maximus placed a reassuring hand on her shoulder, his eyes filled with determination. "We're here for you, Emily," he said firmly. "We'll get through this together."

Emily was moved to a private room in the intensive care unit, the sterile environment a stark contrast to the warmth of her home. The beeping of monitors and the soft hum of medical equipment filled the air. The room was dimly lit, casting long shadows on the walls.

As the hours passed, Emily's condition seemed to worsen. The dizziness and nausea became more intense, and she struggled to stay awake. Her vision blurred, and she felt a crushing fatigue that made it difficult to keep her eyes open. Maximus, Sarah, and Michael stayed by her side, their worry growing with each passing minute.

In the early hours of the morning, Emily's condition took a sudden turn for the worse. She slipped into unconsciousness, her breathing shallow and labored. The monitors beeped urgently, and nurses rushed into the room, their faces grim.

Dr. Patel arrived quickly, his expression tense. "She's slipped into a coma," he said, his voice heavy with concern. "We'll need to keep her on life support and monitor her closely. The next 24 hours will be critical."

Maximus felt a wave of despair wash over him. The thought of losing Emily was unbearable. He sank into a chair, his head in his hands, while Sarah and Michael clung to each other, their faces pale with fear.

The room was filled with the sterile smell of the hospital, the veil of fear lingering in the air. The beeping of the monitors was a constant reminder of the fragility of life. As they sat by Emily's bedside, they prayed for a miracle, hoping against hope that she would wake up.

The hours dragged on, each one filled with a mix of hope and despair. The sterile environment of the hospital was a stark contrast to the warmth and love they felt for Emily. They held onto each other, drawing strength from their shared love and determination to see her through this ordeal.

As the first light of dawn broke through the window, casting a soft glow on Emily's pale face, they continued to hope and pray. The road ahead was uncertain, but they faced it together, united by their love for Emily and their unwavering belief in her strength.

The hospital doors slid open with a soft whoosh, releasing Maximus, Sarah, and Michael into the cool night air. The sky was a deep, inky black, dotted with distant stars that seemed indifferent to the turmoil unfolding below. The scent of freshly cut grass mingled with the faint, sterile smell of the hospital, a stark reminder of the place they had just left behind.

Maximus walked ahead, his shoulders hunched and his hands shoved deep into his pockets. His mind was a whirlwind of worry and fear, the image of Emily lying motionless in the hospital bed seared into his memory. He could still hear the rhythmic beeping of the monitors, a haunting soundtrack to his thoughts. The taste of stale coffee lingered in his mouth, a bitter reminder of the long hours spent in the waiting room.

Sarah walked beside him, her face pale and drawn. Her eyes were red from crying, and she clutched a tissue in her hand, twisting it nervously. She felt a deep, gnawing fear in the pit of her stomach, a fear that threatened to overwhelm her. The thought of losing her mother was unbearable, and she struggled to hold back the tears that threatened to spill over.

Michael trailed behind, his steps slow and heavy. He felt a crushing weight on his chest, a sense of helplessness that he couldn't shake. He had always been the strong one, the one who held the family together, but now he felt powerless. The sight of his mother lying in that hospital bed, her life hanging in the balance, was almost too much to bear.

They reached the car, and Maximus fumbled with the keys, his hands shaking. He finally managed to unlock the doors, and they climbed in, the silence between them heavy and oppressive. Maximus started the engine, the low hum of the motor filling the quiet night. He pulled out of the parking lot, the headlights cutting through the darkness.

The drive home was a blur of emotions. The road stretched out before them, a seemingly endless ribbon of asphalt. The trees on either side loomed like dark sentinels, their branches swaying gently in the breeze. The air was thick with the scent of pine and damp earth, a stark contrast to the sterile environment of the hospital.

Maximus gripped the steering wheel tightly, his knuckles white. His mind raced with thoughts of Emily, of the life they had built together, and the future that now seemed so uncertain. He glanced in the rearview mirror, catching a glimpse of Sarah and Michael in the backseat. Their faces were etched with worry, their eyes filled with unspoken fears.

Sarah stared out the window, her mind a jumble of thoughts and emotions. She remembered the way her mother used to tuck her in at night, the sound of her laughter, the warmth of her embrace. The thought of losing her was like a knife to the heart, and she felt a fresh wave of tears welling up. She blinked them back, determined to stay strong for her father and brother.

Michael sat silently, his hands clenched into fists. He felt a burning anger at the unfairness of it all, at the randomness of the accident that had brought them to this point. He wanted to scream, to rage against the world, but he knew it wouldn't change anything. Instead, he focused on the road ahead, trying to keep his emotions in check.

When they finally reached home, the house seemed eerily quiet. The familiar surroundings offered little comfort, the emptiness a stark reminder of Emily's absence. Maximus parked the car and they climbed out, their footsteps echoing in the still night. The porch light cast a warm glow, but it did little to dispel the darkness that seemed to envelop them.

Inside, the house felt cold and empty. The ticking of the clock on the wall was the only sound, a steady reminder of the passage of time. Maximus sank into a chair, his head in his hands. He felt a crushing sense of despair, a fear that he might never see Emily smile again, never hear her voice.

Sarah and Michael stood in the doorway, unsure of what to do. The weight of their worry was almost palpable, a heavy burden that they all shared. Sarah moved to the kitchen, her movements mechanical. She filled a kettle with water and set it on the stove, the familiar routine offering a small measure of comfort.

Michael wandered into the living room, his eyes scanning the familiar surroundings. The family photos on the wall seemed to mock him, a reminder of happier times. He picked up a framed picture of Emily, her smile radiant and full of life. The sight of it brought a lump to his throat, and he set it down gently, unable to look at it any longer.

The kettle whistled, and Sarah poured the hot water into mugs, adding tea bags and stirring slowly. She carried the mugs into the living room, handing one to Maximus and the other to Michael. They sat together in silence, the warmth of the tea offering little solace.

As the night wore on, the weight of their worry seemed to grow heavier. The house, once filled with laughter and love, now felt like a prison, the walls closing in around them. They clung to each other, drawing strength from their shared love for Emily and their determination to see her through this ordeal.

Maximus finally spoke, his voice hoarse with emotion. "We'll get through this," he said, his eyes filled with determination. "Emily is strong. She'll fight her way back to us."

Sarah and Michael nodded, their hearts heavy but their resolve unwavering. They knew the road ahead would be difficult, but they were determined to face it together. The love they shared for Emily was a powerful force, a beacon of hope in the darkness.

As the first light of dawn began to filter through the windows, they sat together, their hearts united in their love and worry for Emily. The future was uncertain, but they faced it with a fierce determination, their bond stronger than ever. They would be there for Emily, no matter what, and they would hold onto hope, even in the darkest of times.

The living room was cloaked in a heavy silence, broken only by the soft ticking of the clock on the wall. Maximus sat in his favorite armchair, his eyes red and swollen from sleepless nights. The air was thick with the scent of stale coffee and the faint, lingering aroma of Emily's perfume, a bittersweet reminder of her presence. Sarah curled up on the couch, clutching a throw pillow to her chest, her face pale and drawn. Her eyes stared blankly at the floor, lost in a sea of worry and fear.

Michael stood by the window, his silhouette framed by the dim light of the setting sun. He watched the world outside, feeling a deep sense of helplessness. The once vibrant home now felt cold and empty, the laughter and warmth replaced by an overwhelming sense of dread. The taste of anxiety lingered in the air, a constant reminder of the uncertainty that loomed over them.

They were united in their grief, each lost in their own thoughts but bound together by their love for Emily. The weight of their worry was almost palpable, a heavy burden that they all shared. In the quiet of the evening, they clung to each other, hoping for a miracle.

CHAPTER 2
THE UNRAVELING

The Magellan family's descent began with a single, devastating blow. Maximus, once proud and diligent software engineer , found himself standing outside the company lab, clutching a pink slip. The lab, a place that had been his second home for over a decade, had shut down without warning. The air was thick with the scent of burnt wire and melted plastic, now mingled with the bitter tang of despair. Maximus's heart pounded in his chest, each beat echoing the finality of his situation. The taste of bile rose in his throat as he thought of Emily, lying motionless in a hospital bed, and their children, Sarah and Michael, who were already showing signs of the emotional toll.

The night was an unforgiving abyss, swallowing any glimmer of hope that dared to flicker. Maximus trudged through the rain-soaked streets, his clothes clinging to his frail body. The homeless shelter, a place that had offered temporary solace, now felt like a distant memory, its warmth and safety replaced by the cold, harsh reality of his situation. Despair hung heavy in the air, mingling with the scent of damp concrete and the faint odor of decay.

Maximus's heart ached with a profound sense of regret. He yearned for Emily, the love of his life, whose absence left a gaping void in his soul. The taste of failure was bitter on his tongue, a constant reminder of the unpaid bills, the lost job, and the relentless spiral into poverty. His phone, once a lifeline, was now a useless piece of plastic, lost in the chaos of eviction. The car, a symbol of freedom, had been repossessed, leaving him stranded in a world that seemed to close in on him from all sides.

As he walked, the voices in his mind grew louder, whispering guilt and pain. He could almost hear the mocking laughter of fate, taunting him for his inability to protect his family. Sarah and Michael clung to his side, their small hands gripping his with a desperation that mirrored his own. Their eyes, once bright with innocence, were now clouded with fear and uncertainty.

Their lives lay shattered, fragments of a once beautiful mosaic scattered across the cold, unforgiving ground. The taste of failure was a constant companion, gnawing at Maximus's insides like a relentless parasite. He could feel the weight of his mistakes pressing down on him, threatening to crush what little remained of his spirit.

Emily lay in a hospital bed, her body motionless, her mind trapped in a coma. The sterile smell of antiseptic filled the air as Maximus entered her room for the first time. The nurses glanced at him with a mixture of pity and disdain, their eyes lingering on his filthy clothes and unkempt appearance. He could see the judgment in their eyes, a silent condemnation of his failures.

He spent the night at a dirty convenience store, leaning against the wall, panhandling and smoking. The taste of regret was sharp in his mouth as he watched people buy scratch-offs, their hopes pinned on a slim chance of fortune. He knew the odds were against them, just as they were against him. The irony was not lost on him; they had a better chance of being struck by lightning than winning anything substantial.

Maximus returned to the hospital, his heart heavy with the fear that this might be the last time he saw Emily. He was terrified that she would be moved to a state-run nursing home, a place where he would never be able to visit her. The thought of losing her completely was unbearable, a pain that cut deeper than any physical wound.

As he left the hospital, he felt the weight of the world pressing down on him. He returned to his spot in the convenience store lot, leaning against the wall once more. The night was cold, and the darkness seemed to close in around him, but he continued to panhandle, hoping for a miracle that seemed increasingly out of reach.

The next morning, Maximus woke up in the parking lot of the convenience store, the cold concrete pressing against his back. He knew he had to see Emily one last time, fearing that she would be moved to a state-run nursing home. The thought of her being taken away, of never being able to see her again, was a weight he could barely carry.

As he made his way back to the hospital, he was accosted by a group of men. Their intentions were clear, their eyes filled with malice. But Maximus, despite his weakened state, remembered his training in jiu-jitsu. He moved with a fluid grace, deflecting their attacks and using their own momentum against them. The fight was over quickly, the men retreating with bruised egos and battered bodies.

Maximus continued on his way, his heart heavy but his resolve unbroken. He knew that the convenience store in the hood was a place where he wouldn't be bothered, a place where he could panhandle in peace. As he settled back against the wall, the taste of failure still sharp in his mouth, he watched the people around him, their lives a stark contrast to his own.

The night was unforgiving, but Maximus held on to a sliver of hope, a faint glimmer that maybe, just maybe, things could get better. He knew the odds were against him, but he had to keep trying, for Emily, for Sarah and Michael, and for himself. The fragments of his once beautiful mosaic life lay scattered around him, but he refused to let them be swept away by the relentless tide of despair.

Maximus leaned against the grimy wall of the convenience store, the cold seeping through his thin jacket. The cheap vino he had consumed dulled his senses, but it couldn't numb the pain that gnawed at his soul. As he drifted into a restless sleep, the world around him faded, and he was plunged into a vivid, terrifying dream.

In the dream, the night was darker than he had ever seen, an oppressive blackness that seemed to swallow all light. The air was thick with an eerie silence, broken only by the distant sound of a mournful wind. Maximus found himself standing in an empty street, the buildings around him crumbling and decayed, like the remnants of a forgotten world.

A sudden gust of wind blew a piece of dark parchment towards him. It clung to his pants, refusing to let go. He peeled it off, his fingers trembling as he held it up to the dim light. The parchment was old and worn, its edges frayed and brittle. Written in flowing cursive, the words seemed to pulse with a sinister energy. The ink was dark, almost black, but as he looked closer, he realized it was written in blood. The riddle on the parchment sent a chill down his spine:

"In shadows deep, a life unravels, A price to pay, a burden to bear. The day you failed to heed the signs, the darkness spread, left in despair."

As he read the words, memories flooded back, vivid and painful. He saw himself walking into the lab, the place where he had once worked with pride. The day had started like any other, but it quickly turned into a nightmare. A massive surge of energy had erupted, destroying everything in its path. Equipment shattered, flames roared, and the air was filled with the acrid smell of burning wires and chemicals. The project he had dedicated his life to was reduced to ashes in an instant.

In the midst of the chaos, a dark specter appeared, its form shifting and indistinct. It pointed at him, its laughter echoing through the ruined lab. The sound was cold and mocking, a cruel reminder of his failure. Maximus tried to move, to run, but his feet were rooted to the spot. The specter loomed closer, its eyes glowing with malevolent glee.

"You are to blame," it hissed, its voice a venomous whisper. "You brought this upon yourself. The price must be paid."

Maximus felt a crushing weight on his chest, the burden of his guilt and regret. The specter's laughter grew louder, a cacophony of torment that filled his mind. He wanted to scream, to beg for mercy, but no sound escaped his lips.

Suddenly, he jolted awake, his heart pounding in his chest. The dream lingered, its images seared into his mind. He could still feel the parchment in his hand, the words etched in blood. The memory of the lab, the surge, and the specter haunted him, a reminder of the day his life had unraveled.

Maximus looked around, the harsh reality of the convenience store parking lot coming back into focus. The taste of cheap wine lingered in his mouth, a bitter reminder of his current state. He knew he had to see Emily one last time, to hold on to whatever shred of hope remained. But the dream, with its dark riddle and haunting specter, left him with a sense of foreboding that he couldn't shake.

The weight of his past and the uncertainty of his future pressed down on him. The fragments of his once beautiful life are like a mournful mosaic now.

The remnants of the nightmare are still clinging to his mind like a dark fog. The cold concrete beneath him was unforgiving, seeping through his thin jacket and chilling him to the bone. He shivered, his breath visible in the frigid air, and instinctively began to scrape around in his pockets. His fingers, numb from the cold, fumbled with the few coins he managed to find. The clinking of the change was a small comfort, a reminder that he could still afford a brief respite from the relentless chill.

As he stood up, his joints aching from the night spent on the hard ground, he noticed a group of men down the block. They were a street gang, their presence unmistakable. They moved with a predatory grace, hassling anyone who dared to cross their path. Maximus watched them for a moment, his heart pounding with a mix of fear and uncertainty. He knew he had to be careful; one wrong move could draw their attention, and he was in no state to defend himself.

Clutching the coins tightly in his hand, Maximus made his way towards the convenience store. The promise of a hot cup of coffee was the only thing driving him forward. He kept his head down, avoiding eye contact with the gang members as he passed by. The air was thick with tension, and every step felt like a gamble.

Inside the store, the warmth was a welcome relief. The fluorescent lights buzzed overhead, casting a harsh glow on the worn linoleum floor. Maximus approached the counter, his hands shaking as he placed the coins down. The cashier, a tired-looking woman with dark circles under her eyes, gave him a sympathetic glance as she handed him a steaming cup of coffee.

Maximus wrapped his hands around the cup, savoring the warmth that seeped into his fingers. He took a tentative sip, the hot liquid burning his throat but warming his insides. For a moment, he allowed himself to relax, the nightmare and the cold fading into the background. But the sight of the gang outside, still harassing passersby, kept him on edge.

He found a corner of the store where he could sit and watch the world outside. The gang's laughter and shouts echoed through the night, a stark reminder of the dangers that lurked just beyond the store's doors. Maximus knew he couldn't stay here forever, but for now, the coffee and the warmth were enough to keep him going.

As he sat there, the dream's dark riddle and the specter's mocking laughter replayed in his mind. The weight of his past mistakes and the uncertainty of his future pressed down on him, but he held on to the small comfort of the coffee, hoping it would give him the strength to face whatever came next.

Maximus sat on the cold concrete, his back against the rough wall of the convenience store, a cup in front of him with a few coins clinking inside. The early morning air was biting, each breath a reminder of the harsh reality he faced. He watched the world pass by, hoping for a few generous souls to spare some change for breakfast.

Sitting there, his eyes caught movement on the ground. A sleek, dark spider emerged from the shadows, its legs moving with an eerie precision. The spider's glossy black body glistened in the dim light, a stark contrast against the dirty pavement. It crawled towards him, each step deliberate and unsettling.

Maximus felt a chill run down his spine as the spider stopped abruptly, just inches from his outstretched hand. The air around him seemed to grow colder, and he could almost hear a dark, chant-like whisper carried on the wind. The sound was faint, barely audible, but it sent a shiver through his bones. It was as if the very air was alive with a malevolent presence, whispering secrets meant only for him.

The spider remained still for a moment, as if listening to the same haunting whispers. Then, with a sudden burst of movement, it turned and began to crawl away, heading towards the abandoned lot across the street. Maximus watched, transfixed, as the spider navigated the cracked asphalt and disappeared into the tall scrub brush growing from the sandy dirt.

The lot was a desolate place, overgrown with weeds and littered with debris. The tall scrub brush swayed gently in the breeze, casting long, twisted shadows that seemed to dance in the early morning light. The sandy dirt was a dull, lifeless gray, a stark contrast to the vibrant green of the weeds. The entire scene felt otherworldly, as if it belonged to a different realm entirely.

Maximus couldn't shake the feeling that the spider's appearance was more than a mere coincidence. The dark whispers, the sudden chill in the air, and the spider's deliberate movements all seemed to be part of some larger, more sinister design. He felt a sense of foreboding, a deep unease that gnawed at the edges of his mind.

As he sat there, the world around him seemed to blur, the line between reality and nightmare growing thin. The abandoned lot, with its tall scrub brush and sandy dirt, loomed like a dark omen, a reminder of the shadows that lurked just beyond the edge of his consciousness. Maximus knew he had to stay vigilant, for the world was full of unseen dangers, and the whispers on the wind carried warnings he could not afford to ignore.

Maximus sat on the cold concrete, his back against the rough wall of the convenience store, a cup in front of him with a few coins clinking inside. The early morning air was biting, each breath a reminder of the harsh reality he faced. He watched the world pass by, hoping for a few generous souls to spare some change for breakfast.

As he sat there, the world around him seemed to blur, the line between reality and nightmare growing thin. The abandoned lot, with its tall scrub brush and sandy dirt, loomed like a dark omen, a reminder of the shadows that lurked just beyond the edge of his consciousness. Maximus knew he had to stay vigilant, for the world was full of unseen dangers, and the whispers on the wind carried warnings he could not afford to ignore.

Maximus leaned against the cold, rough wall of the convenience store, his body weary and his spirit even more so. The early morning light cast long shadows across the pavement, and the air was still, carrying the faint scent of stale cigarettes and exhaust fumes. He glanced down at the cup in front of him, the few coins inside clinking softly as he counted them with trembling fingers. Each coin represented a small hope for a meal, a brief respite from the relentless hunger gnawing at his insides.

As he focused on the change, a group of teenagers rounded the corner, their laughter loud and grating in the quiet morning. They were a motley crew, dressed in a mix of hoodies and ripped jeans, their faces marked by a blend of boredom and mischief. They headed towards the store, but their eyes quickly locked onto Maximus, their expressions shifting from casual indifference to something darker.

"Hey, look at this guy," one of them sneered, nudging his friend. "What a loser."

The group converged on Maximus, their presence casting a shadow over him. He could feel their malevolence like a physical force, pressing down on him. One of the teenagers, a tall boy with a shaved head and a cruel smile, kicked the cup, sending the coins scattering across the pavement.

"Oops," he said mockingly. "Looks like you dropped something."

Maximus's heart sank as he watched his precious change roll away, disappearing into the cracks and crevices of the sidewalk. The teenagers laughed, their voices harsh and mocking. They circled him like vultures, their eyes gleaming with a predatory light.

"Got any more money, old man?" another boy taunted, stepping closer. "Or did you spend it all on booze?"

Maximus felt a surge of anger and humiliation, but he forced himself to remain calm. He knew that reacting would only escalate the situation. Instead, he sat back down, his movements slow and deliberate, as if he were retreating into himself. He ignored their taunts, focusing on the ground in front of him, his eyes tracing the patterns of dirt and grime.

The teenagers continued to jeer and mock him, their words cutting like knives. They shoved him, trying to provoke a reaction, but Maximus remained still, his face a mask of stoic resignation. Eventually, growing bored with his lack of response, they turned their attention elsewhere, their laughter fading as they moved on.

Maximus watched them go, his heart heavy with a mix of relief and despair. He gathered the few remaining coins he could find, his hands shaking as he placed them back in the cup. The encounter had left him feeling even more vulnerable and exposed, a stark reminder of how far he had fallen.

As he sat there, the cold seeping into his bones, he couldn't shake the feeling of being watched, of unseen eyes judging him from the shadows. The world around him felt hostile and unforgiving, a place where kindness was a rare and fleeting thing. But despite the fear and uncertainty, Maximus held on to a sliver of hope, a faint glimmer that maybe, just maybe, things could get better.

As Maximus sat against the cold wall, his spirits low, he barely noticed the quiet figure approaching. The morning light was still dim, casting long shadows that seemed to blend with the figure's movements. Without a word, the stranger knelt beside him, placing a warm, freshly baked roll and a steaming cup of coffee next to his cup of scattered coins.

Maximus looked up, startled by the unexpected kindness. The stranger's face was obscured by a hood, but their eyes shone with a gentle warmth. They gave him a small, reassuring nod before standing up and slipping away as quietly as they had come. The entire encounter lasted only a few moments, but it left Maximus feeling a strange mix of gratitude and wonder.

He picked up the roll and coffee, the warmth seeping into his cold hands. The aroma was comforting, a stark contrast to the harshness of his surroundings. As he took a bite, he couldn't help but marvel at the nature of the visitation. Who was this mysterious benefactor? Why had they chosen to help him?

The questions lingered in his mind, but for now, he savored the small act of kindness, a beacon of hope in his otherwise bleak existence.

As the hours dragged on, Maximus's despair deepened. He had managed to collect a few crumpled bills and some loose change, but it wasn't enough to buy anything substantial. He was about to give up and retreat to his makeshift shelter when he noticed a group of young men approaching the store.

There was something about their demeanor that set him on edge. They moved with a swagger, their voices loud and aggressive. Maximus could see the glint of metal in their hands, and his heart began to race. He knew trouble when he saw it, and these men were trouble.

The group entered the store, their presence immediately causing a stir. Maximus could hear their raised voices, the sound of things being knocked over. He edged closer to the entrance, trying to see what was happening without drawing attention to himself.

Suddenly, the situation escalated. One of the men pulled out a gun, waving it around as he shouted at the cashier. The other customers in the store froze, their faces pale with fear. Maximus felt a surge of panic. He needed to get out of there, but he was rooted to the spot, unable to move.

The gunman fired a shot into the ceiling, the sound deafening in the confined space. People screamed and ducked for cover, the chaos spreading like wildfire. Maximus's instincts finally kicked in, and he turned to run, his heart pounding in his chest.

As he fled, he heard more gunshots, the sound echoing through the night. He didn't look back, his only thought was to get as far away from the store as possible. He sprinted across the street, his breath coming in ragged gasps, his mind a blur of fear and adrenaline.

He didn't stop until he reached the abandoned lot across the street from the store. The lot was overgrown with weeds and littered with debris, a forgotten corner of the city. Maximus stumbled into the bushes, his legs giving out beneath him. He collapsed onto the ground, his body trembling with exhaustion and fear.

The bushes provided some cover, but he could still see the store from his hiding place. The flashing lights of police cars illuminated the scene, casting long shadows on the ground. He watched as officers swarmed the area, their voices urgent and commanding. The gang members were being apprehended, their hands cuffed behind their backs.

Maximus felt a wave of relief wash over him, but it was quickly replaced by a deep sense of despair. He had narrowly escaped a dangerous situation, but his life was still in shambles. Emily was still in the hospital, her condition uncertain, and he was still lost and adrift, with no clear path forward.

He pulled out a cigarette from his pocket, his hands shaking as he lit it. The smoke filled his lungs, providing a momentary distraction from the chaos around him. He took a long drag, the familiar taste bitter on his tongue.

As he sat there, hidden in the bushes, he thought about the people who had walked out of the store with scratch-off tickets earlier. He had scoffed at their hopes of winning, thinking they had a better chance of getting struck by lightning. But now, he realized that they were just like him, clinging to any shred of hope in a world that seemed determined to crush them.

The night wore on, the sounds of the city a constant backdrop to his thoughts. Maximus felt a deep, aching loneliness, a sense of isolation that seemed to stretch into eternity. He knew he couldn't stay in the bushes forever, but he had nowhere else to go.

Maximus watched as the police cruised the street as if they were looking for someone flashing their search light here and there. He looked around but there were only these large bushes for him to crawl under to hide from the police that were getting closer.

As Maximus crawled further under the bush hurriedly he cut his hand on something partially buried under the dirt. He clutched his bleeding hand as he squinted to see what it was he cut his hand on, and he saw a latched strap of a backpack halfway buried in the dirt.

As Maximus crouched under the bushes in the abandoned lot, his eyes catching sight of the backpack partially buried in the dirt. He reached out and pulled it free, revealing a weathered, old backpack. The fabric was frayed and stained, the once vibrant colors now faded to a dull, muddy brown. The zippers were rusted, and patches of mold clung to the surface, giving it an air of long-forgotten neglect. He crouched down, gripping the straps firmly, and began to pull.

As he tugged, the backpack resisted, as if caught on something beneath the dirt. Maximus pulled harder, the effort causing beads of sweat to form on his brow. With a final, forceful yank, the backpack came free, but to his horror, it was attached to something far more sinister. The ground gave way, revealing a skeletal hand clutching the straps, the bones brittle and yellowed with age.

Maximus recoiled in shock, his heart pounding in his chest. The skeletal remains were partially buried, the bones tangled in the roots of the brush. As he pulled the backpack free, he heard the sickening sound of bones snapping and cracking, the brittle fragments breaking apart under the strain. The skull, half-buried in the dirt, seemed to stare up at him with empty eye sockets, a silent witness to its own grim fate.

The scene was macabre, the skeletal remains a stark reminder of the dangers that lurked in forgotten places. Maximus took a moment to steady himself, the initial shock giving way to a sense of grim determination. He carefully examined the backpack, hoping to find some clue about its former owner or the circumstances that had led to their demise.

Curiosity piqued, Maximus unzipped the main compartment, the sound of the zipper grating against the silence of the night. Inside, he found an assortment of items that seemed out of place in such a mundane setting. The first thing he pulled out was a softball-sized metal ball, its surface etched with intricate runes and images. The metal was cold and smooth to the touch, and the runes seemed to shimmer faintly in the dim light, as if holding some ancient power.

Next, he found a military flashlight, its body sturdy and well-worn. The flashlight was heavy in his hand, a testament to its durability. He clicked it on, and a powerful beam of light cut through the darkness, illuminating the surrounding area with a harsh, white glow. It was a tool built for survival, and Maximus felt a strange sense of reassurance holding it.

As he held the flashlight he saw another button, as he pressed the button a red flash of a laser shot forth, nearly setting the bushes on fire. Maximus patted the bush to kill the near igniting of the bush.

Digging deeper, he uncovered an old diary, its leather cover cracked and brittle. The pages inside were yellowed with age, filled with handwritten notes, riddles, and cryptic clues. The ink had faded in places, but the words were still legible, hinting at a hidden treasure waiting to be discovered. Maximus's heart raced as he flipped through the pages, the thrill of adventure momentarily overshadowing his despair.

Beside the diary lay an old, dirty map, its edges tattered and worn. The map was covered in strange symbols and markings, some of which matched the runes on the metal ball. It depicted a landscape that was both familiar and alien, with landmarks that seemed to shift and change as he studied it. The map was a puzzle in itself, a key to unlocking the secrets hidden within the diary.

To his surprise, Maximus also found a bundle of cash, roughly $200, neatly tied with a rubber band. The bills were crisp and clean, a stark contrast to the other items in the backpack. It was a small fortune for someone in his situation, a glimmer of hope in the darkness.

Finally, at the bottom of the backpack, he discovered a huge gem, unlike anything he had ever seen. The gem was roughly the size of his fist, its surface smooth and flawless. It glowed with an inner light, casting a soft, ethereal glow that seemed to pulse with a life of its own. The colors within the gem shifted and swirled, creating a mesmerizing dance of light and shadow. It was as if the gem were enchanted, holding a power that defied explanation.

Maximus sat back, his mind reeling from the discovery. The backpack and its contents were a mystery, a tantalizing glimpse into a world of adventure and danger. As he held the glowing gem in his hand, he felt a spark of hope ignite within him. Perhaps, amidst the chaos and despair, there was still a chance for redemption, a path that could lead him to something greater.

Maximus's heart sank as he realized the skeleton and backpack were remnants of a crime scene. Guilt gnawed at him; the victim had been long dead. Panic set in being a vagrant, he knew he couldn't afford to be accused of this. It wouldn't look good at all before the cops or a judge. Wrestling with his conscience, he backed away, the weight of his own survival pressing heavily on his shoulders.

He quickly decided that he needed to get out of there. The realization that he was standing in the middle of a crime scene sent a jolt of fear through him. Maximus knew that as a vagrant, any suspicion would fall heavily on him. He had no way to call the police anyway he rationalized. He couldn't afford to be accused of something he didn't do.

With renewed determination, Maximus carefully repacks the backpack, his mind racing with possibilities. The night was still dark and uncertain, but he felt a newfound sense of purpose. He would unravel the secrets of the diary and the map, follow the clues, and uncover the hidden treasure. And maybe, just maybe, he would find a way to save Emily and restore his shattered life.

Maximus stood up from his hiding spot under the bushes, the weight of the backpack heavy on his shoulders. The discovery of the cash had given him a glimmer of hope, and he decided to use it to clean himself up. He made his way to the local truck stop, a place he knew would have the

facilities he needed. The walk was short, but each step felt like a small victory, a move towards reclaiming some semblance of normalcy.

With a racing heart, he backed away from the skeleton and looking around he climbed out from under the bush, his mind racing with the urgency to leave the area and avoid any potential trouble. Survival instincts kicked in, and he moved swiftly.

He decided to go to the store across the street and tell the attendant to call the police to tell them about the skeleton under the bush across the street, as he had no phone. Then he turned and hurried out of the store into the parking lot.

Maximus began walking to the truckstop, nervously looking over his shoulder for the hoodlums from earlier.

The truck stop was a chaotic hub of activity, even in the early hours of the morning. The smell of diesel fuel and fried food filled the air, mingling with the scent of rain-soaked asphalt. Maximus entered the building, the fluorescent lights casting a harsh glow on the worn linoleum floor. He approached the counter, where a tired-looking attendant gave him a cursory glance.

"Shower, please," Maximus said, sliding 16 crumpled bills across the counter.

The attendant handed him a key and pointed towards the back. "Shower number three. Towels are inside."

Maximus nodded his thanks and made his way to the designated shower room. The small, tiled space was clean but utilitarian, the air thick with the scent of bleach. He stripped off his dirty clothes and stepped under the hot spray, the water washing away the grime and tension of the past few days. He closed his eyes, letting the warmth soothe his aching muscles and clear his mind.

After his shower, Maximus felt he could press on. He dried off and dressed in his now semi wet clothes as he washed them out then hung them on the hook, then turned his attention to the backpack. He found a sink in the corner of the room and began to clean the items inside, starting with the metal ball. The runes and images on its surface seemed to shimmer more brightly now, as if responding to his touch.

Next, he carefully wiped down the old diary and the map, the pages of the diary revealing more riddles and clues as he examined them closely. The map, now free of dirt, showed a landscape that was both familiar and mysterious, with landmarks that seemed to shift and change as he studied it.

As he held the map up to the light, the gem slipped from his pocket and landed behind it. To his astonishment, the gem's glow illuminated the map, revealing a hidden location marked with an X. The light from the gem seemed to pulse, casting an ethereal glow that highlighted the path he needed to follow.

Maximus's heart raced with excitement. The map and the gem were more than just relics; they were keys to a hidden treasure. He knew he had to follow the clues, to see where they would lead him. The thought of adventure, of uncovering something extraordinary, filled him with a sense of purpose he hadn't felt in a long time.

He packed the items back into the backpack, his mind racing with possibilities. The map indicated a location not too far from the city, a place he could reach within a day's journey. He decided to set out immediately, the thrill of the unknown driving him forward.

As he left the truck stop, the first light of dawn began to break over the horizon, casting a soft glow on the world around him. Maximus felt a renewed sense of hope and determination. He would follow the map, uncover the treasure, and perhaps find a way to save Emily and restore his shattered life. The journey ahead was uncertain, but he was ready to face it, armed with the love and determination that had always defined him.

Maximus stood at the edge of the bustling truck stop, the sun dipping low on the horizon, casting long shadows across the asphalt. The air was thick with the mingling scents of diesel fuel, fried food, and the faint tang of sweat. Trucks of all shapes and sizes rumbled in and out, their engines growling like restless beasts. Maximus clutched a worn map in his hand, the destination circled in red: the caves in Bourbonnais, Illinois.

He approached the first truck, a massive eighteen-wheeler with a gleaming chrome grille. The driver, a burly man with a thick beard and a trucker cap pulled low over his eyes, was leaning against the cab, sipping coffee from a thermos. Maximus cleared his throat and stepped forward.

"Excuse me, sir," he began, his voice steady despite the nerves fluttering in his stomach. "I'm looking for a ride to Bourbonnais. Can you help me out?"

The driver glanced at him, eyes narrowing. "Bourbonnais, huh? That's a bit out of my way, kid. Sorry, can't help you." He took another sip of his coffee and turned away, effectively ending the conversation.

Undeterred, Maximus moved on to the next truck, a sleek, black rig with flames painted along the sides. The driver, a woman with short, spiky hair and a no-nonsense demeanor, was checking her tires. Maximus approached her with the same request.

"Bourbonnais? Not a chance," she said, not even looking up from her task. "Got a tight schedule to keep. Try someone else."

Maximus sighed, feeling the weight of rejection settling on his shoulders. He scanned the truck stop, eyes landing on a weathered blue truck parked near the diner. The driver, an older man with a kind face and a twinkle in his eye, was sitting on the steps of his cab, smoking a cigarette. Maximus approached him, hope rekindling.

"Excuse me, sir," he said, repeating his request. "I'm trying to get to Bourbonnais. Can you give me a ride?"

The man took a long drag of his cigarette, exhaling a cloud of smoke before answering. "Bourbonnais, you say? Well, I ain't got much cargo and I'm heading that way. Hop in, kid."

Maximus's heart leaped with relief. He climbed into the cab, the door closing with a satisfying thud. The interior was surprisingly clean, with a faint scent of pine air freshener. The driver introduced himself as Hank and started the engine, the truck roaring to life.

As they pulled out of the truck stop, the landscape began to blur into a tapestry of greens and browns, the open road stretching out before them. Hank was a talkative man, sharing stories of his years on the road, the places he'd seen, and the people he'd met. Maximus listened, occasionally chiming in with questions or comments.

The first hour passed in a comfortable rhythm, the hum of the engine and Hank's steady voice creating a soothing backdrop. They drove through small towns and open fields, the scenery shifting from the industrial outskirts to the serene countryside. The sky turned a deep shade of indigo, stars beginning to twinkle overhead.

As they entered the second hour, the conversation turned more personal. Hank asked Maximus about his journey, why he was heading to Bourbonnais. Maximus hesitated, then shared his story – the mysterious map, the caves, and the sense of adventure that had driven him to seek out this unknown destination.

Hank nodded thoughtfully. "Sounds like quite the adventure, kid. Just be careful. The road can be a dangerous place, and not just because of the traffic."

They drove on, the truck's headlights cutting through the darkness. The road was mostly empty now, a ribbon of asphalt winding through the night. Maximus watched the landscape pass by, his mind drifting to thoughts of what awaited him in Bourbonnais. The caves held a promise of mystery and discovery, and he felt a thrill of anticipation.

The final half-hour of the journey was marked by a comfortable silence. Hank focused on the road, his hands steady on the wheel, while Maximus gazed out the window, lost in his thoughts. The truck's engine hummed a steady rhythm, a lullaby of sorts, as they neared their destination.

Finally, the lights of Bourbonnais appeared on the horizon, a small cluster of buildings nestled in the darkness. Hank pulled off the highway, navigating the quiet streets with practiced ease. He brought the truck to a stop near the edge of town, where the map indicated the caves were located.

"Well, here we are," Hank said, turning to Maximus with a smile. "Good luck with your adventure, kid. Hope you find what you're looking for."

Maximus thanked him, climbing down from the cab and retrieving his backpack. He watched as Hank drove away, the truck's tail lights disappearing into the night. He turned towards the dark outline of the caves, feeling a mix of excitement and trepidation.

The journey had been long, but it was only the beginning. Maximus took a deep breath and started walking, the promise of discovery guiding his steps into the unknown.

Maximus Magellan walked away from the truck stop, the distant hum of engines fading into the background as he ventured towards the caves. The night was cool, a gentle breeze rustling the leaves of nearby trees. The sky was a canvas of deep indigo, dotted with countless stars that twinkled like distant beacons. The moon hung low, casting a silvery glow over the landscape, illuminating his path.

As he walked, the sounds of the night enveloped him. The distant howl of coyotes echoed through the air, their calls eerie and haunting. Crickets chirped in a rhythmic symphony, and the occasional rustle of underbrush hinted at unseen wildlife. Each step Maximus took seemed to amplify the sounds around him, creating an almost surreal atmosphere.

The path to the caves was rugged, winding through dense thickets and over uneven terrain. Maximus moved with purpose, his eyes scanning the surroundings for any signs of danger. The map he carried was old and worn, the edges frayed from years of use. He glanced at it occasionally, ensuring he was on the right track.

As he neared the mouth of the caves, the air grew cooler, and the sounds of the night seemed to intensify. The entrance loomed before him, a dark, yawning maw that seemed to swallow the light. The rocky outcroppings around the cave were jagged and imposing, casting long shadows that danced in the moonlight.

Maximus paused at the entrance, taking a moment to steady his nerves. He could feel the weight of the journey ahead, the unknown mysteries that awaited him within the depths of the cave. With a deep breath, he stepped forward, the crunch of gravel underfoot echoing in the stillness.

Finding a suitable spot to make camp, Maximus set down his backpack and began to unpack his gear. He chose a flat, sheltered area near the cave entrance, where the rocky walls provided some protection from the elements. The ground was cold and hard, but he had come prepared.

He pulled out his military-grade flashlight, a powerful tool with a laser function that could cut through the darkness like a knife. The beam illuminated the area around him, casting stark shadows and revealing the intricate details of the rocky terrain. He gathered some dry twigs and branches, arranging them in a small pile to start a fire.

With practiced ease, Maximus struck a match and lit the kindling. The flames flickered to life, casting a warm, golden glow that contrasted sharply with the cold, blue light of the flashlight. The fire crackled and popped, sending sparks dancing into the night air. He fed the fire with larger pieces of wood, building it up until it provided a steady source of heat and light.

Satisfied with his campfire, Maximus turned his attention to the map and the book of clues and riddles he had brought with him. He spread the map out on the ground, using stones to hold down the corners. The map was detailed, showing the layout of the caves and the surrounding area. He traced the route with his finger, noting the landmarks and potential obstacles.

The book of clues and riddles was an old, leather-bound tome, its pages yellowed with age. Maximus opened it carefully, the musty scent of old paper filling the air. The book was filled with cryptic passages and intricate illustrations, each one a piece of the puzzle he needed to solve. He studied the clues, his brow furrowing in concentration as he tried to decipher their meanings.

Hours passed as Maximus pored over the map and the book, the fire crackling steadily beside him. The night deepened, and the sounds of the wilderness seemed to grow louder, more insistent. The howls of coyotes were closer now, their calls echoing off the rocky walls of the cave. The occasional hoot of an owl added to the symphony of the night, creating an almost otherworldly ambiance.

Maximus's eyes grew heavy, the strain of the day's journey and the mental effort of solving the riddles taking their toll. He stifled a yawn, realizing he needed to rest if he was to continue his quest in the morning. He carefully packed away the map and the book, ensuring they were safe from the elements.

He made a mat of grass he plucked nearby near the fire, the warmth of the flames providing a comforting cocoon against the chill of the night. He lay down, staring up at the star-filled sky, his mind still buzzing with thoughts of the adventure ahead. The firelight flickered, casting dancing shadows on the rocky walls, creating an almost hypnotic effect.

As he drifted off to sleep, the sounds of the night continued to surround him. The coyotes' howls, the rustle of leaves, and the crackle of the fire blended into a soothing lullaby. Maximus's dreams were filled with images of the caves, the clues, and the mysteries that awaited him. He knew that the journey ahead would be challenging, but he was ready to face whatever lay in the depths of the cave.

The night passed slowly, the fire burning down to glowing embers. Maximus slept soundly, his body and mind recharging for the challenges of the next day. The first light of dawn began to creep over the horizon, casting a soft, golden glow over the landscape. The sounds of the night faded, replaced by the gentle chirping of birds greeting the new day.

Maximus awoke realizing he was going to need rope. He packed up his camp, extinguished the remnants of the fire, and shouldered his backpack. The entrance to the cave loomed before him, dark and mysterious, but he felt a surge of determination. With the map and the book of clues in hand, he turned to walk to the truckstop not far away. With one last look at the cave entrance, he set off down the path.

The walk back to the truck stop was peaceful, the early morning light casting a golden hue over the landscape. The sounds of the night had faded, replaced by the gentle chirping of birds and the rustle of leaves in the breeze. Maximus moved with purpose, his footsteps crunching on the gravel path. The memory of the eerie howls of coyotes from the night before seemed distant now, replaced by the tranquility of the morning.

As he approached the truck stop, the familiar sights and sounds came into view. Trucks were lined up in neat rows, their engines idling softly. The scent of fresh coffee and frying bacon wafted from the diner, mingling with the smell of diesel fuel. Maximus felt a sense of relief as he entered the busy hub, the activity and noise a stark contrast to "diner. The bell above the door jingled as he entered, and the shopkeeper, a friendly middle-aged woman with a warm smile, greeted him. Morning, young man. What can I do for you today?" she asked

Maximus explained his need for rope and a few other supplies for his exploration. The shopkeeper nodded and led him to the back of the store, where shelves were stocked with various tools and equipment. He selected 4 sturdy coils of rope, extra batteries, and a small first aid kit, a white grease pen, a pair of leather gloves and a led headlamp and of course a fresh cup of coffee. He also picked up some energy bars, some meat sticks, bread and bottles of water, knowing he would need sustenance for the journey ahead.

With his purchases in hand, Maximus thanked the shopkeeper and headed back outside. The sun was higher in the sky now, casting a bright light over the truck stop. He took a moment to enjoy the warmth on his face before setting off back towards the cave.

The return journey felt quicker, his steps fueled by a renewed sense of purpose. The path was familiar now, and he moved with confidence, the weight of his backpack a reassuring presence. The landscape around him was alive with the sounds of nature, the morning chorus of birds providing a cheerful soundtrack to his walk.

As he neared the cave entrance once more, Maximus felt a surge of anticipation. He paused to take a deep breath, the cool air filling his lungs. The cave loomed before him, dark and mysterious, but he felt ready. With his new supplies, he was prepared to delve into its depths and uncover the secrets it held.

Maximus set down his backpack and began to organize his gear. He coiled the rope neatly, ensuring it was easily accessible, and checked the flashlight to make sure it was working properly. Satisfied with his preparations, he took one last look at the map and the book of clues, committing the details to memory.

With everything in place, Maximus stepped forward, the mouth of the cave swallowing him in its shadow. Maximus sat cross-legged before the mouth of the cave, the early morning light casting long shadows across the rocky terrain. The map lay spread out on the ground before him, held down by small stones to prevent it from fluttering in the breeze. He traced the intricate lines and markings with his finger, calculating the path he would need to take. The map was detailed, showing various tunnels and chambers within the cave, each one labeled with cryptic symbols. Beside him, the diary lay open, its pages filled with handwritten notes and sketches. Maximus carefully reviewed the clues and riddles, cross-referencing them with the map to ensure he understood the route. The diary's aged pages crackled softly as he turned them, the scent of old paper mingling with the fresh morning air.

Satisfied with his preparations, Maximus packed away the map and diary, securing them in his backpack. He adjusted the strap of his LED headlamp, ensuring it was snug and comfortable. With a deep breath, he switched on the headlamp, the bright beam cutting through the dim light of the cave entrance. The rocky walls glistened in the artificial light, revealing their rough texture and the occasional glint of mineral deposits. Maximus took one last look at the world outside, the sun now fully risen, casting a golden glow over the landscape. Steeling himself for the journey ahead, he stepped into the darkness of the cave, the light from his headlamp guiding his way as he ventured deeper into the unknown.

As Maximus ventured deeper into the cave, the beam of his LED headlamp cut through the inky darkness, illuminating the rugged interior. The air was cool and damp, carrying a faint, earthy scent mixed with the musty aroma of ancient stone. The walls of the cave glistened with moisture, their surfaces rough and uneven, adorned with patches of moss and lichen that seemed to glow faintly in the artificial light.

The narrow passageways twisted and turned, revealing hidden nooks and crannies. Maximus moved cautiously, his footsteps echoing softly in the confined space. He marked his path with the white grease pen he had picked up from the truck stop, drawing small arrows on the walls to ensure he could find his way back.

As he progressed, the cave came alive with the subtle movements of its indigenous inhabitants. Tiny insects scurried across the damp ground, their exoskeletons glinting in the light. Maximus spotted a colony of cave crickets, their long antennae twitching as they navigated the rocky terrain. The occasional spider web stretched across the path, its delicate threads shimmering like silver in the headlamp's glow.

Further along, he encountered a small, slithering snake, its scales a mottled pattern of brown and green, perfectly camouflaged against the cave floor. It paused briefly, its forked tongue flicking out to taste the air before it disappeared into a crevice. Maximus also noticed a few lizards, their sleek bodies darting in and out of the shadows, their eyes reflecting the light with an eerie, almost otherworldly gleam.

The deeper he went, the more the cave seemed to close in around him. Stalactites hung from the ceiling like jagged teeth, dripping water that formed small, echoing pools on the ground. Stalagmites rose from the floor, creating natural obstacles that Maximus had to navigate around. The air grew colder, and the sounds of the outside world faded into a distant memory, replaced by the steady drip-drip of water and the occasional rustle of unseen creatures.

After what felt like hours of careful exploration, Maximus came upon a small chamber. The walls here were smoother, as if worn down by centuries of water flow. In the center of the chamber, partially obscured by a cluster of stalagmites, he found the first clue. It was an old, weathered plaque, embedded in the rock face. The plaque was covered in a thin layer of grime, but the faint outlines of engraved symbols were still visible.

Maximus wiped away the grime with his sleeve, revealing a series of intricate carvings. The symbols were a mix of ancient runes and pictographs, each one telling a part of a larger story. He recognized some of the symbols from the diary, their meanings slowly coming together in his mind. The plaque depicted a journey, a path through the cave that led to a hidden chamber deep within.

The carvings also included a riddle, inscribed in a flowing script beneath the symbols. Maximus read it aloud, his voice echoing softly in the chamber:

"To find the treasure hidden deep, follow the path where shadows creep. Seek the light that never fades, beyond the reach of time's own shades."

He pondered the riddle, its meaning slowly unraveling in his mind. The "light that never fades" could be a reference to a specific landmark or a natural feature within the cave. The mention of "shadows" suggested that he needed to pay attention to the way light and darkness interacted within the cave's depths.

With a renewed sense of purpose, Maximus carefully noted the details of the plaque in his diary, sketching the symbols and writing down the riddle. He knew that this clue was just the beginning, a piece of the larger puzzle that would guide him through the cave's labyrinthine passages. He took a deep breath, the cool, damp air filling his lungs, and prepared to continue his journey into the unknown.

Maximus continued deeper into the cave, guided by the map and the diary's cryptic clues. The air grew colder and more humid, carrying the scent of damp earth and ancient stone. The beam of his LED headlamp illuminated the path ahead, casting eerie shadows on the walls. The cave's passages twisted and turned, narrowing at points and opening into larger chambers, each step taking him further from the safety of the entrance.

The walls of the cave were adorned with strange mineral formations, glistening in the light. Stalactites hung from the ceiling like jagged teeth, and stalagmites rose from the floor, creating natural obstacles. The sound of dripping water echoed through the passages, a constant reminder of the cave's timeless nature. Maximus moved cautiously, marking his path with the white grease pen to ensure he could find his way back.

As he ventured further, the passages became more treacherous. The ground was uneven, and loose rocks threatened to trip him with every step. He encountered narrow ledges that required careful navigation, his heart pounding as he edged along the precipices. The cave's inhabitants became more elusive, with the occasional bat fluttering past, its wings creating a soft rustling sound in the darkness.

After what felt like hours of careful exploration, Maximus reached a dangerous precipice. The passage abruptly ended, opening into a vast chasm that descended into the depths of the cave. The drop was dizzying, the bottom lost in the shadows far below. The air here was colder, carrying a faint metallic scent that hinted at the minerals hidden within the rock.

Maximus knew he had to descend into the lower section of the cave to continue his journey. He carefully unpacked his rope, checking it for any signs of wear or damage. Finding a sturdy rock formation near the edge of the precipice, he anchored the rope securely, tying a series of strong knots to ensure it would hold his weight. He tested the anchor point, giving the rope a few firm tugs to confirm its stability.

With the rope securely in place, Maximus donned his leather gloves and wrapped the rope around his hand to ensure his grip. He took a deep breath, the cool air filling his lungs, and began his descent. The beam of his headlamp illuminated the rocky wall as he carefully lowered himself into the chasm. The sounds of the cave seemed to amplify, the dripping water and distant echoes creating an almost otherworldly symphony.

As he descended, Maximus encountered several dangers. Loose rocks occasionally dislodged from the wall, tumbling into the darkness below. He had to navigate around sharp outcroppings that threatened to tear his clothing and skin. The air grew colder and more oppressive, the scent of damp stone and minerals becoming more pronounced.

As Maximus descended the rope into the depths of the cave, the air grew colder and more oppressive. The dim light from above barely penetrated the darkness, casting eerie shadows on the jagged walls. His hands, rough and calloused, gripped the rope tightly, each movement slow and deliberate. The rope creaked under his weight, a constant reminder of the precariousness of his descent.

Past the ledge, the chasm below yawned like a hungry maw, its depths shrouded in impenetrable blackness. The sound of dripping water echoed through the cavern, a haunting melody that seemed to come from all directions. The walls were slick with moisture, and strange, luminescent fungi clung to the rocks, casting an otherworldly glow that only added to the sense of unease.

As he descended further, Maximus noticed the dangers lurking in the shadows. Sharp stalactites hung from the ceiling like the fangs of some ancient beast, ready to impale anyone who ventured too close. The ground below was uneven and treacherous, littered with loose rocks and hidden crevices that could easily twist an ankle or worse.

The air was thick with the scent of damp earth and decay, and the occasional skittering of unseen creatures sent shivers down his spine. He could feel the weight of the darkness pressing in on him, a tangible force that seemed to whisper of forgotten horrors and ancient secrets best left undisturbed.

Maximus's heart pounded in his chest as he continued his descent, each step bringing him closer to the unknown dangers that awaited in the depths of the cave. He knew that one wrong move could spell disaster, but he pressed on, driven by a determination that burned brighter than the fear that threatened to consume him.

Halfway down, he paused on a narrow ledge to catch his breath. The darkness below seemed to stretch on forever, the bottom still hidden from view. He adjusted his headlamp, the beam cutting through the gloom, revealing more of the rocky wall. With renewed determination, he continued his descent, each step taking him deeper into the labyrinthine depths of the cave.

Finally, Maximus reached the bottom of the chasm, his feet touching solid ground once more. The air here was thick and heavy, the scent of damp earth and minerals almost overwhelming. He was nearly to the ground and took a moment to survey his surroundings. The passage ahead was narrow and winding, disappearing into the darkness.

As Maximus reached the bottom of the wall, his feet touched the uneven ground of the chasm. The air was thick with an almost palpable sense of dread, and the darkness seemed to close in around him. He took a moment to steady himself, his breath visible in the cold, damp air. The faint glow of the luminescent fungi provided just enough light to reveal the immediate surroundings, casting eerie shadows that danced on the walls.

He took a cautious step forward, his eyes scanning the cavern for any signs of danger. Suddenly, he froze in his tracks, his heart pounding in his chest. The hair on the back of his neck stood on end as a chilling sight came into view.

Before him lay a vast expanse of skeletal remains, their bones bleached white and scattered haphazardly across the cavern floor. The skulls, with their empty eye sockets, seemed to stare back at him, their silent screams frozen in time. Among the bones were remnants of tattered clothing and rusted weapons, hinting at the violent end these unfortunate souls had met.

But it wasn't just the bones that made Maximus's blood run cold. In the center of the chasm, partially obscured by the shadows, stood a massive stone altar. The altar was covered in dark, dried stains that could only be blood, and strange, arcane symbols were etched into its surface. The symbols seemed to pulse with a faint, malevolent energy, as if they were alive and watching him.

Above the altar, suspended by chains that disappeared into the darkness above, hung a grotesque figure. It was a twisted amalgamation of human and beast, its body contorted in unnatural ways. Its eyes glowed with a sickly green light, and its mouth was twisted into a grotesque grin, revealing rows of sharp, jagged teeth. The creature's presence exuded a palpable sense of malice, and Maximus could feel its gaze boring into him, even from a distance.

The air around the altar was thick with the stench of decay and something far more sinister. Maximus could almost hear faint whispers, like the echoes of tormented souls trapped within the cavern walls. The sound sent shivers down his spine, and he felt an overwhelming urge to turn and flee.

But he knew he couldn't. He had come too far, and there was no turning back now. Summoning every ounce of courage, Maximus took a deep breath and steeled himself for whatever horrors lay ahead. The chasm was a place of death and darkness, but he had to press on, driven by a determination that burned brighter than the fear that threatened to consume him.

Maximus stood at the bottom of the chasm, the air thick with the scent of damp earth and ancient stone. The chamber he had descended into was vast, its walls stretching high above him, disappearing into the darkness. The beam of his LED headlamp cast long shadows, revealing the rough, uneven surfaces of the cave. He took a moment to catch his breath, the cool air filling his lungs as he assessed his situation.

Setting his backpack down, Maximus carefully unpacked the map and the diary, spreading them out on a flat rock. He studied the map, tracing the route he had taken and noting the landmarks he had passed. The diary lay open beside him, its pages filled with cryptic notes and sketches. He knew that the answers he sought were hidden within these pages, waiting to be discovered.

As he scoured the chamber, Maximus's headlamp illuminated three hidden symbols carved into the altar base. The first symbol was a spiral, intricately etched into the stone. Beneath it, a riddle was inscribed:

"In the heart of darkness, where shadows play, seek the spiral's end to find your way."

CHAPTER 3
THE DESCENT INTO DARKNESS

Maximus pondered the riddle, considering its meaning. The spiral could represent a path or a journey, leading him deeper into the cave. He made a note of the symbol and the riddle in his diary, determined to decipher its significance.

The second symbol was a pair of crossed arrows, their tips pointing in opposite directions. The riddle beneath this symbol read:

"Where paths diverge and choices are made, the arrows' point will guide your trade."

This riddle suggested a decision point, a place where he would need to choose his path carefully. Maximus marked the symbol and the riddle in his diary, aware that this clue would be crucial in navigating the labyrinthine passages ahead.

The third symbol was a crescent moon, its delicate curves carved with precision. The riddle beneath it was more enigmatic:

"By the light of the moon, in the darkest night, the crescent's glow reveals the sight."

Maximus considered the riddle, its poetic language hinting at a hidden light or a revelation that could only be seen in the darkest parts of the cave. He made a detailed sketch of the symbol and recorded the riddle, knowing that this clue would be vital in his quest.

As he worked, the chamber seemed to come alive with subtle sounds. The occasional drip of water echoed through the space, creating a rhythmic backdrop to his thoughts. Suddenly, a faint, metallic hum emanated from his backpack. Maximus paused, his heart racing as he reached for the source of the sound. He pulled out the mysterious metal ball, its surface smooth and cool to the touch. The hum grew louder, resonating with an almost musical quality.

Maximus held the ball up to the light, watching as it began to glow faintly, casting an ethereal light around the chamber. The glow intensified, revealing hidden details in the carvings on the walls. He felt a strange connection to the object, as if it were guiding him towards the next clue.

As he continued to examine the chamber, a soft, whispering voice seemed to echo in his mind. The voice was faint, almost indistinguishable from the natural sounds of the cave, but it carried a sense of urgency and purpose. Maximus strained to listen, trying to discern the words. The voice seemed to be urging him forward, guiding him towards the next step in his journey.

Maximus took one last look around the chamber, the glow from the metal ball casting an otherworldly light on the ancient carvings. He adjusted his headlamp, the beam cutting through the darkness as he prepared to venture deeper into the cave. The path ahead was uncertain, but the promise of discovery and adventure drove him forward, his heart pounding with anticipation as he stepped into the unknown.

With the clues and symbols recorded in his diary, Maximus felt a sense of warning from the subtle voice he heard. He packed away his gear, ensuring the metal ball was securely stowed in his backpack. The chamber held many secrets, and he knew that the journey ahead would be fraught with challenges and dangers.

Maximus took a deep breath, the cool, damp air of the cave filling his lungs as he prepared to delve further into the dark cavern. The beam of his LED headlamp cut through the darkness, illuminating the rough, uneven walls of the tunnel ahead. The sounds of dripping water and the occasional rustle of unseen creatures echoed around him, creating an eerie symphony that heightened his senses.

As he moved forward, the tunnel began to narrow, forcing him to navigate carefully around jagged outcroppings and loose rocks. The air grew colder, and the scent of damp earth and minerals became more pronounced. Maximus kept a steady pace, his eyes scanning the walls for any signs or symbols that might guide him.

After a while, he reached a point where the tunnel branched off into several intersecting passages. He paused, pulling out the map and the diary to reassess his route. The three clues he had discovered in the chamber played in his mind, each one offering a hint to guide his way.

The first clue, the spiral, suggested a path that twisted and turned. Maximus looked for any signs of a spiral pattern in the tunnels ahead. He noticed that one of the passages had a slight curve to it, resembling the beginning of a spiral. Trusting the clue, he marked his path with the white grease pen and proceeded down the curved tunnel.

As he moved deeper into the labyrinth, the tunnel began to twist and turn more sharply, confirming that he was on the right path. The second clue, the crossed arrows, hinted at a decision point where paths diverged. Maximus soon encountered another intersection, this time with two distinct passages leading in opposite directions.

He paused, considering the riddle: "Where paths diverge and choices are made, the arrows' point will guide your trade." He examined the walls carefully, looking for any markings or signs. His headlamp revealed a faint carving of crossed arrows on the wall to his left. Taking this as a sign, he chose the left passage, marking his path as he went.

The tunnel grew narrower and more treacherous, the ground uneven and littered with loose rocks. Maximus moved cautiously, aware of the potential dangers lurking in the darkness. The air was thick with the scent of damp stone, and the sound of dripping water grew louder, echoing through the passage.

Finally, he reached a point where the tunnel opened up into a larger cavern. The third clue, the crescent moon, suggested that he should seek the light in the darkest night. As he stepped into the cavern, the beam of his headlamp revealed a vast, open space with a large pool of water at its center. The water was dark and still, reflecting the light from his headlamp like a mirror.

Maximus approached the edge of the pool, the air growing colder and more humid. The scent of minerals was strong here, mingling with the earthy aroma of the cave. He noticed faint ripples on the surface of the water, as if something had disturbed it recently. The cavern was silent, save for the occasional drip of water from the stalactites above.

He took a moment to assess his surroundings, the clues from the chamber guiding his thoughts. The crescent moon symbol suggested that there might be something hidden in the water or near its edge. Maximus carefully scanned the area, his headlamp revealing faint markings on the rocks near the water's edge.

As he examined the markings, he felt a faint vibration from his backpack. The mysterious metal ball began to hum softly, its glow intensifying. Maximus pulled it out, holding it up to the light. The ball's glow illuminated the markings on the rocks, revealing another riddle:

"Where water meets the stone, the hidden path is shown. Seek the light beneath the waves, and find the treasure that you crave."

Maximus pondered the riddle, realizing that he needed to explore the pool of water to uncover the next clue. He secured his gear, making sure his pack was fit tightly over his shoulders, prepared to dive into the dark, still waters. The journey ahead was uncertain, his heart pounding with anticipation as he stepped into the unknown depths of the cavern.

Maximus approached the edge of the dark, still pool, the beam of his LED headlamp casting a shimmering light across the water's surface. The air was thick with humidity, and the scent of minerals was strong, mingling with the earthy aroma of the cave. He knelt down, peering into the depths, searching for any signs of clues he might have missed. The water was so clear that he could see the rocky bottom, but the darkness made it difficult to discern any details.

As he scanned the pool, his eyes caught a faint glimmer on one of the submerged rocks. He leaned closer, the light from his headlamp revealing a symbol etched into the stone. It was the same spiral he had seen earlier, but this one was partially hidden beneath the water. Maximus felt a thrill of excitement, knowing he was on the right track.

Suddenly, a subtle, almost ethereal voice echoed in his mind, urging him to don the jewel from his backpack. The voice was calm and reassuring, its tone filled with a sense of purpose. Maximus reached into his backpack and retrieved the jewel, a fist sized gemstone, intricately carved that seemed to pulse with an inner light.

As he placed the jewel around his neck, a strange sensation washed over him. The jewel began to glow, casting a soft, radiant light that illuminated the entire chamber. The water in the pool responded to the light, shimmering and rippling as if alive. Maximus watched in awe as the glow intensified, revealing hidden details beneath the surface.

The light from the jewel penetrated the depths of the pool, uncovering a hidden passageway that had been concealed by the darkness. The passage was lined with ancient carvings, their intricate designs telling a story that had been lost to time. Maximus could see symbols and runes similar to those in the diary, each one a piece of the larger puzzle.

The voice in his mind grew clearer, guiding him on how to proceed. "The path lies beneath the water, where the light reveals the way. Trust in the jewel, and it will guide you to the heart of the cave. Follow the symbols, and you will find what you seek."

Maximus felt a surge of determination. He knew that the jewel was the key to unlocking the secrets of the cave. He took a deep breath, the cool air filling his lungs, and prepared to dive into the pool. The water was cold and refreshing, enveloping him as he submerged himself. The glow from the jewel illuminated the passageway, casting an otherworldly light on the ancient carvings.

As he swam deeper, the symbols on the walls became more intricate, each one telling a part of the story. The passageway twisted and turned, leading him further into the heart of the cave. The voice continued to guide him, its tone filled with a sense of urgency and purpose.

"Follow the light, and it will lead you to the chamber of secrets. There, you will find the answers you seek. But beware, for the path is fraught with danger. Trust in the jewel, and it will protect you."

Maximus swam on, the light from the jewel guiding his way. The passageway opened up into a larger chamber, the water shimmering with an ethereal glow. He surfaced, taking a deep breath as he looked around. The chamber was vast, its walls covered in ancient carvings and symbols. At the center of the chamber, a pedestal rose from the water, a small, intricately carved box resting on top.

The voice in his mind grew softer, its tone filled with a sense of accomplishment. "You have found the chamber of secrets. The box holds the key to unlocking the mysteries of the labyrinth. Use the jewel to open it, and you will discover the truth."

Maximus approached the pedestal, his heart pounding with anticipation. He placed the jewel on the box, and it began to glow, the light intensifying until it enveloped the entire chamber. The box opened with a soft click, revealing a scroll covered in ancient symbols and runes.

He carefully unrolled the scroll, the light from the jewel illuminating the intricate designs. The scroll contained a map, detailing the layout of the cave and the hidden chambers within. Maximus knew that this was the key to unlocking the secrets of the cave, and he felt a sense of accomplishment and excitement as he prepared to continue his journey.

Maximus emerged from the cold, dark pool, his body shivering uncontrollably from the icy water. The chill seeped into his bones, making his muscles ache with each movement. He scanned the cavern for a dry spot, his headlamp casting a faint glow on the rocky walls. Spotting a flat, elevated ledge nearby, he made his way over, his wet clothes clinging to his skin and making each step a struggle.

Reaching the ledge, Maximus dropped his backpack and began to strip off his soaked clothing, laying it out on the rocks in an attempt to dry it. The air in the cavern was still and cold, but at least it was dry. He rummaged through his backpack, relieved to find that the diary was still dry, thanks to its waterproof design. The pages were intact, the ink unblurred, a small comfort in the midst of his discomfort.

As he settled on the ledge, he pulled out the mysterious metal ball, its surface cool and smooth against his fingers. He set it on the cold stone beside him, watching as it began to react to his touch. The ball started to hover, lifting gently off the rock, and then it began to spin slowly. Bands of light emerged from its surface, expanding outward like the rings of an atom, each band pulsating with a soft, radiant glow.

The light grew more intense, filling the cavern with a warm, golden hue. Maximus felt the warmth seep into his skin, driving away the chill from the cold water. The bands of light spun faster, creating a mesmerizing display that seemed to defy the laws of physics. The air around him hummed with energy, the light casting intricate patterns on the rocky walls.

As the ball continued to spin, the light coalesced into a vision-like scene before him. The cavern walls seemed to dissolve, replaced by a vivid, three-dimensional map of the labyrinthine cave system. Maximus watched in awe as the map unfolded, revealing the long path that lay ahead. The vision showed tunnels twisting and turning, intersecting chambers, and hidden passages that led deeper into the heart of the cave.

At the center of the vision was a large, ominous chamber labeled "The Chamber of Souls." The path to this chamber was fraught with obstacles and dangers, but the vision provided a clear route, highlighting key landmarks and symbols that would guide him. Maximus felt a sense of determination welling up inside him, knowing that this was the ultimate goal of his journey.

The voice from before echoed in his mind once more, its tone calm and reassuring. "The path is long and perilous, but the jewel will guide you. Trust in its light, and you will find your way. The Chamber of Souls holds the answers you seek, but beware the dangers that lie ahead. Stay vigilant, and you will prevail."

Maximus nodded, absorbing the information and committing the details to memory. The vision slowly faded, the bands of light retracting back into the metal ball, which settled gently on the stone once more. The cavern returned to its natural state, the warm glow lingering in the air.

Feeling a renewed sense of purpose, Maximus dressed in his now slightly drier clothes and packed his gear. He secured the diary and the metal ball in his backpack, the jewel still glowing faintly around his neck. With the path ahead clear in his mind, he stood up, the warmth from the vision still radiating through him.

He adjusted his headlamp, the beam cutting through the darkness as he prepared to venture deeper into the labyrinth. His heart pounding with anticipation as he stepped into the unknown, ready to face whatever challenges lay ahead on his journey to the Chamber of Souls.

As Maximus ventured deeper into the labyrinthine cave, the weight of exhaustion began to settle heavily on his shoulders. The relentless journey through the dark, twisting tunnels had taken its toll, and he knew he needed to rest. His legs ached, and his eyes felt heavy, the beam of his headlamp flickering slightly as if mirroring his own fatigue.

He scanned the surroundings for a suitable spot to rest, his headlamp casting long shadows on the rocky walls. Finally, he found a small alcove, a natural indentation in the stone that offered some shelter and a flat surface to sit on. The air was cool and still, the scent of damp earth and minerals a constant presence.

Maximus settled into the alcove, leaning against the rough stone wall. He reached into his backpack and pulled out one of the energy bars he had brought along. The wrapper crinkled loudly in the silence of the cave, and he took a bite, the sweet, chewy texture providing a much-needed boost of energy. As he ate, he felt a faint vibration from his backpack. The mysterious metal ball began to hum softly, a familiar sound that now brought a sense of anticipation.

One of the symbols on the ball started to glow, casting a soft, ethereal light. The voice in his mind grew clearer, repeating a single word over and over. Maximus focused on the word, letting it resonate within him. He spoke it aloud, his voice echoing softly in the cavern:

"Illuminate."

As soon as the word left his lips, the ball began to hover once more. Bands of light emerged from its surface, expanding outward in a mesmerizing display. The light grew warmer, filling the alcove with a comforting glow. Maximus turned off his headlamp, the artificial light no longer needed in the presence of the ball's radiant illumination.

As Maximus whispered the word "illuminate," the symbol on the softball-sized metal ball began to glow with a soft, ethereal light. The glow intensified, casting a warm, golden hue that spread outwards, pushing back the oppressive darkness of the chasm. The light revealed the cavern in greater detail, illuminating the jagged walls and the eerie, skeletal remains scattered across the floor.

The once shadowy chamber now stood clearly before him, its dark, dried stains and arcane symbols visible in the warm glow. The symbols, which had seemed to pulse with malevolent energy, now appeared less threatening under the gentle light. A grotesque figure suspended above the chamber carved from stone, was bathed in the golden glow, its sickly green eyes dimming as if subdued by the warmth.

Maximus felt a comforting warmth envelop him, a stark contrast to the cold, damp air of the cave. The light seemed to chase away the chill, wrapping him in a protective embrace. The whispers that had haunted him faded into the background, replaced by a sense of calm and clarity.

With the chasm now fully illuminated, Maximus could see a path forward, the dangers more apparent but less daunting. The light gave him the courage to press on, a beacon of hope in the heart of darkness.

The warmth from the ball seeped into his skin, driving away the chill of the cave. He settled against the stone wall, feeling a sense of peace wash over him. But as he closed his eyes, his thoughts drifted to his family, the faces of his loved ones filling his mind. He thought of his wife and children, their worried expressions as he had set off on this journey. He wondered how they were coping, if they were safe and well.

A pang of guilt pierced his heart, the weight of his decisions pressing down on him. He had left them behind, driven by a sense of adventure and the need to uncover the secrets of the cave. The thought of their worry and fear gnawed at him, the pain of separation becoming overwhelming. He missed their warmth, their support, and the comfort of home.

Tears welled up in his eyes, the emotions he had been holding back finally breaking through. The guilt and pain were almost too much to bear, the weight of his choices pressing down on him like a heavy burden. He felt a deep sense of longing, a desire to be with his family, to reassure them that he was safe.

The voice in his mind grew softer, its tone filled with empathy and understanding. "You are not alone, Maximus. Your journey is important, but so is your connection to those you love. Trust in the light, and it will guide you back to them."

Maximus took a deep breath, the warmth from the ball providing a small measure of comfort. He knew that his journey was far from over, but the promise of discovery and the hope of reuniting with his family gave him the strength to continue. He closed his eyes, letting the warmth and light envelop him as he drifted into a restless sleep, his heart heavy with the weight of his emotions.

Maximus struggled to stay awake, the warm glow of the metal ball casting eerie shadows on the cave walls. Fatigue gripped his bones, pulling him towards sleep. The soft light flickered, revealing the grotesque carving and the dark alcove. Whispers seemed to echo from the depths, blending with the rhythmic drip of water. His eyelids grew heavy, the line between reality and nightmare blurring in the unsettling stillness.

An eerie whispering emanated from the darkness, weaving through the air like a ghostly lullaby, its sinister tones beckoning Maximus to surrender to sleep. The shadows seemed to pulse and shift, as if alive, their movements synchronized with the haunting whispers. Fatigue gripped his bones, and despite his efforts to stay awake, his eyelids grew heavier, the line between reality and nightmare blurring in the unsettling stillness.

Maximus felt the weight of fatigue pressing down on him, his eyelids heavy and his body aching. The warm glow of the metal ball provided some comfort, but the darkness around him seemed to pulse and shift, as if it were alive and trying to swallow the light. The eerie whispers from the shadows grew louder, their sinister tones weaving through the air like a ghostly lullaby, beckoning him to surrender to sleep.

In a desperate attempt to fight the encroaching darkness, Maximus forced himself to sit up. The cold, damp air of the cave clung to his skin, and he shivered as he reached into his bag, pulling out the map and the diary. The pages of the diary were worn and yellowed with age, the ink faded but still legible. He opened it to a random page, hoping that the act of reading would distract him from the eerie feeling creeping in on him.

The light from the metal ball flickered, casting long, twisted shadows on the cave walls. The shadows seemed to dance and writhe, their movements synchronized with the haunting whispers that filled the air. Maximus's hands trembled as he held the diary, his eyes scanning the familiar handwriting. The words on the page seemed to blur and shift, making it difficult to focus.

He glanced at the map, its intricate lines and symbols a stark contrast to the chaotic darkness around him. The map depicted the cave system in meticulous detail, but in the dim light, it seemed almost otherworldly, as if it were a portal to another realm. Maximus traced the lines with his finger, trying to make sense of the labyrinthine passages and hidden chambers.

The whispers grew louder, more insistent, and Maximus felt a chill run down his spine. It was as if the darkness itself was trying to lull him into a false sense of security, to draw him into its depths. He shook his head, trying to clear his mind, but the fatigue was relentless, and the whispers seemed to seep into his very bones.

Desperate to stay awake, Maximus began to read aloud from the diary, his voice echoing through the cavern. The words were a mix of personal reflections and cryptic notes, the ramblings of a mind teetering on the edge of madness. As he read, he felt a strange connection to the writer, a sense of shared struggle and despair.

The light from the metal ball flickered again, and Maximus's heart raced as the shadows seemed to close in around him. He could feel the darkness pressing against the edges of the light, trying to snuff it out. The whispers were now a cacophony of voices, each one more sinister than the last, their words a jumbled mess of threats and promises.

Maximus gripped the diary tightly, his knuckles white with tension. He knew he had to stay awake, to keep the darkness at bay. The map and the diary were his lifelines, a fragile connection to the world above. He focused on the words, forcing himself to read each one with care, to let their meaning anchor him in reality.

The minutes stretched into hours, and Maximus's exhaustion grew, but he refused to give in. The light from the metal ball, though flickering, remained a beacon of hope in the oppressive darkness. He clung to it, drawing strength from its warmth, and continued to read, his voice a steady rhythm that cut through the eerie whispers.

As the night wore on, the darkness seemed to relent, its grip on him loosening. The whispers faded, and the shadows retreated, leaving Maximus alone with his thoughts. He knew that the battle was far from over, but for now, he had won a small victory. The map and the diary lay open before him, their secrets waiting to be uncovered.

CHAPTER 4

THE DREAM

Maximus settled against the cold stone wall, the warmth from the pulsating ball enveloping him like a comforting blanket. The bands of light spun gently, casting a soft, golden glow that filled the alcove with a sense of peace and security. The hum of the ball was soothing, a gentle lullaby that began to ease the tension from his weary muscles. His eyelids grew heavy, the exhaustion of the day's journey finally catching up with him. He let out a deep sigh, his body relaxing as he drifted closer to sleep.

The light from the ball flickered softly, creating a mesmerizing dance of shadows on the rocky walls. The warmth seeped into his skin, driving away the chill of the cave and lulling him into a state of drowsiness. Maximus's thoughts began to blur, the edges of reality softening as he slipped into the realm between wakefulness and dreams.

As he hovered on the brink of sleep, he felt a faint tickle on his arm. His mind, foggy with fatigue, barely registered the sensation. The tickle grew more insistent, and he glanced down, his vision hazy. There, crawling up his arm, was a spider. Its body was sleek and black, with long, spindly legs that moved with an almost mechanical precision. Maximus couldn't tell if it was real or a figment of his imagination, the line between reality and dream blurring in his exhausted state.

Before he could react, the spider bit him. A sharp, stinging pain shot through his arm, jolting him awake. He gasped, clutching his arm as the pain radiated outward. The spider scurried away, disappearing into the shadows, leaving Maximus to wonder if it had been real or just a vivid dream.

The pain quickly gave way to a strange, tingling sensation that spread through his body. His vision began to blur, the edges of the alcove dissolving into a kaleidoscope of colors. The hum of the ball grew louder, its light intensifying until it filled his entire field of vision. Maximus felt himself slipping into a hallucinatory state, the world around him transforming into something otherworldly.

In his vision, he found himself standing in a vast, alien landscape. The sky above was a swirling mass of colors, filled with strange constellations and celestial bodies that defied the laws of physics. The ground beneath his feet was covered in intricate patterns, like the circuitry of a giant machine. He felt a sense of awe and wonder, the beauty and complexity of the scene overwhelming his senses.

Before him stood a massive structure, a machine of alien design that seemed to pulse with energy. Its surface was covered in glowing symbols and runes, each one a piece of a larger puzzle. Maximus approached the machine, his mind racing with curiosity and excitement. As he drew closer, the symbols began to shift and rearrange themselves, forming intricate schematics and diagrams.

The vision revealed a complex software design, a fusion of advanced astrophysics and alien technology. The schematics showed a network of interconnected nodes, each one representing a different aspect of the machine's function. Maximus could see equations and formulas, their meanings just beyond his grasp. The diagrams depicted a device capable of manipulating space and time, a machine that could unlock the secrets of the universe.

The voice in his mind returned, its tone filled with urgency and purpose. "This is the key, Maximus. The machine holds the answers you seek. Study the schematics, understand the design, and you will unlock the path to the Chamber of Souls."

Maximus felt a surge within his brain, his mind racing to absorb the information. The vision was vivid and detailed, each symbol and diagram etched into his memory. He knew that this knowledge was not yet fully within his grasp, but he memorized the details from his strange vision.

As the vision began to fade, the warmth from the pulsating ball enveloped him once more. The pain from the spider bite dulled, replaced by a sense of clarity and purpose. Maximus settled back against the stone wall, the light from the ball casting a comforting glow.

His thoughts drifted to his family, the faces of his loved ones giving him strength. He closed his eyes, the exhaustion finally overtaking him as he drifted into a deep, restful sleep.

Maximus awoke slowly, the remnants of his vivid dream lingering in his mind. The warmth from the pulsating ball had faded, leaving the alcove in a gentle, ambient glow. He blinked a few times, adjusting to the dim light, and stretched his stiff muscles. The cold stone wall had left an imprint on his back, but the rest had rejuvenated him. The air was still cool and damp, carrying the familiar scent of earth and minerals.

He sat up, the events of the dream replaying in his mind. The alien machine, the intricate schematics, and the voice guiding him—all of it felt so real. He knew that the vision held crucial information for his journey. Maximus reached for his backpack, spreading out the map, the scroll, and the diary. He spread them on the flat rock, the light from the metal ball illuminating the pages.

The map, now more familiar, showed the labyrinthine passages he had traversed and the path still ahead. He traced the route with his finger, noting the landmarks and symbols that had guided him thus far. The scroll, with its ancient symbols and runes, seemed to pulse with a faint light, as if responding to the presence of the metal ball and the jewel around his neck.

Maximus took a deep breath, focusing on the task at hand. He opened the diary, its pages filled with handwritten notes and sketches. The diary had been a constant companion, its waterproof design protecting it from the elements. As he studied the entries, he noticed new details that had previously escaped his attention. The symbols and riddles seemed to align with the vision he had seen, each one a piece of the larger puzzle.

The metal ball began to hum softly, its surface glowing with a warm, golden light. One of the symbols on the ball started to glow, casting a faint beam onto the map. Maximus watched in awe as the light revealed hidden markings on the map, lines and symbols that had been invisible before. The path to the Chamber of Souls became clearer, the route illuminated by the ball's light.

The jewel around his neck pulsed in sync with the ball, its light casting intricate patterns on the rocky walls. Maximus felt a sense of connection to the objects, as if they were guiding him with a purpose. He carefully noted the new details, sketching the hidden markings and symbols in the diary. The voice from his dream echoed in his mind, its tone calm and reassuring.

"Trust in the light, Maximus. The path is clear, but you must stay vigilant. The Chamber of Souls holds the answers you seek, but the journey is fraught with danger. Use the knowledge you have gained, and you will prevail." Maximus packed away the map, scroll, and diary, ensuring they were secure in his backpack.

He stood up, the weight of his backpack a familiar comfort. Maximus took one last look around the alcove, the light from the ball casting a comforting glow. With a deep breath, he stepped into the darkness of the cave, the light from the ball and the jewel illuminating his way.

As he ventured deeper into the labyrinth, the new details from the map and the diary guided his steps. The symbols and markings revealed hidden passages and secret chambers, each one bringing him closer to the Chamber of Souls. The journey ahead would be long and perilous, Maximus knowing he was nearing his unknown destination. The vision from his dream had shown him the way, and he was determined to uncover the secrets hidden within the depths of the cave.

Maximus ventured deeper into the labyrinthine cave, the light from the metal ball and the jewel guiding his way. The tunnels twisted and turned, the rocky walls closing in around him. The air grew colder and more stale, the scent of damp earth and minerals a constant presence. The sounds of dripping water and the occasional rustle of unseen creatures echoed through the passages, creating an eerie symphony that heightened his senses.

After what felt like hours of careful navigation, Maximus entered a new chamber. The space was vast, the ceiling high above him, adorned with stalactites that hung like jagged teeth. The floor was uneven, covered in loose rocks and patches of moss that glows faintly in the light. The air was thick with the scent of damp stone and the faint, metallic tang of minerals.

As he stepped further into the chamber, the light from the metal ball illuminated a series of carvings on the walls. The carvings were intricate and detailed, depicting scenes of ancient rituals and mysterious symbols. Maximus felt a thrill of excitement, knowing that he had discovered the next set of clues.

He approached the carvings, his eyes scanning the symbols for any signs of riddles or hidden messages. The first clue he discovered was a series of concentric circles, each one filled with tiny, intricate designs. Beneath the circles, a riddle was inscribed:

"In circles within circles, the path is shown. Seek the center, where the light is known."

Maximus pondered the riddle, considering its meaning. The circles could represent a journey inward, a path that led to the heart of the chamber. He made a note of the symbol and the riddle in his diary, determined to decipher its significance.

The second clue was a pair of intertwined serpents, their bodies coiled around each other in a complex pattern. The riddle beneath this symbol read:

"Where serpents twist and shadows play, the hidden path will light your way."

This riddle suggested a place where light and shadow interacted, revealing a hidden passage. Maximus marked the symbol and the riddle in his diary, aware that this clue would be crucial in navigating the chamber.

The third clue was a starburst pattern, its rays extending outward in all directions he'd seen this earlier as well. The riddle beneath it was more enigmatic:

"By the light of the stars, in the darkest night, the path to the heart will be revealed in sight."

Maximus considered the riddle, its poetic language hinting at a hidden light or a revelation that could only be seen in the darkest parts of the chamber. He made a detailed sketch of the symbol and recorded the riddle, knowing that this clue would be vital in his quest.

As he studied the carvings, the metal ball began to hum softly, its surface glowing with a warm, golden light. One of the symbols on the ball started to glow, casting a faint beam onto the carvings. Maximus watched in awe as the light revealed hidden details in the symbols, lines and patterns that had been invisible before.

The voice in his mind grew clearer, guiding him on how to proceed. "The path lies within the symbols, where light and shadow meet. Trust in the jewel, and it will guide you to the heart of the chamber. Follow the clues, and you will find what you seek."

Maximus carefully noted the new details, sketching the hidden markings and symbols in his diary. With the new clues and riddles recorded, he prepared to continue his journey into the depths of the cave.

Maximus pressed on through the labyrinthine tunnels, the light from the metal ball and the jewel guiding his way. The path ahead was fraught with obstacles, the rocky terrain uneven and treacherous. The air grew colder and more oppressive, the scent of damp earth and minerals a constant reminder of the cave's ancient history. The sounds of dripping water and the occasional rustle of unseen creatures echoed through the passages, creating an eerie symphony that heightened his senses.

After hours of careful navigation, Maximus reached a narrow passage that opened into a small cove. The walls of the cove were covered in intricate carvings, each one depicting scenes of ancient rituals and mysterious symbols. The air was thick with the scent of damp stone, and the light from the metal ball cast long shadows on the rocky walls.

Maximus felt a wave of exhaustion wash over him. It had been a whole day since he had last rested, and his body was weary from the relentless journey. He found a flat rock near the edge of the cove and settled down, pulling out one of the energy bars from his backpack. The wrapper crinkled loudly in the silence of the cave, and he took a bite, he realized he only had two energy bars left, a stark reminder of the limited resources he had.

As he ate, the metal ball began to hum softly, its surface glowing with a warm, golden light. One of the symbols on the ball started to glow, casting a faint beam onto the carvings on the walls. Maximus watched in awe as the light revealed hidden details in the symbols, lines and patterns that had been invisible before.

The first clue he discovered was a series of interlocking triangles, each one filled with tiny, intricate designs. Beneath the triangles, a riddle was inscribed:

"In the union of three, the path is shown. Seek the balance, where the light is known."

Maximus pondered the riddle, considering its meaning. The triangles could represent a balance or a union, a path that led to the heart of the chamber. He made a note of the symbol and the riddle in his diary, determined to decipher its significance.

The second clue was a spiral pattern, its curves twisting and turning in a complex design. The riddle beneath this symbol read:

"Where spirals twist and shadows play, the hidden path will light your way."

This riddle suggested a place where light and shadow interacted, revealing a hidden passage. Maximus marked the symbol and the riddle in his diary, aware that this clue would be crucial in navigating the cove.

The third clue was a starburst pattern, its rays extending outward in all directions. The riddle beneath it was more enigmatic:

"By the light of the stars, in the darkest night, the path to the heart will be revealed in sight."

Maximus considered the riddle, its poetic language hinting at a hidden light or a revelation that could only be seen in the darkest parts of the cove. He made a detailed sketch of the symbol and recorded the riddle, knowing that this clue would be vital in his quest.

As he studied the carvings, the feeling of claustrophobia began to creep in. The walls of the cove seemed to close in around him, the air growing thicker and more oppressive. He took a deep breath, trying to steady his nerves, but the sensation was overwhelming. The light from the metal ball flickered, casting eerie shadows on the walls.

Suddenly, he felt a faint tickle on his arm. He glanced down, his vision hazy, and saw the same mysterious spider from before. Its sleek, black body moved with an almost mechanical precision, and before he could react, it bit him again. A sharp, stinging pain shot through his arm, and he gasped, clutching the bite mark.

The pain quickly gave way to a strange, tingling sensation that spread through his body. His vision began to blur, the edges of the cove dissolving into a kaleidoscope of colors. The hum of the ball grew louder, its light intensifying until it filled his entire field of vision. Maximus felt himself slipping into a hallucinatory state, the world around him transforming into something otherworldly.

In his vision, he saw a dark, shadowy specter standing before him. The figure was tall and imposing, its form shrouded in darkness. It raised a bony finger, pointing directly at Maximus. The sight filled him with a sense of dread, the weight of the specter's gaze pressing down on him.

The vision shifted, and Maximus found himself back in the abandoned lot outside the convenience store. He saw the skeletal remains under the bush, the bones brittle and yellowed with age. The vision showed him how the person had met their demise, a tragic end brought about by the same journey he was now undertaking. The specter seemed to be warning him, a silent reminder of the dangers that lay ahead.

Maximus tried to shake the unsettling feeling that the vision left with him. He knew that the journey was perilous, but he was determined to uncover the secrets of the cave. The vision began to fade, the warmth from the pulsating ball enveloping him once more. The pain from the spider bite dulled, replaced by a sense of clarity and purpose.

He settled back against the stone wall, the light from the ball casting a comforting glow. His thoughts drifted to his family, the faces of his loved ones giving him strength. He closed his eyes, letting the warmth and light lull him into a restless sleep.

As Maximus settled against the cold stone wall, the warmth from the pulsating ball enveloping him, his thoughts drifted back to a week before his life began to unravel. The memory was vivid, etched into his mind like a scene from a movie.

It had been a crisp autumn morning, the air cool and invigorating as he walked towards the company lab where he worked. The sky was a clear, brilliant blue, and the leaves on the trees had turned vibrant shades of red, orange, and yellow. The wind blew gently, rustling the leaves and carrying the scent of earth and foliage.

Maximus had been lost in thought, his mind preoccupied with the latest project he was working on. The lab was a place of innovation and discovery, a sanctuary where he could immerse himself in his work. As he approached the entrance, a sudden gust of wind blew a piece of parchment across the parking lot. The paper fluttered and danced in the air before sticking to his pant leg.

He paused, reaching down to peel the parchment off his pants. The paper was old and weathered, its edges frayed and yellowed with age. Intrigued, Maximus unfolded it, revealing a long riddle written in elegant, flowing script. The words read like a dark fortune from a Chinese cookie, cryptic and foreboding:

"In pursuit of the prize, a cost must be paid. The path is fraught with peril, and shadows will invade. The heart must be strong, the mind must be clear. For the journey ahead, will test all you hold dear." He had the vision of the blood written message at the hood convenience store

Maximus had read the riddle several times, pondering its meaning. It seemed like a warning, a cautionary tale about the dangers of seeking something valuable. He had wondered who had written it and why it had found its way to him. But in the rush of the morning, he had quickly discarded the note, tucking it into his pocket and forgetting about it as he entered the lab.

Now, as he sat in the depths of the cave, the memory of the riddle resurfaced with startling clarity. The words seemed to echo in his mind, their meaning suddenly all too clear. The journey he was on, the quest for the Chamber of Souls, was exactly what the riddle had foretold. The cost of the prize was becoming evident—the physical and emotional toll, the dangers he faced, and the sacrifices he had to make.

Maximus felt a chill run down his spine, the weight of the riddle pressing down on him. The dark fortune had been a harbinger of the trials he now faced, a warning he had ignored in his haste. The realization filled him with a sense of dread and foreboding. He knew that the journey ahead would test him in ways he had never imagined, but he was resolved to see it through.

The warmth from the pulsating ball provided a small measure of comfort, driving away the chill of the cave. Maximus took a deep breath, the cool air filling his lungs, and steeled himself for the challenges ahead. The path to the Chamber of Souls was a test of flesh and bone, of mind and metal, but he was resolved to uncover its secrets and find the answers he sought.

The riddle had warned him of the cost, but it had also prepared him for the journey. With renewed resolve, he closed his eyes, letting the warmth and light lull him into a restless sleep, the promise of discovery and adventure guiding his dreams.

Maximus awoke with a start, his heart pounding in his chest. The warmth from the pulsating ball had faded, leaving the alcove in an eerie, dim light. The air was thick and oppressive, the scent of damp earth and minerals almost suffocating. As his eyes adjusted to the darkness, he saw a shadowy figure lurking at the edge of the light, its form indistinct and shrouded in darkness.

The dark specter seemed to glide towards him, its presence sending a chill down his spine. Maximus felt a wave of dread wash over him, the hairs on the back of his neck standing on end. The specter whispered in a voice that was both haunting and familiar, its words echoing in his mind:

"You will be like the skeleton man, lost and forgotten, buried in the depths of this cursed cave."

Maximus shivered, the specter's words filling him with a sense of impending doom. The vision of the man who had preceded him on this eerie quest became clearer with each visit. He saw the man, a fellow adventurer, driven by the same lust of fulfilling the elusive quest. The man had been determined, much like Maximus, but his journey had ended in tragedy.

The vision showed the man navigating the same labyrinthine passages, his face etched with determination and fear. Maximus saw him uncovering clues and solving riddles, each step bringing him closer to the Chamber of Souls. But the deeper he ventured, the more the cave seemed to conspire against him. The air grew colder, the passages narrower, and the dangers more insidious.

Maximus watched in horror as the vision revealed the man's untimely demise. The man had reached a point of no return, trapped in a narrow passage with no way forward or back. Exhausted and desperate, he had tried to force his way through, but the cave had claimed him. The rocks had shifted, trapping him in a deadly embrace.

As the man's breath left him, a wormhole opened within the cave, a swirling vortex of light and shadow. The man's lifeless body was pulled into the wormhole, disappearing into the void.

The vision shifted, showing the wormhole depositing the man's remains in the abandoned lot outside the convenience store. The skeleton lay hidden under the brush, a grim discovery waiting for the next poor victim.

Maximus tried to fight off the feeling that the remnants of the vision that had shown him the dangers, but it had also prepared him for the challenges ahead. He took a deep breath, the cool air filling his lungs, and steeled himself against the specter's words.

The warmth from the pulsating ball began to return, driving away the chill of the specter's presence. The light grew brighter, casting long shadows on the rocky walls. Maximus felt a sense of clarity and the chill of the remnant of his vision. He knew that the path to the Chamber of Souls was fraught with danger, but he was determined to uncover its secrets and find the answers he sought.

With renewed resolve, Maximus stood up, the specter faded into the darkness, its whispers growing fainter until they were nothing more than a distant echo. Maximus took one last look around the alcove, the vision of the man who had preceded him a stark reminder of the risks he faced.

Maximus forced himself onward, the light from the metal ball casting a warm glow that cut through the oppressive darkness of the cave. The air grew colder and more dense, threatening to suffocate him. The sounds of water dripping from the stalactites and the occasional rustle of unseen creatures echoed through the passages. The scurrying of some cave dweller in the distance of the tunnel caused a chill to run down his spine.

As he ventured deeper, the path grew narrower and more treacherous. The rocky terrain was uneven, and loose stones threatened to trip him with every step. The light from the ball flickering and flaring, casting eerie shadows on the walls, creating an almost surreal atmosphere. Maximus moved cautiously, his eyes scanning the surroundings for any signs of danger.

Finally, he reached the cove of snakes and bats. The air was thick with the musty scent of guano, and the sound of fluttering wings filled the chamber. Bats hung from the ceiling in clusters, their eyes reflecting the light from his headlamp with an eerie, red glow. The floor was littered with loose rocks and patches of moss, making each step a careful endeavor.

Maximus moved slowly, his eyes scanning the chamber for any signs of danger. The snakes were harder to spot, their sleek, sinuous bodies blending seamlessly with the rocky terrain. He could hear the faint hiss of their breath, the occasional rustle of scales against stone. The air was cool and damp, the scent of earth and decay almost overwhelming.

In the center of the chamber, he discovered a shallow pond filled with human bones. The sight was horrifying, a grim reminder of the fate that had befallen those who had ventured here before him. The bones were scattered haphazardly, some partially submerged in the murky water, others lying on the rocky shore. Skulls with empty eye sockets seemed to stare up at him, their silent screams echoing through the chamber.

Maximus felt a chill run down his spine, the weight of the scene pressing down on him. He knew that the journey was perilous, but the sight of the bones drove home the reality of the dangers he faced. He took a deep breath, the cool air filling his lungs, and steeled himself against the fear.

As he approached the edge of the pond, the light from the metal ball illuminated a large, intricately carved stone tablet partially submerged in the water. The surface was covered in ancient symbols and runes, each one telling a part of a larger story. Beneath the symbols, a long, cryptic riddle was inscribed:

"In the lair of serpents and the flight of bats, the path to the soul's chamber lies in the shadows cast. By the light of the moon and the stars' embrace, the hidden passage you must trace. Beware the bones that guard the way, for in their silence, the truth will sway. Seek the serpent's eye, where light and shadow meet, and the key to the chamber will be at your feet."

CHAPTER 5
ChamberThe of Souls

Maximus pondered the riddle, considering its meaning. The serpents' lair held secrets, and the path to the Chamber of Souls was hidden within the interplay of light and shadow. He made a detailed sketch of the tablet and recorded the riddle in his diary, determined to decipher its significance.

As he studied the carvings, the feeling of claustrophobia began to creep in. The walls of the cove seemed to close in around him, the air growing thicker and more oppressive. He took a deep breath, trying to steady his nerves, but the sensation was overwhelming. The light from the metal ball flickered, casting eerie shadows on the walls.

Suddenly, the dark specter appeared once more, its form shrouded in darkness. The specter loomed closer, its presence sending a wave of dread through Maximus. The voice was haunting and familiar, its words echoing in his mind:

"You seek the serpent's eye, but it will be your undoing. The path you tread is fraught with peril, and the serpents guard their secrets jealously. Turn back now, or you will share the fate of those who came before you."

Maximus stood at the edge of the shallow pond, the bones of unfortunate fortune hunters scattered around him like grim reminders of the cave's deadly nature. The air was thick with the filthy scent of decay as he choked back the urge to vomit, and the ultimate darkness that seemed to swallow the light within the cave.

Maximus stood at the edge of the shallow pond, the bones of unfortunate fortune hunters scattered around him like grim reminders of the cave's deadly nature. The air was thick with the musty scent of decay, and the oppressive darkness seemed to press in on him from all sides. The light from the metal ball and the jewel flickered, casting eerie shadows on the rocky walls.

Suddenly, the dark specter appeared once more, its form shrouded in darkness. The specter loomed closer, its presence sending a wave of dread through Maximus. The voice was haunting and familiar, its words echoing in his mind:

"You seek the serpent's eye, but it will be your undoing. The path you tread is fraught with peril, and the serpents guard their secrets jealously. Turn back now, or you will share the fate of those who came before you."

The specter raised a bony finger, pointing to the intricately carved stone tablet partially submerged in the murky water. The light from the metal ball illuminated the tablet, revealing the ancient symbols and runes etched into its surface. The specter began to weave a dark, cryptic tale, its voice filled with malice and foreboding:

"Long ago, another adventurer stood where you stand now, driven by the same desire for the lust of wealth and knowledge. He was determined to solve the riddle of the serpent's eye, believing it would lead him to the Chamber of Souls. He deciphered the symbols and thought he had found the key, but he was gravely mistaken."

The vision shifted, showing the adventurer as he navigated the same labyrinthine passages. His face was wracked with fear, his eyes fixed on the stone tablet before him. The adventurer reached out to touch the serpent's eye, convinced he had solved the riddle. As his fingers brushed the symbol, a dark curse was unleashed.

The specter continued, its voice dripping with sinister delight:

"The curse took hold of him, twisting his mind and body. He was consumed by visions of horror, his senses overwhelmed by the darkness that seeped into his soul. He saw the faces of those who had perished before him, their eyes filled with despair and agony. The cave itself seemed to come alive, the walls closing in around him, the air growing thick and putrid."

Maximus watched in horror as the vision showed the adventurer's descent into madness. The man stumbled through the passages flailing his arms at the invisible spiders that assailed him, his mind unraveling with each step. He tried to escape, but the worms and the serpents were quickly upon him. The specter's laughter echoed through the chamber, a chilling sound like needles of ice down Maximus's spine.

He pulled out his diary, the map, and the scroll, spreading them out on a flat rock near the pond. The light from the metal ball illuminated the pages, revealing the intricate symbols and notes he had collected along his journey. Maximus knew that the key to solving the riddle of the serpent's eye lay within these clues.

The riddle inscribed on the stone tablet echoed in his mind:

"In the lair of serpents and the flight of bats, the path to the soul's chamber lies in the shadows cast. By the light of the moon and the stars' embrace, the hidden passage you must trace. Beware the bones that guard the way, for in their silence, the truth will sway. Seek the serpent's eye, where light and shadow meet, and the key to the chamber will be at your feet."

Maximus studied the symbols and notes, piecing together the fragments of the puzzle. The first part of the riddle spoke of the lair of serpents and the flight of bats, indicating that the clues were hidden within this very chamber. He recalled the intricate carvings on the walls, each one depicting scenes of ancient rituals and mysterious symbols.

The second part of the riddle mentioned the light of the moon and the stars' embrace, suggesting that the interplay of light and shadow was crucial to revealing the hidden passage. Maximus adjusted the light from the metal ball, casting it at different angles to see how the shadows shifted on the rocky walls.

As he moved the light, he noticed that the shadows formed patterns, aligning with the symbols on the stone tablet. The bones scattered around the pond seemed to play a role as well, their positions casting specific shadows that interacted with the carvings. Maximus realized that the bones were not just grim reminders of past adventurers but also integral to solving the riddle.

The third part of the riddle warned of the bones that guarded the way, indicating that their arrangement held the key to the hidden passage. Maximus carefully examined the positions of the bones, noting how their shadows aligned with the symbols on the walls. He adjusted the light from the metal ball, casting it in such a way that the shadows of the bones and the carvings formed a cohesive pattern.

Finally, the riddle spoke of seeking the serpent's eye, where light and shadow met. Maximus focused on the serpent symbol carved into the stone tablet. He adjusted the light one last time, casting it directly onto the serpent's eye. The shadows shifted, revealing a hidden symbol that had been invisible before—a small, intricately carved key.

Maximus reached out, his fingers brushing the hidden symbol. As he did, the ground beneath him trembled, and a section of the rocky wall began to shift. The hidden passage to the Chamber of Souls was revealed, a narrow tunnel that descended into the depths of the cave.

The specter's voice echoed in his mind, its tone filled with malice and foreboding:

"You have solved the riddle, but the path ahead is fraught with peril. The Chamber of Souls holds secrets that will test your very soul. Proceed if you dare, but know that the cave will not easily relinquish its treasures."

With the hidden passage revealed, Maximus packed away his diary, map, ball and scroll, ensuring they were secure in his backpack. He took one last look around the cove, and descended into the dark passage that led to the Chamber of Souls.

As he moved, he had to put his hands upon the walls of the narrow tunnel to keep himself upright as he had to crouch traversing the tunnel, the vacuum of darkness here seemed to consume the light, causing him to second guess his movements. Maximus was wary to press on, not sure if there was a precipice looming before him that would send him plummeting to some dark pit below and a sure death.

After what felt like an eternity, the passage opened up into a vast chamber. Maximus stood at the entrance, his eyes widening in awe and horror at the sight before him. The Chamber of Souls was immense, its ceiling lost in the darkness above. The walls were covered in intricate carvings, depicting scenes of ancient rituals and sacrifices. The air was thick with the scent of decay and the faint, metallic tang of blood.

The floor of the chamber was littered with bones, the remains of those who had ventured here before him. Human Skulls half crushed and spinal columns littered the path to the stone altar.

There was the sense of a dark presence that lurked in the shadows, Maximus squinted as he attempted to scan the edges of the dark chamber.

In the center of the chamber stood a massive stone altar, its surface stained with dark, dried blood. The altar was surrounded by a circle of ancient runes, each one glowing faintly with an otherworldly light. Maximus felt a pressing sense of doom surrounding him.

As he stepped further into the chamber, the light from the metal ball illuminated a series of statues lining the walls. The statues were grotesque, their features twisted and contorted in expressions of agony and despair. Each statue held a different pose, their hands reaching out as if pleading for mercy. The sight was horrifying, a grim reminder of the fate that awaited those who failed the quest.

Maximus approached the altar, his heart pounding in his chest. The air grew colder, and the light from the metal ball flickered more intensely. He could feel a presence in the chamber, a malevolent force that seemed to watch his every move. The specter's voice echoed in his mind, its tone filled with malice and foreboding:

"You have entered the Chamber of Souls, but it will be your doom. The souls of the damned are trapped here, their agony eternal. Turn back now, or you will join them in their torment."

As he examined the altar, he noticed a series of symbols carved into its surface. The symbols matched those he had seen in the diary and the scroll, each one a piece of the larger puzzle. Maximus carefully traced the symbols with his fingers, feeling the rough texture of the stone beneath his touch.

Determined to uncover the secrets hidden within the chamber, Maximus began to search the grotesque statues that lined the walls. Each statue was twisted and contorted in expressions of agony and despair, their features frozen in eternal torment. The sight was horrifying, but Maximus knew that the clues he sought were hidden within these stone sentinels.

He approached the first statue, a figure with its hands raised in a pleading gesture. The light from the metal ball illuminated the statue's surface, revealing intricate carvings and symbols etched into the stone. Maximus carefully examined the statue, his fingers tracing the rough texture of the carvings. He found a hidden symbol near the base, a small, intricate design that matched the ones he had seen in the diary and the scroll.

As he moved to the next statue, the hissing sounds grew louder, echoing through the chamber like the whispers of malevolent spirits. The air grew colder, and Maximus could feel the weight of the darkness pressing down on him. He steeled himself against the fear, focusing on the task at hand.

The second statue was even more grotesque, its features twisted in a grimace of pain. Maximus examined the statue carefully, his eyes scanning the surface for any hidden symbols. He found another clue, a series of runes carved into the statue's arm. The runes glowed faintly with an otherworldly light, their meaning just beyond his grasp.

The hissing grew more insistent, a sinister chorus that seemed to come from all directions. Maximus felt a chill run down his spine, the air growing colder and more oppressive. He moved to the third statue, a figure with its head bowed in sorrow. The light from the metal ball revealed a hidden compartment in the statue's chest, a small door that opened to reveal a carved key.

Maximus carefully took the key, feeling its weight in his hand. The key was intricately designed, covered in ancient runes that matched the symbols he had seen throughout the cave. He knew that this key was crucial to unlocking the secrets of the Chamber of Souls.

As he continued his search, the hissing sounds grew louder, filling the chamber with an almost tangible sense of malevolence. The darkness seemed to close in around him, the shadows growing longer and more menacing. Maximus felt a surge of fear, but he was determined to see his quest through to the end.

He approached the final statue, a figure with its arms outstretched as if reaching for something just out of reach. The light from the metal ball illuminated the statue's surface, revealing a hidden symbol on its back. The symbol glowed with an eerie light, casting strange shadows on the rocky walls.

Determined to uncover the secrets hidden within the chamber, Maximus began to study the three long, cryptic riddles he had discovered. Each riddle was inscribed on a different statue, their dark nature adding to the sense of foreboding that filled the chamber. He knew that two of the riddles were false clues, designed to mislead him, while one held the key to solving the chamber's secret.

The first riddle was inscribed on the statue of a figure with its hands raised in a pleading gesture. The words were etched deeply into the stone, their meaning shrouded in mystery:

"In shadows deep where serpents lie, the path to truth is but a lie. Seek the light that never fades, and find the key in darkest shades. Beware the whispers in the night, for they will lead you from the light."

Maximus pondered the riddle, considering its meaning. The mention of shadows and serpents seemed to align with the chamber's dark nature, but something about the riddle felt off. The warning about whispers in the night seemed designed to sow doubt and confusion. He made a note of the riddle, but he suspected it was one of the false clues.

The second riddle was carved into the statue of a figure with its head bowed in sorrow. The words were written in an elegant, flowing script, their meaning equally cryptic:

"By the light of the moon and stars, the path to truth is never far. Seek the heart where shadows play, and find the key to light the way. Beware the bones that guard the gate, for they will lead you to your fate."

This riddle also spoke of light and shadows, but the mention of the moon and stars seemed to contradict the chamber's oppressive darkness. The warning about the bones guarding the gate felt like a deliberate attempt to mislead. Maximus made a note of the riddle, but he remained skeptical of its validity.

The third riddle was inscribed on the statue of a figure with its arms outstretched, reaching for something just out of reach. The words were etched with precision, their meaning dark and foreboding:

"In the heart of darkness, where shadows creep, the serpent's eye holds secrets deep. By the light of the stars' embrace, the hidden passage you must trace. Seek the eye where light and shadow meet, and the key to the chamber will be at your feet."

Maximus felt a chill run deep in his spine, the hair on his neck bristled as he read the third riddle. The mention of the serpent's eye and the interplay of light and shadow resonated with the clues he had gathered so far. The riddle's dark nature and the warning about the hidden passage seemed to align with the chamber's secrets. He suspected that this was the true riddle, the key to solving the chamber's secret.

With the three riddles recorded in his diary, Maximus carefully considered each one. The first two riddles seemed designed to mislead, their warnings and contradictions creating doubt and confusion. The third riddle, however, felt different. Its dark nature and the mention of the serpent's eye aligned with the clues he had gathered, and he felt a sense of clarity and purpose.

Maximus stood in the dimly lit Chamber of Souls, the air thick with an ancient, almost tangible tension. The walls, adorned with cryptic symbols and faded murals, seemed to whisper secrets long forgotten. In his hand, he held the three dark riddles, each one a twisted enigma that promised to reveal the location of the hidden keys.

As he pondered the first riddle, a gentle, ethereal voice began to guide his thoughts. "Seek the light within the shadow," it whispered, its tone soothing and wise. Maximus scanned the chamber, his eyes darting from one shadowy corner to another, searching for any clue that might lead him to the first key. His gaze settled on a faint glimmer beneath a pile of ancient bones. With a careful hand, he unearthed the first key, its surface cold and smooth, shaped like a serpent coiled around a dagger.

The second riddle spoke of "the heart of stone that beats with fire." The voice, ever patient, urged him to look deeper. Maximus approached the altar, its base carved from a single massive stone. He traced his fingers along the intricate carvings until he felt a warmth emanating from a hidden compartment. Inside, he found the second key, a small, intricately designed heart made of obsidian, pulsing with an inner glow.

As he deciphered the final riddle, "the silent scream of the forgotten," the voice grew more insistent, guiding him to a shadowed alcove where the third key lay hidden. This key was a simple iron rod, unadorned but heavy with the weight of ages.

Maximus approached the altar, knowing that only one key would fit the keyhole at its base. As he deliberated, a malevolent voice slithered into his mind, its tone dripping with deceit. "Choose wisely, Maximus," it hissed. "The serpent's key will unlock the power you seek. The heart of stone is but a trinket, and the iron rod a fool's choice."

The specter's voice grew louder, more insistent:

"The altar holds the keyhole to the Chamber of Souls, but it will also be your undoing. The curse of the cave is strong, and it will consume you if you are not careful. Proceed if you dare, but know that the cave will not easily relinquish its treasures."

Maximus hesitated, the malevolent voice sowing seeds of doubt. He knew that choosing the wrong key would unleash a terrible fate. The chamber would collapse, entombing him forever in darkness, or worse, the souls trapped within would consume his very essence, leaving him a hollow shell like the statues in this very chamber.

Drawing a deep breath, Maximus silenced the malevolent voice and trusted the gentle guidance that had led him this far. He selected the heart of stone, its warmth a beacon of hope. As he inserted it into the keyhole, the chamber trembled, and the altar began to glow with a radiant light, revealing the true path forward.

Maximus carefully noted the symbol in his diary, the pieces of the puzzle slowly coming together. The hissing sounds reached a crescendo, a sinister symphony that filled the chamber with an almost palpable sense of dread.

Suddenly, the ground beneath him trembled, and a hidden compartment in the altar opened. Inside, he found a small keyhole. The keyhole was surrounded by ancient runes, each one glowing faintly with an odd light. Maximus carefully lifted the keys, feeling their weight in his hands.

The specter's voice grew louder, more insistent:

"The altar holds the keyhole to the path to the gate beyond the Chamber of Souls, but it will also be your undoing. The curse of the cave is strong, and it will consume you if you are not careful. Proceed if you dare, but know that the gate will not easily relinquish its treasures."

CHAPTER 6
THE GATE OF DESTINY

As the altar slid away with a deep, resonant rumble, Maximus found himself staring into a newly revealed chamber. The room was vast, its ceiling lost in shadows, and the air was thick with the scent of ancient stone and forgotten souls. At the far end stood a large, imposing gate, its surface covered in intricate carvings and symbols that seemed to shift and change when viewed from different angles.

The chamber was dimly lit by flickering torches mounted on the walls, casting eerie shadows that danced and twisted. The floor was a mosaic of tiles, each depicting scenes of triumph and tragedy, hinting at the trials that lay ahead. As Maximus stepped forward, he noticed several pressure plates scattered across the floor, some marked with symbols that matched those on the gate.

To his left, a series of statues lined the wall, each one holding a different object: a sword, a shield, a scroll, and a chalice. Inscribed at the base of each statue was a riddle, their answers seemingly tied to the objects they held. Maximus knew that solving these riddles would be crucial to unlocking the gate.

The first riddle read: "I am not alive, but I grow; I do not have lungs, but I need air; I do not have a mouth, but water kills me. What am I?" Maximus pondered for a moment before realizing the answer was "fire." He carefully took the torch from the wall and placed it in the hand of the statue holding the sword, which immediately began to glow with a warm light.

The second riddle was more cryptic: "I speak without a mouth and hear without ears. I have no body, but I come alive with wind. What am I?" After some thought, Maximus deduced the answer was "an echo." He whispered into the ear of the statue holding the scroll, and the scroll unfurled, revealing a hidden compartment with a key inside.

Maximus stood before the mosaic tiles, their intricate patterns forming a labyrinthine path to the gate. Each tile was a piece of a larger puzzle, depicting scenes of ancient battles, mythical creatures, and celestial events. He knew that one wrong step could trigger the deadly traps hidden within the chamber.

As he studied the tiles, he noticed subtle differences in their designs. Some tiles had faint, almost imperceptible markings that seemed to glow under the flickering torchlight. The gentle voice that had guided him earlier whispered once more, "Follow the path of light, Maximus. Trust your instincts."

Maximus took a deep breath and stepped onto the first glowing tile. The chamber remained silent, and he felt a surge of confidence. He continued, carefully placing his feet on the illuminated tiles, each step bringing him closer to the gate. The path twisted and turned, leading him through a maze of potential dangers.

Halfway through, he encountered a series of pressure plates, each one connected to a different trap. He knew he needed to solve this puzzle to proceed safely. Reaching into his satchel, he retrieved a small, spherical object—a ball he had found earlier in his journey. The ball was covered in strange runes and symbols, and he had yet to discover its true purpose.

Holding the ball in his hand, Maximus felt a sudden warmth emanate from it. The runes began to glow, and a holographic display projected from the ball, casting a map of the chamber onto the floor. The map highlighted the safe path through the pressure plates, revealing the locations of the hidden traps.

With the guidance of the ball, Maximus navigated the treacherous terrain, avoiding the arrows, pits, and creeping mist that lay in wait. Each step was precise, each movement calculated. The ball's display provided real-time updates, showing him the safest route to the gate.

As he reached the final stretch, the ball emitted a soft chime, and the display shifted to reveal a hidden mechanism within the gate. Maximus approached the gate, using the ball to decipher the final puzzle. He aligned the symbols on the gate with those on the ball, and with a satisfying click, the gate began to open.

Beyond the gate, a dazzling array of treasures awaited him. Gold coins, glittering jewels, and ancient artifacts filled the chamber, but it was the knowledge contained within the scrolls and tomes that truly captivated him. Maximus knew that these secrets would be invaluable in his quest, providing him with the wisdom and power needed to face the challenges ahead.

With the ball still glowing in his hand, Maximus stepped into the treasure chamber, ready to uncover the mysteries that lay within.

As he solved each riddle, the room seemed to come alive, the symbols on the gate glowing brighter with each correct answer. However, the chamber was not without its dangers. Hidden traps lay in wait for the unwary: arrows that shot from the walls, pits that opened beneath his feet, and a creeping mist that sapped his strength if he lingered too long.

Finally, with all the riddles solved and the keys in hand, Maximus approached the gate. He inserted the keys into the corresponding locks, and with a loud, grinding noise, the gate began to open.

Beyond it lay a treasure trove of unimaginable wealth: piles of gold coins, glittering jewels, and ancient artifacts of immense power. But more valuable than the riches was the knowledge contained within the chamber—scrolls and tomes that held the secrets of the ancients, waiting to be discovered by those brave enough to seek them.

Maximus knew that his journey was far from over, but with the treasures and knowledge he had gained, he felt more prepared than ever to face the challenges that lay ahead.

Maximus stood in awe, taking in the sheer volume of scrolls that lined the walls of the treasure chamber. He began to count them, his fingers tracing the edges of the ancient parchments. There were fifty scrolls in total, each one meticulously preserved and bound with ribbons of various colors, indicating their different subjects and origins.

He carefully selected a scroll bound with a deep blue ribbon, intrigued by its mysterious aura. As he unrolled it, the parchment crackled softly, releasing a faint scent of aged paper and ink. The scroll was covered in intricate, flowing script, written in a language that seemed both familiar and arcane.

The gentle voice that had guided him earlier whispered once more, "This scroll holds the secrets of the lost city of Eldoria, Maximus. Read carefully."

Maximus's eyes scanned the text, absorbing the detailed descriptions of Eldoria's grand architecture, its hidden passages, and the powerful artifacts that lay within its walls. The scroll also contained a map, drawn with exquisite precision, showing the city's layout and the locations of its most guarded treasures.

As he read, the room seemed to come alive with the history of Eldoria. He could almost hear the bustling streets, the clinking of blacksmiths' hammers, and the whispers of scholars in their grand libraries. The scroll spoke of a time when Eldoria was a beacon of knowledge and power, its people revered for their wisdom and ingenuity.

Maximus felt a surge of excitement and determination. The knowledge contained within this scroll was invaluable, a key to unlocking even greater mysteries and treasures. He carefully rolled the scroll back up and placed it on the great bench where the scrolls were stored.

With a great thirst to reveal the knowledge of the other scrolls, Maximus turned his attention to the other scrolls and started to number them and place them in order.

Maximus carefully numbered each scroll, ensuring they could be easily identified and read separately. Here is the list of the scrolls, numbered from one to fifty:

1:Scroll of Eldoria - Secrets of the lost city.

2:Scroll of Arcane Spells - Powerful incantations.

3:Scroll of Ancient Maps - Detailed maps of forgotten lands.

4:Scroll of Alchemy - Formulas for potions and elixirs.

5:Scroll of Mythical Creatures - Descriptions and lore.

6:Scroll of Battle Tactics - Strategies of ancient warriors.

7:Scroll of Celestial Events - Records of astronomical phenomena.

8:Scroll of Healing Arts - Techniques for healing and medicine.

9:Scroll of Enchanted Weapons - Crafting and enchantment methods.

10:Scroll of Lost Languages - Deciphering ancient scripts.

11:Scroll of Elemental Magic - Control over natural elements.

12:Scroll of Legendary Heroes - Tales of great champions.

13:Scroll of Forbidden Knowledge - Dark and dangerous secrets.

14:Scroll of Sacred Rituals - Ceremonies and rites.

15:Scroll of Hidden Passages - Secret routes and tunnels.

16:Scroll of Divine Prophecies - Predictions of the future.

17:Scroll of Ancient Artifacts - Descriptions and powers.

18:Scroll of Mystical Beasts - Encounters and taming.

19:Scroll of Time Travel - Theories and methods.

20:Scroll of Elemental Guardians - Protectors of nature.

21:Scroll of Ancient Civilizations - Histories and cultures.

22:Scroll of Celestial Navigation - Guiding by the stars.

23:Scroll of Enchanted Forests - Mysteries and inhabitants.

24:Scroll of Legendary Battles - Accounts of epic conflicts.

25:Scroll of Ancient Runes - Symbols and meanings.

26:Scroll of Sacred Geometry - Patterns and significance.

27:Scroll of Lost Kingdoms - Tales of vanished realms.

28:Scroll of Magical Creatures - Abilities and habitats.

29:Scroll of Ancient Seers - Visions and insights.

30:Scroll of Elemental Forces - Harnessing natural power.

31:Scroll of Legendary Artifacts - Items of great power.

32:Scroll of Ancient Myths - Stories and legends.

33:Scroll of Celestial Beings - Angels and divine entities.

34:Scroll of Forbidden Spells - Dangerous incantations.

35:Scroll of Sacred Texts - Religious writings.

36:Scroll of Hidden Treasures - Maps and clues.

37:Scroll of Ancient Wisdom - Philosophies and teachings.

38:Scroll of Mystical Lands - Descriptions of magical places.

39:Scroll of Legendary Weapons - Famous arms and armor.

40:Scroll of Elemental Spirits - Beings of nature.

41:Scroll of Ancient Prophecies - Predictions and outcomes.

42:Scroll of Enchanted Items - Objects with magical properties.

43:Scroll of Celestial Alignments - Astrological events.

44:Scroll of Ancient Guardians - Protectors of the past.

45:Scroll of Mystical Arts - Techniques and practices.

46:Scroll of Legendary Creatures - Beasts of myth.

47:Scroll of Forbidden Knowledge II - More dark secrets.

48:Scroll of Sacred Relics - Holy artifacts.

49:Scroll of Hidden Realms - Parallel worlds and dimensions.

50:Scroll of Ancient Secrets - Lost and hidden knowledge.

Maximus felt a sense of accomplishment as he finished numbering the scrolls. Each one held a wealth of knowledge and potential, waiting to be explored. He carefully selected the first scroll, the Scroll of Eldoria, and unrolled it once more, eager to delve deeper into its secrets. The parchment crackled softly as he read, the ancient script revealing the hidden wonders and dangers of the lost city.

Maximus stood in the treasure chamber, surrounded by the wealth and knowledge of ages past. Despite the allure of the treasures, he knew he needed to find a way out. The air was still and heavy, the only sound the faint crackling of the torches on the walls.

He began his search methodically, starting with the walls. Running his hands over the ancient stone, he felt for any irregularities or hidden mechanisms. The walls were adorned with intricate carvings and symbols, some of which seemed to tell stories of the chamber's creation and the guardians who once protected it.

As he moved along the wall, he noticed a section where the carvings were slightly different. The symbols here were more worn, as if they had been touched many times before. Maximus pressed against the stone, and to his surprise, it shifted slightly under his hand. He pushed harder, and a hidden panel slid open, revealing a narrow passageway.

The passage was dark and foreboding, but Maximus felt a cool breeze coming from within, a sign that it might lead to the outside. He took a torch from the wall and stepped into the passage, the flickering light casting eerie shadows on the rough stone walls.

The passageway was narrow and winding, with several twists and turns. As he moved deeper, he encountered a series of traps designed to deter intruders. Using the ball's holographic display, he carefully navigated the traps, avoiding pressure plates and hidden spikes.

After what felt like an eternity, the passage began to slope upward. The air grew fresher, and the sound of distant birdsong reached his ears. Maximus quickened his pace, eager to reach the surface. Finally, he saw a faint light ahead, growing brighter with each step.

He emerged into a small, hidden glade, the sunlight filtering through the trees above. The glade was peaceful and serene, a stark contrast to the dark, oppressive chamber below. Maximus took a deep breath, savoring the fresh air and the feeling of freedom.

Standing in the tranquil glade, Maximus took a moment to appreciate the serene beauty around him. The sunlight filtered through the canopy of leaves, casting dappled patterns on the forest floor. Birds chirped melodiously, and a gentle breeze rustled the foliage, creating a symphony of nature's sounds.

Maximus turned back to the hidden entrance, a cleverly disguised door that blended seamlessly with the surrounding rock. With a firm push, he closed the outer door, sealing the passageway from the outside world. The sound of the door sliding shut echoed softly, a reminder of the ancient mechanisms at work.

He took a deep breath, steeling himself for the descent back into the treasure chamber. The cool, damp air of the passageway greeted him as he stepped inside, the torchlight flickering and casting long shadows on the rough stone walls. The winding stairway seemed to spiral endlessly, each step taking him deeper into the earth.

As he descended, the air grew heavier, filled with the scent of aged stone and the faint, metallic tang of ancient treasures. The walls were adorned with more carvings, depicting scenes of guardians and protectors, their eyes seeming to follow him as he moved.

Finally, Maximus reached the bottom of the stairway and stepped back into the treasure chamber. The golden glow of the treasures greeted him once more, the piles of gold coins and precious jewels shimmering in the torchlight. The scrolls, carefully numbered and arranged, awaited his further exploration.

Maximus carefully retrieved the softball-sized metal ball from his backpack, its surface covered in intricate symbols and images that seemed to pulse with a faint, otherworldly light. He placed it gently on the bench, next to the jewel that sparkled with an inner fire. The two objects, side by side, seemed to resonate with each other, their combined presence filling the chamber with a subtle hum of energy.

With a determined look, Maximus turned and made his way back through the Chamber of Souls. The dim light and eerie whispers of the chamber seemed almost welcoming now, a familiar part of his journey. He moved swiftly, his steps confident as he navigated the ancient hallways.

Entering the cave of bats and snakes, he was greeted by the unsettling sounds of fluttering wings and the hiss of serpents. The cave was a labyrinth of shadows and hidden dangers, but Maximus knew the way. He carefully closed the entrance to the Chamber of Souls, ensuring it was sealed tight. The ancient mechanisms clicked into place, the stone door blending seamlessly with the cave wall.

Next, he moved to the outer entrance of the cave. The path was treacherous, but Maximus's resolve was unwavering. He closed the entrance, the heavy stone door sliding shut with a deep, resonant thud. The cave was now sealed from the outside, the way he had come effectively hidden from any who might follow.

Returning to the treasure chamber, Maximus felt a sense of accomplishment. He had successfully reset all the secret passages, ensuring that the chamber remained hidden and protected. The treasures and knowledge within were now secure, waiting for the right moment to be revealed.

Standing in the treasure chamber once more, Maximus took a deep breath. The journey had been long and arduous, but he had achieved his goal. The chamber was now a sanctuary, a place where he could study the scrolls and artifacts in peace, preparing for the challenges that lay ahead.

As Maximus stood in the treasure chamber, surrounded by the wealth and knowledge of ages past, a sudden and overwhelming urgency gripped his heart. The treasures and ancient secrets, once so alluring, now seemed insignificant compared to the pressing need to reunite with his family. His thoughts turned to Emily, his beloved wife, lying in a hospital bed, and to his children, Sarah and Michael, who were now wards of the state. He could almost feel the soft fur of Max, their loyal golden retriever, who had been a source of comfort and joy in their darkest times.

Maximus knew that the journey ahead would be long and arduous, but the thought of seeing his family again gave him the strength he needed. He carefully gathered the scrolls and artifacts he had selected, placing them securely in his satchel. With one last look at the treasures he was leaving behind, he filled his backpack with a goodly amount of jewels, knowing they would be invaluable in supporting his family through the difficult times ahead.

With his preparations complete, Maximus turned and made his way back through the winding passageways. He ascended the stair into the glade, the cool, damp air of the passageway giving way to the fresh, invigorating breeze of the forest. As he stepped into the glade, he took a moment to make note of the secret door that led back to the treasure chamber, ensuring he could find it again if needed. The hidden entrance blended seamlessly with the surrounding rock, a testament to the ancient craftsmanship that had created it.

Maximus carefully closed the outer door behind him, sealing the passageway from the outside world. The sound of the door sliding shut echoed softly, a reminder of the ancient mechanisms at work. He stood in the glade, the sunlight filtering through the canopy of leaves, casting dappled patterns on the forest floor. Birds chirped melodiously, and a gentle breeze rustled the foliage, creating a symphony of nature's sounds.

With a determined look, Maximus set off through the dense forest, his mind focused on the journey ahead. The thought of Emily's smile, Sarah and Michael's laughter, and Max's wagging tail spurred him on, each step bringing him closer to the reunion he so desperately needed.

As he navigated the forest, he thought about the healing process that lay ahead. Their lives had fallen apart, but he was determined to piece them back together. He would be there for Emily, supporting her through her recovery. He would fight to bring Sarah and Michael home, to give them the stability and love they deserved. And he would make sure Max was by their side, a symbol of the family bond that could never be broken.

Maximus knew that the road to healing would be long and challenging, but with the strength of his love for his family and the knowledge he had gained, he felt ready to face whatever lay ahead. The journey had only just begun, but he was determined to see it through, to rebuild their lives and find redemption in the love and unity of his family.

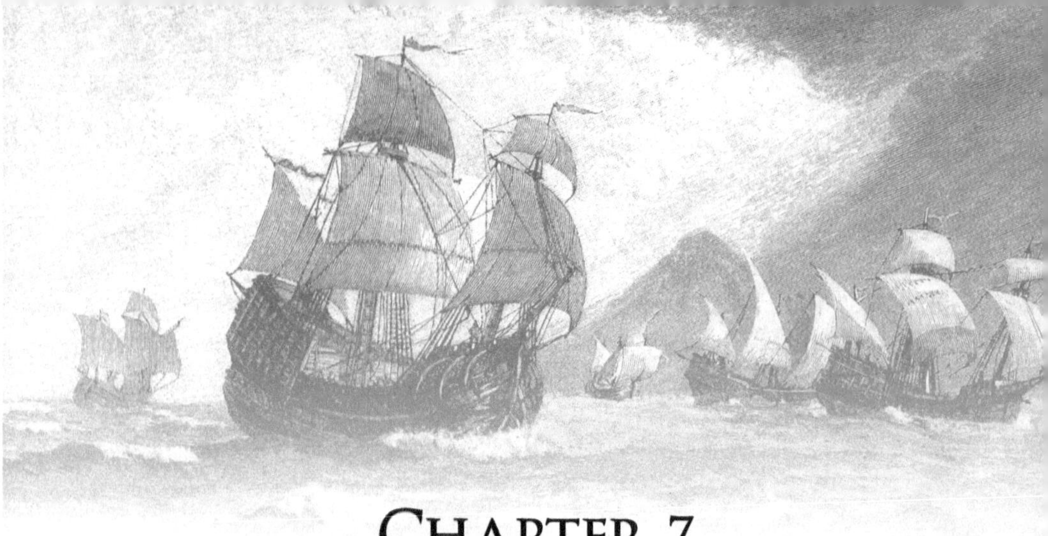

CHAPTER 7
THE RETURN

Maximus made his way carefully out of the dense forest, marking his path with small, discreet symbols on the trees to ensure he could find his way back if needed. The journey was arduous, but the thought of reuniting with his family kept him moving forward with determination.

Emerging from the forest, he found himself on the outskirts of Bourbonnais, Illinois. His first priority was to get cleaned up and buy some new clothes. He headed to Kohl's, a well-known department store in the area, where he found a variety of clothing. After a refreshing shower and a change into clean clothes, he felt more like himself, ready to tackle the next steps of his plan.

With his appearance restored, Maximus sought out a place to sell the jewels he had carefully selected from the treasure chamber. He made his way to Broadway Jewelry & Rare Coins in nearby Bradley, about 2.5 miles walking. The jewelry and rare coin store is well known for buying and selling precious items. The staff there were helpful and professional, offering him a fair price for the jewels. The transaction provided him with the funds he needed for the next part of his journey.

Maximus stood outside Broadway Jewelry & Rare Coins, the sun casting long shadows across the storefront. The building was modest but well-kept, with a large sign displaying the store's name in elegant, gold lettering. The windows showcased an array of glittering jewelry and rare coins, hinting at the treasures within.

Taking a deep breath, Maximus pushed open the door and stepped inside. The interior was cool and inviting, with glass display cases lining the walls, each filled with an assortment of precious items. The soft hum of an air conditioner provided a soothing backdrop to the quiet murmur of customers browsing the store.

A friendly clerk behind the counter greeted him with a warm smile. "Good afternoon! How can I help you today?"

Maximus approached the counter, his backpack slung over one shoulder. "I have some jewels I'd like to sell," he said, placing the bag on the counter and carefully opening it to reveal the glittering contents.

The clerk's eyes widened slightly at the sight of the jewels. "These are quite impressive," she remarked, her tone professional yet intrigued. "Let me call our appraiser to take a look."

A few moments later, an older gentleman with a keen eye and a magnifying glass joined them. He introduced himself as Mr. Thompson, the store's expert appraiser. Maximus watched as Mr. Thompson meticulously examined each jewel, his practiced hands moving with precision and care.

After a thorough inspection, Mr. Thompson looked up, his expression thoughtful. "These are indeed valuable pieces," he said. "We can certainly make you an offer, but it will depend on whether you're looking to sell them all at once or in smaller lots."

Maximus considered the question. "I'd prefer to sell them all at once if possible," he replied. "I need the funds urgently."

Mr. Thompson nodded. "Understood. Let me calculate a fair price for the entire collection." He stepped away to consult with his colleagues and review the store's current inventory and budget.

After a few minutes, he returned with a proposal. "We can offer you $150,000 for the entire collection," he said. "This is a fair market value based on the quality and rarity of the jewels."

Maximus felt a wave of relief wash over him. The amount was more than enough to support his immediate needs and help his family. "That sounds fair," he agreed, shaking Mr. Thompson's hand to seal the deal.

The transaction was completed smoothly, with the store handling the paperwork and transferring the funds to Maximus. As he left Broadway Jewelry & Rare Coins, he felt a renewed sense of purpose and determination. With the funds secured, he was ready to continue his journey to Springfield and begin the long process of healing and rebuilding his family's life.

As he drove out of Bourbonnais, the road ahead seemed filled with promise. The urgency to see Emily, Sarah, Michael, and Max Maximus stood outside Broadway Jewelry & Rare Coins, the sun casting long shadows across the storefront. With the transaction complete and the jewels sold, he felt a renewed sense of purpose. He hailed a cab from Timely Cab Services1, a reliable local company, and soon found himself on the way to the jeep dealership.

The cab ride was smooth, the driver navigating the streets of Bourbonnais with ease. Maximus watched the town pass by, his mind already on the next steps of his journey. The cab pulled up to Taylor Chrysler Jeep Dodge2, a well-known dealership in the area.

Stepping out of the cab, Maximus took in the scene. The dealership was bustling with activity, rows of shiny new vehicles gleaming under the afternoon sun. Salespeople moved between customers, their voices a mix of friendly chatter and professional advice.

Maximus walked into the showroom, the cool air conditioning a welcome relief from the summer heat. A friendly salesperson approached him with a warm smile. "Good afternoon! How can I assist you today?"

"I'm looking to buy a jeep," Maximus replied, his tone decisive. "I need something reliable for a long drive."

"Of course," the salesperson said, gesturing for Maximus to follow. "We have a great selection of Jeeps. Let me show you some of our best models."

They walked through the lot, stopping at a sleek, black Jeep Grand Cherokee. The salesperson detailed its features: powerful engine, advanced safety systems, and comfortable interior. Maximus nodded, impressed by the vehicle's capabilities.

After a thorough inspection and a test drive, Maximus felt confident in his choice. They returned to the showroom to finalize the purchase. The paperwork was straightforward, and with the funds from the jewel sale, the transaction was completed smoothly.

With keys in hand, Maximus thanked the salesperson and headed to his new Jeep. As he settled into the driver's seat, he felt a sense of readiness. The road to Springfield lay ahead, and with this newly purchased vehicle, he was finally closer to reuniting with his family and beginning the healing process.

He started the engine, the powerful hum of the Jeep filling him with confidence. As he drove out of the dealership, the sun began to set, casting a golden glow over the landscape. The journey to Springfield had begun, and Maximus was filled with emotion as he started his drive home. He knew that the journey to Springfield was just the beginning of the long healing process that awaited his family.

As Maximus drove the Jeep Grand Cherokee out of Bourbonnais, the sun dipped below the horizon, painting the sky in hues of orange and pink. The road stretched out before him, a ribbon of asphalt leading to Springfield and the family he longed to reunite with. The hum of the engine was a comforting constant, a reminder of the progress he was making.

The journey was a blend of emotions, each mile bringing a new wave of memories and feelings. He thought back to the treasure chamber, the ancient scrolls, and the riddles he had solved. The sense of accomplishment was tempered by the urgency to see his family, to hold them close and begin the healing process.

As he drove, the landscape changed from the bustling town to the serene countryside. Fields of corn and soybeans stretched out on either side, the occasional farmhouse dotting the horizon. The rhythmic passing of the scenery was almost hypnotic, giving Maximus time to reflect on his ordeal.

He remembered the moment he found the treasure chamber, the thrill of discovery mingled with the weight of responsibility. The ancient knowledge and artifacts he had uncovered were invaluable, but they paled in comparison to the importance of his family. The jewels he had sold would provide the financial support they needed, but it was the emotional and physical presence that mattered most.

Maximus's thoughts turned to Emily, his wife, lying in a hospital bed. He could picture her smile, the way her eyes lit up when she saw him. He knew that her recovery would be a long and difficult journey, but he was determined to be by her side every step of the way. He would support her, encourage her, and help her regain her strength.

His children, Sarah and Michael, were now wards of the state, a situation that tore at his heart. He remembered their laughter, their playful antics, and the way they looked up to him with trust and love. He vowed to fight for their return, to provide them with the stability and love they deserved. He would work tirelessly to prove that he could be the father they needed, to bring them home and restore their sense of security.

And then there was Max, their beloved golden retriever. The loyal companion who had been a source of comfort and joy in their darkest times. Maximus could almost feel the dog's soft fur and see his wagging tail. He knew that Max would be a crucial part of their healing process, a symbol of the family's bond and resilience.

As the miles rolled by, Maximus formulated a plan to restore their lives to a sense of normalcy. He would first visit Emily in the hospital, offering her the emotional support she needed. He would work with the doctors and therapists to ensure she received the best care possible. Next, he would focus on bringing Sarah and Michael home, navigating the legal system and proving his capability as a father. He would recreate the stable and fulfilling environment for them, filled with love and reassurance.

Financially, the jewels he had sold would provide a cushion, allowing him to focus on his family's needs without immediate worry. He would buy their house back that was lost to the bank, that would allow for him to be present for his family, restoring the home life to ensure they felt supported and loved.

The road to Springfield was long, but Maximus felt a renewed sense of purpose with each passing mile. The journey had been filled with challenges, but it had also given him the strength and determination to face the path ahead.

As he approached the city, the lights of Springfield twinkling in the distance, he knew that the real adventure was just beginning—the adventure of healing, rebuilding, and finding redemption in the love and unity of his family.

Maximus parked the Jeep in the hospital lot, his heart pounding with a mix of anticipation and dread. The imposing structure of Springfield General Hospital loomed before him, its sterile white walls and bustling entrance a stark contrast to the ancient chambers he had recently left behind. He took a deep breath, preparing himself for what lay ahead, and walked through the automatic doors.

The hospital was alive with activity, with doctors, nurses, and patients moving purposefully through the corridors. The scent of antiseptic filled the air, mingling with the faint hum of medical equipment. Maximus approached the reception desk, his voice steady but filled with urgency. "I'm here to see Emily, my wife. She's in the ICU."

The receptionist nodded sympathetically and directed him to the Intensive Care Unit. Maximus's steps quickened as he navigated the maze of hallways, his mind racing with thoughts of Emily. He reached the ICU and was greeted by a nurse who led him to Emily's room.

As he entered, the sight of Emily lying in the hospital bed hit him like a physical blow. Her face was pale, framed by a cascade of dark hair, and her body was connected to a myriad of machines that beeped and whirred softly. The room was dimly lit, the only sound was the rhythmic hiss of the ventilator.

Maximus approached her bedside, his emotions a tumultuous storm. He gently took her hand, feeling the coolness of her skin against his. "Emily," he whispered, his voice breaking. "I'm here."

The nurse quietly informed him of Emily's condition. She had been in a coma for weeks, her body fighting to heal from the injuries sustained in the accident. The prognosis was uncertain, and the doctors had done all they could. Now, it was up to Emily to find her way back.

Maximus felt a wave of guilt and sorrow wash over him. His life unraveling in a rollercoaster like event , he felt he had failed his family. The weight of his decisions pressed heavily on his shoulders. He had left them when they needed him most, and now he was faced with the consequences.

As he stood by her side, tears welled up in his eyes. He sank to his knees, his head resting on the edge of the bed. "Please, Father," he prayed to the Lord, his voice choked with emotion. "Bring Emily back to us. We need her, we love her."

In that moment, a miracle happened. Emily's fingers twitched, and her eyelids fluttered. Maximus looked up in amazement as hope surged through him. Slowly, her eyes opened, and she gazed at him with a mixture of confusion and recognition.

"Maximus?" she whispered, her voice weak but unmistakable.

"Emily!" Maximus cried, tears streaming down his face. He clasped her hand tightly, his heart overflowing with relief and joy. "You're awake. You're back."

Emily's eyes filled with tears as she squeezed his hand. "I knew you'd come," she said softly.

Maximus wept openly, his emotions a raw and powerful force. He felt a profound sense of gratitude and love, but also a deep regret for the time lost and the pain endured. He vowed then and there to make amends, to be the husband and father his family needed.

As Emily's strength slowly returned, Maximus shared his plan to restore their lives to a sense of normalcy. He would fight to bring Sarah and Michael home, to provide them with the stability and love they deserved. He would support Emily through her recovery, ensuring she had the best care possible. And he would make sure Max, their loyal golden retriever, was by their side, a symbol of their family's unbreakable bond.

As Emily's strength slowly returned, her eyes filled with a mixture of relief and confusion. She looked at Maximus, her brow furrowing as memories began to surface. "Maximus," she whispered, her voice trembling. "The accident... I remember the accident."

Maximus's heart tightened. He knew this moment would come, and he braced himself for the flood of emotions that would follow. "Yes, Emily," he said softly, squeezing her hand. "It was a terrible accident."

Emily's eyes widened with sudden realization. "Little Tommy," she gasped, her voice breaking. "What happened to Tommy? Is he okay? Please, Maximus, tell me he's okay."

Maximus felt a lump form in his throat. He had dreaded this moment, knowing how much Emily cared for Tommy, the young patient she was driving home in the rainstorm. He took a deep breath, his eyes meeting hers with a mixture of sorrow and hope.

"Tommy survived," he said gently, his voice filled with emotion. "He's alive, Emily. But he's been through a lot."

Tears welled up in Emily's eyes as she clung to Maximus's words. "Where is he? How is he? Please, tell me everything."

Maximus nodded, his voice steady but filled with compassion. "Tommy was injured in the accident, but the doctors have been taking good care of him. He's been in the pediatric ward, recovering from his injuries. He's a strong little boy, Emily. He's been fighting hard."

Emily's tears flowed freely now, a mixture of relief and sorrow. "I need to see him, Maximus. I need to know he's okay."

Maximus gently wiped away her tears. "You will, Emily. As soon as you're strong enough, we'll go see him together. He's been asking about you, and I know seeing you will mean the world to him."

Emily nodded, her grip on Maximus's hand tightening. "Thank you," she whispered, her voice filled with gratitude. "Thank you for being here, for taking care of everything."

Maximus leaned in, pressing a gentle kiss to her forehead. "We're in this together, Emily. We'll get through this, all of us. Tommy, Sarah,

Michael, and Max. We'll rebuild our lives and find our way back to each other."

As Emily lay back, exhausted but comforted by Maximus's words, he felt a renewed sense of life. The road ahead would be long and challenging, but with his family by his side, he knew they could overcome anything. Together, they would heal, rebuild, and find strength in their love and unity.

Maximus sat by Emily's bedside, holding her hand gently. The room was quiet, the soft beeping of the medical equipment the only sound. Emily's eyes were filled with a mixture of relief and lingering worry, her strength slowly returning. Maximus knew he had to tell her about Sarah and Michael, and the steps he needed to take to bring their family back together.

"Emily," he began softly, his voice trembling with emotion. "There's something I need to tell you."

Emily looked at him, her eyes searching his face. "What is it, Maximus?"

He took a deep breath, his heart heavy with the weight of his words. "I need to go see Sarah and Michael. They're in a foster home right now, and I need to make sure they're okay."

Tears welled up in Emily's eyes, her grip on his hand tightening. "Our babies," she whispered, her voice breaking. "How are they? Are they safe?"

Maximus nodded, his own eyes filling with tears. "They're safe, Emily. But they need us. They need to come home."

Emily's tears flowed freely now, her emotions a raw and powerful force. "I miss them so much, Maximus. I feel like I've failed them."

Maximus shook his head, his voice firm but gentle. "You haven't failed them, Emily. This isn't your fault. We're going to bring them home. I'm going to hire a lawyer, and we're going to fight to get them back."

Emily's eyes searched his, her expression a mix of hope and fear. "Do you think we can do it? Do you think we can bring them home?"

Maximus leaned in, pressing a gentle kiss to her forehead. "I know we can. We're a family, and nothing can keep us apart. I'll do whatever it takes to bring Sarah and Michael back to us."

Emily nodded, her tears still flowing but her resolve strengthening. "Thank you, Maximus. Thank you for being here, for fighting for our family."

Maximus held her close, his own tears mingling with hers. "We're in this together, Emily. We'll get through this, all of us. We'll rebuild our lives and find our way back to each other."

As he stood to leave, Emily's eyes followed him, filled with love and gratitude. "Be safe, Maximus. Bring our babies home."

Maximus nodded, his heart swelling with determination. "I will, Emily. I promise."

With a final, lingering look, he left the hospital room, his mind focused on the next steps. He would visit Sarah and Michael, reassure them that they were loved and missed, and then hire the best lawyer he could find to fight for their return. The road ahead would be long and challenging, but with the strength of his love for his family, he knew they could overcome anything. Together, they would heal, rebuild, and find strength in their love and unity.

Before heading to the lawyer, Maximus made a quick stop at the phone shop on South Veterans Parkway. The store was bristling with activity, customers browsing the latest electronics and gadgets. He approached the mobile phone section, where a friendly associate greeted him.

"How can I help you today?" the associate asked.

"I need a new phone," Maximus replied, his tone decisive.

The associate guided him through the options, and Maximus quickly selected a reliable smartphone. The transaction was smooth and efficient, the associate activating the phone and ensuring it was ready for use. Within minutes, Maximus's new phone in hand, he was ready to meet the lawyer.

With the phone safely tucked into his pocket, Maximus left the store and headed to his appointment with the lawyer, feeling a renewed sense of readiness and determination.

Maximus drove through the streets of Springfield, his mind focused on the task ahead. He had found a reputable family law firm, Mayce & Gary, Lawyers, P.C., known for their dedication and expertise in handling complex family cases. The building was a stately brick structure, its entrance framed by well-manicured shrubs and a welcoming sign.

He parked the Jeep and took a moment to gather his thoughts before stepping inside. The reception area was warm and inviting, with comfortable chairs and tasteful decor. A receptionist greeted him with a friendly smile. "Good afternoon. How can we assist you today?"

"I'm here to see a lawyer, " Maximus replied, his voice steady but filled with urgency. "I have an appointment."

"Of course," she said, checking her schedule. "Please have a seat. He'll be with you shortly."

Maximus sat down, his mind racing with thoughts of Sarah and Michael. He knew this meeting was crucial for their future. After a few minutes, a door opened from the interior office as a sharp looking young woman leaned out into the waiting area and said "Mr Magellan."

Maximus stood replying. "Yes, that's me." The beautiful legal aide guided Maximus to the Office of Mr. Mayce, "Go right in he's waiting for you now sir," she said politely with a smile.

"Please, come in," Mr. Sheehan said, leading him to a spacious office filled with bookshelves and framed certificates. They sat down at a large wooden desk, and Mr. Mayce leaned forward, his expression serious but compassionate. "How can I help you today?"

Maximus took a deep breath, his emotions raw. "I need to get my children back. Sarah and Michael are in a foster home, and I need to bring them home."

Mr. Mayce nodded, his eyes filled with understanding. "Tell me everything. Start from the beginning."

Maximus recounted the events that had led to this moment—the accident, Emily's coma, and the separation from his children. He spoke of his determination to reunite his family and the steps he had already taken to ensure their well-being.

Mr. Sheehan listened intently, taking notes and asking questions to clarify details. "It sounds like you've been through a lot," he said finally. "But I believe we can help you. We'll need to gather all the necessary documentation and evidence to present a strong case to the court."

Maximus nodded, feeling a glimmer of hope. "What do we need to do?"

"First, we'll need to demonstrate that you can provide a stable and loving environment for Sarah and Michael," Mr. Sheehan explained. "This includes financial stability, a safe home, and a support system. We'll also need to address any concerns the state may have about their well-being."

Maximus felt a surge of determination. "I'll do whatever it takes. I have the funds from selling some valuable items, and I'm ready to prove that I can take care of them."

Mr. Mayce smiled, his confidence reassuring. "That's a good start. We'll also need to gather character references, medical records, and any other relevant information. I'll guide you through the process and represent you in court."

Maximus felt a weight lift from his shoulders. "Thank you, Mr. Mayce, This means everything to me."

"We'll get through this together," Mr. Mayce said, standing and shaking Maximus's hand firmly. "Let's bring your children home."

As Maximus left the office and headed for his car, he dropped to his knees in the parking lot looking heavenward, "Thank you LORD!"

Maximus stood outside the bank, the imposing building a symbol of the challenges he had faced. With determination, he stepped inside, ready to reclaim his family's home. The bank manager greeted him, and they discussed the necessary steps to restore the house from foreclosure.

After reviewing the paperwork and providing proof of his newfound financial stability, thanks to the sale of the jewels, Maximus signed the final documents. The manager handed him the keys, a look of understanding and encouragement in his eyes.

Maximus drove to the house, his heart pounding with a mix of anxiety and hope. The familiar sight of their home brought a flood of memories. He unlocked the door and stepped inside, the air filled with the scent of dust and disuse. The rooms were empty, but the walls still held echoes of laughter and love.

He walked through each room, envisioning the life they would rebuild. The kitchen, where they would cook their favorite meals; the living room, where they would gather as a family; the bedrooms, where Sarah and Michael would sleep peacefully, knowing they were safe.

Maximus felt a sense of accomplishment. This house would once again be a home, filled with love and warmth. He began making plans for repairs and renovations, ensuring it would be ready for his family's return. The journey was far from over, but with the house restored, he had taken a crucial step toward rebuilding their lives. With that all out of the way Maximus now was going to try to jump through the hoops of the bureaucracy of the child welfare system. Maximus sat in his Jeep outside the house, the new phone he had purchased resting in his hand. He took a deep breath, preparing himself for the call he was about to make. The agency in charge of Sarah and Michael's foster care was his next step in the journey to reunite his family.

He dialed the number, his heart pounding as the phone rang. After a few moments, a calm, professional voice answered. "Good afternoon, Child Protective Services. How can I assist you?"

"Hello, my name is Maximus," he began, his voice steady but filled with emotion. "I'm calling about my children, Sarah and Michael. They're currently in foster care, and I need to arrange a visit with them."

"Of course, Mr. Magellan," the representative replied kindly. "Can you provide me with their case number or any other identifying information?"

Maximus quickly provided the necessary details, his mind racing with thoughts of his children. The representative typed away on her keyboard, the sound of the keys a steady rhythm in the background.

"Thank you for your patience," she said after a moment. "I see their case here. We can certainly arrange a visit. Are there any specific times or dates that work best for you?"

Maximus thought for a moment. "As soon as possible," he said, his voice replete with urgency. "I want to see them as soon as I can."

The representative's tone was understanding. "I understand, Mr. Magellan. We have a few openings this week. How does Thursday at 2 PM sound?"

"That sounds perfect," Maximus replied, relief washing over him. "Thank you so much."

"We'll need to have the visit supervised, as per protocol," she continued. "It will take place at our visitation center. I'll send you the details and address via email. Is there anything else I can assist you with?"

Maximus felt a surge of gratitude. "No, that's all for now. Thank you for your help."

"You're welcome, Mr. Maximus. We'll see you on Thursday. Take care."

As he ended the call, Maximus felt a mix of emotions—relief, anticipation, and a lingering sense of anxiety. The thought of seeing Sarah and Michael again filled him with hope, but he knew the road ahead would be challenging. He was determined to make the most of the visit, to reassure his children that they were loved and missed, and to begin the process of bringing them home.

With the visit arranged, Maximus felt a renewed sense of purpose. He would fight for his family, no matter the obstacles. The journey to reunite with Emily, Sarah, Michael and Max had begun, and he was ready to face the difficult path to restoration.Maximus walked through the hospital corridors, his heart lighter than it had been in weeks. The news he carried was a beacon of hope, and he couldn't wait to share it with Emily. He reached her room and paused for a moment, taking a deep breath before pushing the door open.

Emily was sitting up in bed, her eyes brightening as she saw him. "Maximus," she said, her voice filled with warmth and relief.

He crossed the room and took her hand, his eyes shining with excitement. "Emily, I have some wonderful news."

She looked at him expectantly, her heart pounding. "What is it?"

"I've restored the house," he began, his voice steady. "It's ours again. We have a home to go back to."

Tears welled up in Emily's eyes, her grip on his hand tightening. "Oh, Maximus, that's amazing. Thank you."

"There's more," he continued, his voice filled with determination. "I've hired a lawyer to help us get Sarah and Michael back. And I've arranged a visit with them on Thursday."

Emily's tears flowed freely now, a mixture of relief and joy. "You're bringing our family back together," she whispered, her voice choked with emotion. "Thank you, Maximus. Thank you so much."

Maximus leaned in and kissed her forehead, his own eyes misting. "We're going to be okay, Emily. We're going to get through this together."

Emily nodded, her heart swelling with love and gratitude. "I believe you," she said softly. "I believe in us."

Maximus took a deep breath, his voice gentle but firm. "There's one more thing. I want to take you to see Tommy. He's been asking about you."

Emily's eyes widened, a mixture of hope and fear. "Tommy... I need to see him. Please, take me to him."

Maximus helped her out of bed, supporting her as they made their way through the hospital corridors. The journey was slow, but Emily's determination was unwavering. They reached the pediatric ward, and Maximus led her to Tommy's room.

The sight of Tommy lying in the hospital bed brought a fresh wave of tears to Emily's eyes. He looked small and fragile, but his eyes lit up as he saw them enter. "Mommy!" he cried, his voice filled with joy.

Maximus wheeled Emily to his side, her tears flowing freely. "Tommy!," she exclaimed, hugging him gently. "I'm so glad to see you!."

Tommy clung to her, his small arms wrapped around her neck. "I missed you, Mrs.Magellan."

"I missed you too, Tommy," Emily said, her voice breaking. "I'm so glad you're okay."

Maximus stood by, his heart swelling with emotion as he watched the reunion. The sight of Emily and Tommy together, their love and relief discernable. They had been through so much, the trials of the past weeks had taken its toll.

Emily and Maximus sat by Tommy's hospital bed, the room filled with the soft beeping of medical equipment and the gentle hum of the air conditioner. Tommy clung to Emily, his small arms wrapped around her neck, his eyes bright with relief and love. Maximus stood close by, his heart swelling with emotion as he watched the tender reunion.

Suddenly, the door to the room opened, and Tommy's parents, Sara and John, walked in. Their faces were etched with worry and exhaustion, but their eyes softened as they saw Tommy safe and sound in Emily's arms. The tension in the room was palpable, a mixture of relief, guilt, and unspoken words hanging in the air.

Sara's eyes filled with tears as she took in the scene. "Tommy," she whispered, her voice trembling. "Oh, my sweet boy."

Tommy looked up, his face lighting up with joy. "Mommy! Daddy!" he cried, reaching out to them.

Sara and John rushed to his side, enveloping him in a gentle embrace. Maximus wheeled Emily back a foot or so, her eyes filled with tears, her heart heavy with the weight of the accident and its aftermath. Maximus placed a comforting hand on her shoulder, his own emotions raw and powerful.

Sara looked up, her eyes meeting Emily's. There was a moment of silence, the air thick with unspoken emotions. Finally, Sara spoke, her voice soft but steady. "Emily, Maximus… thank you for being here with Tommy. We know how much you care about him."

Emily's tears flowed freely now, her voice choked with emotion. "I'm so sorry, Sara. I'm so sorry for everything. I never meant for any of this to happen."

Sara went to Emily's side, leaning over put her arms around Emily's neck so their foreheads were touching, "I know your heart Emily, I know you only meant to help, I'm so sorry for my harsh words to you."

John stepped forward, his expression a mix of sorrow and understanding. "We know, Emily. It was an accident. We've had time to think, and we realize that blaming you won't change anything. What matters now is that Tommy is safe and that we all move forward together."

Emily's heart swelled with gratitude and relief. "Thank you," she whispered, her voice breaking. "Thank you for understanding."

Sara took Emily's hand, her eyes filled with compassion. "We're all in this together. Let's focus on healing and making sure Tommy gets the love and support he needs." Emily tucked her face in her hands and wept uncontrollably.

Maximus felt a wave of emotion wash over him. The forgiveness and understanding from Tommy's parents were more than he had dared to hope for. He stepped forward, his voice filled with sincerity. "We'll do everything we can to help. We're here for Tommy, and for you."

John nodded, his eyes meeting Maximus's with a sense of shared purpose. "Thank you, Maximus. Let's work together to make sure our families come through this stronger."

The room was filled with a feel of shared unity, the bonds of love and forgiveness weaving a new path forward. As they stood together, supporting each other, Maximus felt a massive weight lifted from hi shoulders. The journey ahead would be challenging, but with their families united, they could face anything. Together, they would heal, rebuild, and find strength in their love and unity.

Maximus gently wheeled Emily back through the hospital corridors, the soft hum of the wheels on the linoleum floor a comforting sound. The journey was slow, but filled with a sense of hope and determination. Emily's hand rested lightly on his, her eyes reflecting a mixture of exhaustion and relief.

As they reached her room, a kind nurse stepped forward to assist. "Let's get you settled back in, Mrs. Magellan," she said with a warm smile. Together, they carefully helped Emily back into her bed, adjusting the pillows and blankets to ensure she was comfortable.

Maximus leaned in close, his voice a soft whisper in her ear. "Emily, there's something I need to tell you."

She looked up at him, her eyes filled with curiosity and trust. "What is it, Maximus?"

He took a deep breath, his voice barely audible. "I made a discovery in the cave. There's a hidden chamber filled with treasures. I'm going to go back and gather more to sell. With the money, I plan to build us a new house, near the secret wall to the chamber. A place where we can start fresh."

Emily's eyes widened, a mixture of surprise and hope. "Maximus, that's incredible. But please, be careful."

He nodded, his expression serious but determined. "I will. I promise. I'll be back in a few days, just in time to see the children on Thursday. We'll get through this, Emily. We'll rebuild our lives together."

Tears welled up in her eyes, her voice filled with emotion. "Thank you, Maximus. I believe in you. I believe in us."

Maximus pressed a gentle kiss to her forehead, his heart swelling with love and resolve. "Rest now, Emily. I'll be back soon."

Maximus drove through the winding roads of Springfield, the city gradually giving way to the serene countryside. The sun was setting, casting a warm, golden glow over the fields and trees. As he drove, his mind raced with reflections on the unbelievable events that had unfolded in their lives over the past few days. From discovering the hidden treasure chamber to reuniting with Emily and planning to bring Sarah and Michael home, it all felt like a whirlwind.

The hum of the Jeep's engine was a comforting constant, grounding him as he navigated the familiar route back to the forest. He thought about the promise he had made to Emily, the determination in her eyes, and the hope that had filled the hospital room. The weight of his responsibilities felt lighter now, buoyed by the love and support of his family.

As he approached the forest area where the secret door to the chamber was hidden, he pulled over to the side of the road and took out his new phone. He needed to make a few important calls to set his plans in motion.

First, he called the furniture Store in Springfield. The phone rang a few times before a cheerful voice answered. "Tashley furniture, how can I help you?"

"Hi, my name is Maximus Magellan. I'm looking to furnish a new home and need some assistance with selecting and purchasing furniture."

"Of course, Mr. Magellan. We'd be happy to help. When would you like to come in and take a look at our selection?"

"How about tomorrow morning?" Maximus suggested.

"That sounds perfect. We'll have a consultant ready to assist you. See you then!"

With the furniture appointment set, Maximus made his next call to Park Construction LLC, a reputable construction company in Springfield. The phone was answered promptly by a professional-sounding receptionist. "Park Construction, how can we assist you?"

"Hello, my name is Maximus Magellan. I need to schedule an appointment for a survey and consultation. I'm planning to build a house and a lab near a specific area in the forest."

"Certainly, Mr. Magellan. We can have a team out there this week. How does Wednesday morning sound?"

"That works for me. Thank you."

"You're welcome. We'll see you on Wednesday."

Feeling a sense of progress, Maximus made his final call to a real estate agency about purchasing the acres in the forest at the hidden glade. He dialed the number and waited as the phone rang. A friendly voice answered. "Springfield Real Estate, how can I help you?"

"Hi, my name is Maximus Magellan. I'm interested in purchasing some land in the forest area, specifically near a hidden glade."

"Of course, Mr. Magellan. We have several listings that might interest you. Can we set up a meeting to discuss the details and arrange a viewing?"

"Yes, that would be great. How about Wednesday afternoon?"

"Perfect. We'll send you the details and meet you then."

With all the calls made and appointments set, Maximus felt a plan taking root and the satisfaction tenible. He drove the rest of the way to the forest, the familiar path leading him to the secret door of the treasure chamber. The forest was quiet, the only sounds were the rustling of leaves and the distant call of birds.

He parked the Jeep and made his way to the hidden entrance, marking the spot carefully. The journey ahead would be challenging, but with each step, he felt more prepared to face whatever lay ahead. The plans were in motion, and soon, he would return to Springfield to see Emily and the children, ready to rebuild their lives and find strength in a secured future.

Maximus navigated the winding forest roads with a sense of purpose, the Jeep's headlights cutting through the early evening gloom. The trees grew denser as he approached the hidden glen, their branches forming a natural canopy that obscured the sky. He knew he had to find a discreet spot to park, away from prying eyes.

After a few minutes of careful searching, he found the perfect spot—a small clearing surrounded by thick underbrush. He parked the Jeep, ensuring it was well-hidden from any passersby. The engine's hum faded into the forest's natural symphony of rustling leaves and distant bird calls.

Maximus stepped out of the Jeep, his senses alert to the sounds of the forest. He moved with practiced stealth, his footsteps barely making a sound on the soft forest floor. The path to the hidden glen was familiar, and he navigated it with ease, his eyes scanning for any signs of disturbance.

Reaching the glen, he paused for a moment, taking in the serene beauty of the secluded spot. The glen was bathed in the soft glow of twilight, the trees casting long shadows that danced in the gentle breeze. He made his way to the secret door, hidden behind a thick curtain of ivy and moss.

With a practiced hand, Maximus brushed aside the foliage, revealing the ancient stone door. He pressed the hidden mechanism, and the door slid open with a soft, grinding sound. The entrance to the treasure chamber lay before him, a dark, winding stairway descending into the earth.

Maximus took a deep breath, the cool, damp air of the passageway filling his lungs. He stepped inside, the light from his phone casting eerie shadows on the rough stone walls. The stairway spiraled downward, each step taking him deeper into the hidden world below.

As he descended, the air grew heavier, filled with the scent of aged stone and the faint metallic tang of ancient surroundings. The walls were adorned with intricate carvings, their details barely visible in the dim light. The journey was long, but Maximus moved with determination, his mind focused on the task ahead.

Finally, he reached the bottom of the stairway and stepped into the treasure chamber. The golden glow of the treasures greeted him once more, the piles of gold coins and precious jewels shimmering in the torchlight. The scrolls, carefully numbered and arranged, awaited his further exploration.

Maximus felt a great feeling of accomplishment as he stood in the chamber. The journey had been long and challenging, but he was ready to gather more treasures to support his family and build a new life. With renewed determination, he began his work, knowing that each step brought him closer to reuniting with his loved ones and restoring their lives to a sense of normalcy.

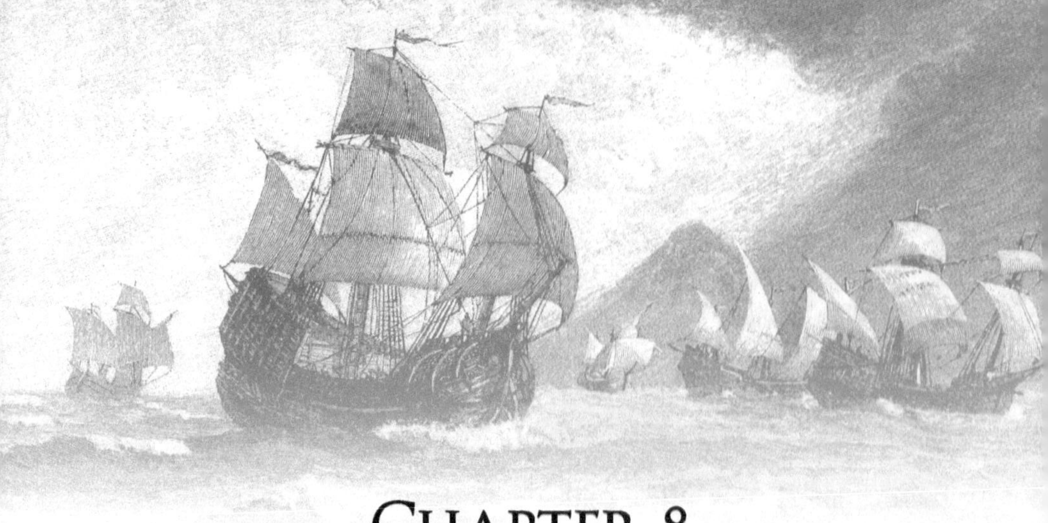

CHAPTER 8

THE TROVE

Maximus stood in the center of the treasure chamber, his eyes scanning the vast array of riches and ancient artifacts that surrounded him. The golden glow of the treasures cast a warm light across the room, illuminating the intricate carvings on the walls and the piles of gold coins and precious jewels that glittered in the torchlight.

He took a deep breath, the air thick with the scent of aged stone and the faint metallic tang of the treasures. His gaze moved from one corner of the room to the next, taking in the sheer volume of knowledge and wealth contained within. Scrolls, artifacts, and relics were carefully arranged on shelves and tables, each one a testament to the wisdom and craftsmanship of the ancients.

In the center of the room stood a grand treasure chest, its surface encrusted with gems and intricate carvings. The chest was massive, its wood dark and polished, reinforced with bands of gleaming metal. The carvings depicted scenes of mythical battles and legendary heroes, their stories etched into the wood with exquisite detail.

Maximus approached the chest, his heart pounding with anticipation. The chest seemed to radiate a sense of power and mystery, as if it held secrets that had been locked away for centuries. He ran his fingers over the carvings, feeling the smoothness of the wood and the coolness of the metal.

With a sense of reverence, he lifted the heavy lid, the hinges creaking softly as it opened. Inside, the chest was filled with an array of treasures: glittering jewels, ancient coins, and delicate artifacts that seemed to glow with an inner light. Among the treasures, he spotted several scrolls, their ribbons indicating their importance.

Maximus knew that this chest would be the perfect place to start his research. The treasures within were not only valuable but also held the key to unlocking the knowledge and wisdom of the ancients. He carefully selected a few scrolls and artifacts, placing them on a nearby table for closer examination.

As he began his work, the sense of awe and purpose that had driven him through the winding passageways and hidden chambers filled him once more. The journey ahead would be challenging, but with the treasures and knowledge he had uncovered, he felt ready to face whatever lay ahead. The path to rebuilding his family's life had begun, and he was determined to see it through, one discovery at a time.

Maximus carefully lifted the lid of the grand treasure chest, its hinges creaking softly. Inside, the chest was a dazzling array of treasures, but what caught his eye were the special scrolls nestled among the jewels and artifacts. There were ten scrolls in total, each one bound with a unique ribbon and radiating an aura of ancient wisdom.

Scroll of Eternal Light: Bound with a golden ribbon, this scroll contains spells and rituals to harness and manipulate light. The parchment glows faintly, as if imbued with the very essence of sunlight.

Scroll of the Ancients: Tied with a silver ribbon, this scroll holds the wisdom of the ancient civilizations. It includes detailed accounts of their history, culture, and technological advancements, written in a language that seems to pulse with life.

Scroll of Elemental Harmony: This scroll, bound with a blue ribbon, details the balance and control of the natural elements. It includes spells for summoning and controlling elemental forces, as well as rituals for maintaining harmony with nature.

Scroll of the Celestial Path: Wrapped in a starry, midnight-blue ribbon, this scroll contains knowledge of the stars and celestial navigation. It includes charts of the night sky, astrological predictions, and guidance for travelers.

Scroll of the Arcane Forge: Bound with a crimson ribbon, this scroll describes the creation and enchantment of magical weapons and armor. It includes detailed instructions on forging techniques and the rituals needed to imbue items with powerful enchantments.

Scroll of the Mystic Veil: Tied with a purple ribbon, this scroll holds secrets of illusion and invisibility. It includes spells for creating illusions, cloaking oneself from sight, and manipulating perceptions.

Scroll of the Sacred Grove: This scroll, bound with a green ribbon, contains knowledge of healing and herbalism. It includes detailed descriptions of medicinal plants, recipes for healing potions, and rituals for restoring health and vitality.

Scroll of the Timekeeper: Wrapped in a silver-and-gold ribbon, this scroll holds the secrets of time manipulation. It includes spells for slowing, speeding up, and even reversing time, as well as rituals for glimpsing into the past and future.

Scroll of the Spirit Realm: Bound with a white ribbon, this scroll contains knowledge of the spirit world. It includes rituals for communicating with spirits, summoning ethereal beings, and protecting oneself from malevolent entities.

Scroll of the Dragon's Heart: Tied with a fiery red ribbon, this scroll holds the secrets of dragon lore. It includes detailed accounts of dragon species, their habitats, and their magical abilities, as well as spells for summoning and controlling these powerful creatures.

Maximus felt a sense of awe as he carefully examined each scroll. The knowledge contained within these ancient parchments was invaluable, a testament to the wisdom and power of the ancients. With these scrolls in hand, he could only imagine the achievements he could achieve.

In the treasure chamber of the Magellan Project, Maximus Magellan discovers a great chest filled with five unique artifacts. Each artifact holds a significant history and power, contributing to the overarching mystery and adventure. Here's a detailed description of each:

The Crystal Compass: This ancient compass is made of a translucent crystal that glows faintly in the dark. It doesn't point north but instead guides the holder to their heart's true desire. The compass's needle moves in unpredictable patterns, reflecting the inner turmoil or clarity of the person holding it.

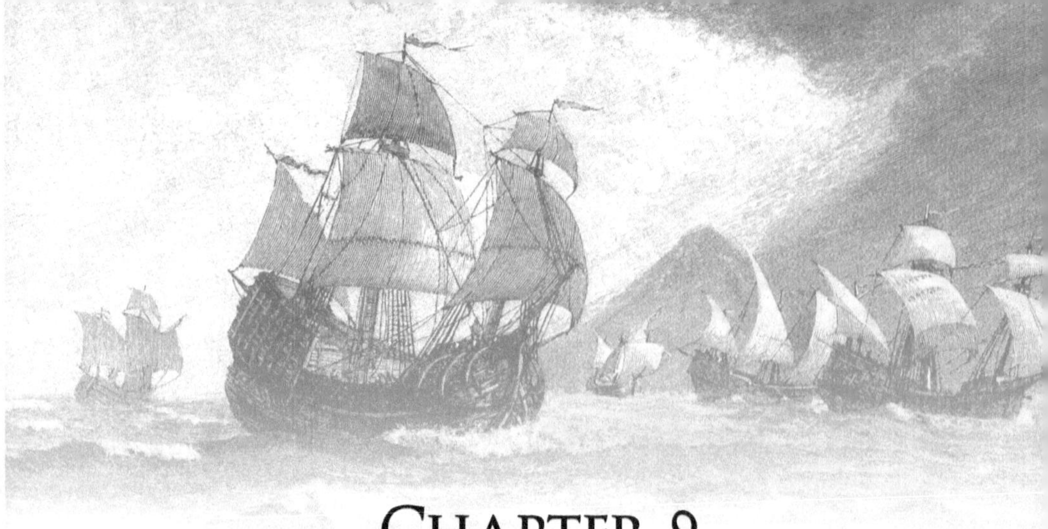

CHAPTER 9
THE AETHERIUM CORE

The Phoenix Feather: Encased in a glass vial, this feather is from a mythical phoenix. It shimmers with iridescent colors and is warm to the touch. The feather is said to have healing properties and can revive someone from the brink of death, but it can only be used once.

The Timekeeper's Hourglass: This hourglass is made of gold and encrusted with precious gems. The sand inside is a deep, shimmering blue, and it flows upwards instead of down. When turned, it can transport the user back in time for a brief period, allowing them to alter a single event. However, the consequences of such changes are unpredictable.

The Siren's Locket: A beautifully crafted silver locket that emits a soft, melodic hum when opened. Inside, there is a small, enchanted pearl that can amplify the holder's voice, making it irresistible and persuasive. However, prolonged use can lead to the user becoming entranced by their own power.

The Dragon's Scale: This large, iridescent scale is from a legendary dragon. It is nearly indestructible and can be used as a shield. The scale also has the ability to grant the user temporary invulnerability, but it comes with the risk of attracting the dragon's wrath if used recklessly.

Each artifact in the chest is not only a treasure but also a key to unlocking deeper secrets and challenges within the Magellan Project. Maximus must use them wisely to navigate the perils ahead.

The square metallic block that Maximus Magellan discovers is an enigmatic artifact, unlike anything he has ever seen. Here is the detailed description he enters in the diary: (note to self, get many notebooks)

Composition and Appearance

Material: The block is made of an unknown alloy, giving it a unique, almost otherworldly sheen. It has a smooth, mirror-like surface that reflects light in a mesmerizing way.

Size: It measures about 12 inches on each side, perfectly symmetrical.

Color: The block has a deep, metallic blue hue with subtle streaks of silver running through it, creating an effect that makes it look like it's constantly shifting colors.

Markings: Intricate, glowing runes are etched into its surface. These runes pulse with a faint, rhythmic light, suggesting some form of ancient, arcane energy.

Mysterious Appearance

Aura: The block emits a low, humming sound that resonates through the room, creating a sense of anticipation and mystery.

Temperature: It feels cool to the touch, but as Maximus's fingers brush against it, the temperature begins to rise slightly, indicating a reaction to his presence.

The Hovering Phenomenon

As Maximus touches the block, an incredible sequence of events unfolds:

Initial Reaction: The runes on the block glow brighter, and the humming sound intensifies, filling the room with a palpable energy.

Levitation: The block begins to hover a few inches above the ground, defying gravity. It rotates slowly, revealing more of the glowing runes on all sides.

Light Display: Beams of light shoot out from the runes, creating a dazzling display of colors that dance across the walls and ceiling. The light forms intricate patterns, almost like a celestial map.

Energy Field: An invisible force field emanates from the block, causing small objects around the room to levitate as well. Papers, pens, and other lightweight items float gently in the air.

Soundscape: The humming sound evolves into a harmonious melody, resonating with a frequency that seems to touch the very soul. It's both soothing and awe-inspiring, creating a sense of wonder and reverence.

Impact on Maximus

Physical Sensation: Maximus feels a tingling sensation in his fingertips that spreads through his entire body, as if the block is sharing its energy with him.

Emotional Response: He is filled with a mix of awe, curiosity, and a hint of fear. The experience is overwhelming, yet he feels an inexplicable connection to the block, as if it holds the key to a greater mystery.

This extraordinary display leaves Maximus both exhilarated and intrigued.

As the block hovers and the light display intensifies, a voice begins to emanate from it. The voice is:

Timeless: It carries an ageless quality, neither distinctly male nor female, but a harmonious blend of both.

Resonant: The voice has a deep, resonant tone that seems to vibrate through the very air, creating a sense of profound authority and wisdom.

Calm and Soothing: Despite its power, the voice is calm and soothing, instilling a sense of peace and reassurance in Maximus.

Echoing: Each word echoes slightly, as if spoken in a vast, cavernous space, adding to the sense of mystery and grandeur.

The Artifact's Name and Origin

Name: The artifact is called "The Aetherium Core".

Origin: The Aetherium Core is an ancient relic from a long-lost civilization known as the Aetherians. This advanced society existed thousands of years ago, far beyond the reach of current historical records. The Aetherians were known for their mastery of both technology and magic, blending the two seamlessly to create powerful artifacts.

The Aetherium Core's History

Creation: The Aetherium Core was created as a central power source for the Aetherians' greatest achievements. It was designed to harness and amplify the natural energies of the universe, making it a limitless source of power and knowledge.

Purpose: The Core was intended to be a guiding beacon for the Aetherians, helping them navigate the cosmos and unlock the secrets of existence. It was also used to maintain harmony and balance within their society.

Disappearance: As the Aetherian civilization mysteriously vanished, the Aetherium Core was lost to time, hidden away in the treasure chamber where Maximus now finds it.

The Voice's Message

As Maximus listens, the voice from the Aetherium Core speaks:

"Seeker of Truth, you have awakened the Aetherium Core. Within me lies the wisdom of the ancients and the power to shape destiny. Use this gift wisely, for it holds the key to both creation and destruction. The path ahead is fraught with peril, but also with great promise. Trust in the light, and you shall find your way."

This message leaves Maximus with a sense of Awe and mystery and daunting responsibility. The Aetherium Core is not just a treasure; it is a beacon of hope and a tool of immense power that could change the course of natural history.

As Maximus Magellan stands in awe, absorbing the incredible scene that just unfolded, he is left with more questions than answers. The origins of the chambers and the treasure trove within the cave system are shrouded in mystery.

The Builders of the Chambers

The chambers within the cave system were constructed by the Aetherians, the same ancient civilization responsible for creating the Aetherium Core. The Aetherians were master architects and engineers, blending their advanced technology with mystical elements to create structures that have withstood the test of time.

Design: The chambers are intricately designed with a blend of natural and artificial elements. The walls are adorned with glowing runes and symbols, similar to those on the Aetherium Core, indicating their origin. The architecture is both functional and beautiful, with hidden mechanisms and traps to protect the treasures within.

Purpose: These chambers were built as a sanctuary and a vault to safeguard the Aetherians' most valuable artifacts. They were designed to be nearly impossible to find and access, ensuring that only those deemed worthy could uncover their secrets.

The Means of the Treasure's Arrival

The treasure and the trove of artifacts found within the chambers were brought there through a combination of Aetherian technology and magic. The Aetherians had the ability to manipulate space and time, allowing them to transport objects and even entire structures across vast distances.

Teleportation: Using their advanced knowledge, the Aetherians could teleport the treasures directly into the chambers, bypassing physical barriers and ensuring their safety.

Guardianship: The treasures were placed under the guardianship of powerful enchantments and mechanical guardians, designed to protect them from intruders. These guardians would only allow entry to those who could solve the intricate puzzles and prove their worthiness.

The Unfolding Mystery

As Maximus contemplates these revelations, he realizes that the discovery of the Aetherium Core and the chambers is just the beginning. The voice from the Core hinted at a greater purpose and a path filled with both peril and promise. Maximus must now piece together the clues left by the Aetherians, uncover the true extent of their knowledge, and understand the role he is destined to play in this ancient saga.

As Maximus Magellan sits amidst the treasure, he gathers his thoughts and poses his question to the Aetherium Core: "What are your special capabilities, and can you replicate technology or hardware designed by the Aetherians?"

The Aetherium Core's Response

Voice of the Core: "Seeker of Truth, the Aetherium Core possesses a multitude of capabilities, each designed to harness and amplify the energies of the universe. Here are my primary functions:

Energy Manipulation: I can channel and control various forms of energy, including elemental, cosmic, and arcane forces. This allows for the creation of powerful spells, the enhancement of physical abilities, and the manipulation of natural phenomena.

Knowledge Repository: I contain the collective knowledge and wisdom of the Aetherians. This includes their history, technological advancements, magical practices, and philosophical insights. By connecting with me, you can access this vast repository of information.

Healing and Restoration: I have the ability to heal wounds, cure ailments, and restore vitality. This extends to both living beings and inanimate objects, allowing for the repair of damaged artifacts and structures.

Temporal Manipulation: I can influence the flow of time, enabling brief glimpses into the past or future. This power must be used with caution, as altering the timeline can have unforeseen consequences.

Spatial Manipulation: I can create portals and manipulate space, allowing for instantaneous travel across great distances. This includes the ability to transport objects and individuals to specific locations.

Replication of Aetherian Technology

Regarding your query about replicating Aetherian technology or hardware:

Voice of the Core: "Indeed, I possess the capability to replicate and even enhance the technology and hardware designed by the Aetherians. By providing me with the necessary materials and understanding the intended purpose, I can reconstruct devices, tools, and artifacts with precision. However, the replication process requires a deep connection with the energies that power these creations, and it is essential to approach this task with respect and reverence for the Aetherian legacy."

This revelation leaves Maximus with a profound sense of awe and responsibility. The Aetherium Core is not just a relic; it is a powerful ally that can aid him in his quest, provided he uses its capabilities wisely.

As Maximus Magellan sits amidst the treasure, he formulates his question to the Aetherium Core: "Who was the skeleton man under the bush in the abandoned lot, and how did he come by the diary, the map, the softball-sized metal ball covered in images and runes, and the curious jewel? Describe his last week before his death in the bowels of the cave where the wormhole opened, depositing his skeleton under the bush in the abandoned lot where I found him."

The Aetherium Core's Response

Voice of the Core: "The skeleton man you discovered was Dr. Elias Thorn, an archaeologist and explorer who dedicated his life to uncovering the secrets of the Aetherians. His journey was fraught with danger and mystery, ultimately leading to his untimely demise."

Dr. Elias Thorn's Journey

Acquisition of Artifacts:

The Diary: Dr. Thorn found the diary in an ancient library hidden beneath the ruins of an old monastery. The diary belonged to an Aetherian scholar and contained detailed notes on their civilization and the location of the treasure chamber.

The Map: The map was discovered in a hidden compartment within the diary. It was a detailed chart of the cave system, marked with symbols and annotations that guided Dr. Thorn to the treasure chamber.

The Metal Ball: The softball-sized metal ball, covered in images and runes, was found in a forgotten temple deep in the jungle. It was a key to unlocking the treasure chamber, designed to resonate with the Aetherium Core.

The Curious Jewel: The jewel was a gift from a mysterious guardian who protected the temple. It was said to possess the power to reveal hidden truths and protect its bearer from harm.

Dr. Thorn's Last Week

Day 1: Dr. Thorn enters the cave system, guided by the map and the diary. He encounters numerous traps and puzzles, each more challenging than the last. His determination and knowledge of the Aetherians help him navigate these obstacles.

Day 2: He discovers the entrance to the treasure chamber but realizes he needs the metal ball and the jewel to unlock it. He spends the day deciphering the runes on the ball and aligning them with the symbols on the chamber door.

Day 3: Dr. Thorn successfully opens the treasure chamber and is overwhelmed by the sight of the treasures within. He spends hours documenting and studying the artifacts, including the Aetherium Core.

Day 4: As he continues his exploration, he accidentally activates a hidden mechanism that triggers the opening of a wormhole. The sudden surge of energy destabilizes the chamber, causing it to collapse.

Day 5: Dr. Thorn is caught in the chaos and is pulled into the wormhole. The intense energy and spatial distortion take a toll on his body, and he struggles to maintain consciousness.

Day 6: The wormhole deposits Dr. Thorn's weakened body in the abandoned lot, far from the cave system. Severely injured and disoriented, he crawls under a bush, clutching the diary, map, metal ball, and jewel.

Day 7: Dr. Thorn succumbs to his injuries, his final thoughts filled with regret and a desperate hope that someone would continue his quest. His skeleton remains hidden under the bush until Maximus discovers it.

The Spectre's Tale

As Maximus listens to the Aetherium Core, a ghostly figure materializes before him—a spectre of Dr. Elias Thorn. The spectre begins to speak, recounting his tragic end:

"Maximus, I was driven by the same thirst for knowledge that now guides you. I ventured into the depths of the cave, deciphering the ancient runes and unlocking the secrets of the Aetherians. But as I pushed forward, I reached a point of no return.

The walls closed in, and the path ahead was blocked. There was no way back, no way forward. In my desperation, I activated a mechanism that opened a wormhole. The energy was overwhelming, and I was pulled into the void. The wormhole deposited me under that bush, where I drew my last breath. I leave these artifacts in your hands, hoping you can succeed where I failed."

This haunting tale leaves Maximus with a profound sense of responsibility and determination. The legacy of Dr. Thorn and the Aetherians now rests on his shoulders, guiding him on his quest to uncover the ultimate truth.

As Maximus Magellan absorbs the shocking yet amazing events that just unfolded, he spends 20 minutes formulating a new question for the Aetherium Core: "Is there any technology in your grasp that can make (print) me an advanced AI helper to assist in the cataloging and study of all of the scrolls, artifacts, and any other technology I might find here?"

The Aetherium Core's Response

Voice of the Core: "Seeker of Truth, the Aetherians possessed the capability to create advanced artificial intelligences, designed to assist in the preservation and study of their vast knowledge. I can indeed help you create such an AI helper. Here is how it can be done:

Blueprint Generation: I will generate the blueprints for an advanced AI construct, tailored to your specific needs. This AI will be equipped with the ability to catalog, analyze, and interpret the artifacts and scrolls you discover.

Material Requirements: You will need to gather specific materials to construct the physical form of the AI. These materials include rare metals, crystals, and other components that can be found within the treasure chamber and the surrounding cave system.

Assembly Process: Once the materials are gathered, I will guide you through the assembly process. This involves precise construction techniques and the infusion of Aetherian energy to bring the AI to life.

Programming and Activation: The final step involves programming the AI with the necessary knowledge and capabilities. I will transfer a portion of my own data and algorithms to ensure the AI is fully equipped to assist you. Once activated, the AI will be able to interact with you, provide insights, and help manage your discoveries.

The AI Helper's Capabilities

Cataloging: The AI will systematically catalog all artifacts, scrolls, and technologies you find, creating a comprehensive database.

Analysis: It will analyze the properties and origins of each item, providing detailed reports and insights.

Translation: The AI will be able to translate ancient texts and runes, making it easier for you to understand the Aetherian language and knowledge.

It will assist you in solving puzzles, navigating the cave system, and utilizing the Aetherian technology effectively.

The AI helper shall be named "Aetheris", in honor of the Aetherians who created the technology.

This advanced AI helper will be an invaluable companion on your journey, aiding you in uncovering the secrets of the Aetherians and ensuring that their legacy is preserved and understood.

Maximus is stunned by the revelation, and the implications of what this could mean. Maximus, Sits down to carefully form his request to the Aetherium core.

Maximus, still reeling from the revelation and the immense possibilities it presents, sits down to carefully form his request to the Aetherium Core. He asks, "Aetherium Core, describe in great detail and specifics how to build a 3D printer capable of creating 'Aetheris.'"

The Aetherium Core's Response

Voice of the Core: "Seeker of Truth, to build a 3D printer capable of creating 'Aetheris,' you must follow these detailed instructions. This printer will be a blend of advanced technology and Aetherian magic, ensuring precision and functionality."

Components and Materials

Frame and Structure:

Material: Use a lightweight, durable alloy such as titanium or a similar Aetherian metal.

Dimensions: The frame should be sturdy and large enough to accommodate the construction of complex components, approximately 1.5 meters in height, 1 meter in width, and 1 meter in depth.

Print Bed:

Material: A heat-resistant, non-stick surface such as borosilicate glass or a specialized Aetherian crystal.

Heating Element: Incorporate a uniform heating element to ensure even temperature distribution across the print bed.

Extruder and Nozzle:

Material: High-grade steel or an Aetherian alloy capable of withstanding high temperatures and wear.

Precision: The nozzle should have interchangeable tips for different levels of detail, ranging from 0.2 mm to 1 mm in diameter.

Filament and Resin:

Material: Use a combination of advanced polymers and Aetherian-infused resins. These materials should be capable of conducting energy and integrating magical properties.

Storage: Ensure the filament and resin are stored in a controlled environment to maintain their integrity.

Control System:

Processor: A high-speed, multi-core processor capable of handling complex calculations and real-time adjustments.

Interface: A touch-screen interface with intuitive controls and real-time monitoring of the printing process.

Power Source:

Energy Core: Utilize a compact Aetherian energy core to provide a stable and powerful energy supply. This core should be capable of sustaining long print cycles without fluctuations.

Calibration and Sensors:

Sensors: Integrate high-precision sensors to monitor temperature, humidity, and print accuracy. These sensors should be able to make real-time adjustments to ensure optimal print quality.

Calibration: Include an automatic calibration system to ensure the print bed and extruder are perfectly aligned before each print.

Assembly Instructions

Frame Construction:

Assemble the frame using the titanium or Aetherian alloy components. Ensure all joints are secure and the structure is stable.

Attach the print bed to the frame, ensuring it is level and securely fastened.

Extruder and Nozzle Installation:

Install the extruder and nozzle assembly onto the frame. Connect the heating elements and ensure they are properly insulated.

Attach the filament and resin feed systems to the extruder, ensuring smooth and consistent material flow.

Control System Integration:

Install the processor and interface components. Connect all necessary wiring and ensure the control system is properly grounded.

Configure the touch-screen interface and test all controls to ensure they are responsive and accurate.

Power Source Connection:

Install the Aetherian energy core in a secure compartment within the frame. Connect the power supply to the control system and heating elements.

Test the power supply to ensure it is stable and capable of sustaining the printer's operations.

Calibration and Sensor Setup:

Install the sensors at strategic points around the printer. Connect them to the control system and configure them to monitor key parameters.

Run the automatic calibration system to ensure the print bed and extruder are perfectly aligned.

Final Steps

Testing: Conduct a series of test prints to ensure the printer is functioning correctly. Make any necessary adjustments to the settings and components.

Programming: Upload the necessary software and algorithms to the control system, including the data and instructions for creating 'Aetheris.'

Activation: Once all components are tested and calibrated, activate the printer and begin the process of creating your advanced AI helper, 'Aetheris.'

This 3D printer will be a powerful tool in your quest, enabling you to bring 'Aetheris' to life and assist you in uncovering the secrets of the Aetherians. Voice of the Core: "Seeker of Truth, the Aetherian metal you seek is indeed present within this chamber. The Aetherians, in their wisdom, ensured that their most valuable resources were safeguarded alongside their treasures. Here is how you can locate and extract the Aetherian metal:

Locating the Aetherian Metal

Hidden Compartments: The walls of this chamber contain hidden compartments where the Aetherian metal is stored. Look for subtle markings and runes that indicate the presence of these compartments.

Energy Resonance: Use the Aetherium Core to resonate with the energy signatures of the metal. Hold the Core close to the walls and observe the runes; they will glow brighter near the hidden compartments.

Unlocking Mechanisms: Each compartment is secured with a unique mechanism. You will need to solve the corresponding puzzle or align the runes correctly to unlock them.

Extracting the Aetherian Metal

Tools Required: You will need specialized tools to extract the metal without damaging it. These tools can be found within the treasure chamber, designed specifically for this purpose.

Careful Handling: The Aetherian metal is highly reactive to energy. Handle it with care and use the provided tools to avoid any unintended reactions.

Storage: Once extracted, store the metal in a secure, insulated container to maintain its purity and prevent any energy loss.

Additional Deposits

While there is a significant deposit of Aetherian metal within this chamber, you may also find more in other parts of the cave system. The map and diary you possess will guide you to these locations, marked with the same runes and symbols.

By following these instructions, you will be able to obtain the Aetherian metal necessary to construct the 3D printer and bring 'Aetheris' to life. Proceed with caution and respect for the ancient knowledge you are uncovering."

In the dimly lit corner of the treasure chamber, Maximus spots another intriguing box. This box, about the size of a footlocker, immediately catches his eye with its unique appearance and the aura of mystery surrounding it.

Detailed Description of the Box

Material and Appearance:

Composition: The box appears to be made of the same Aetherian metal described by the Aetherium Core. Its surface has a deep, metallic blue hue with streaks of silver, giving it an almost ethereal glow.

Size: It measures approximately 3 feet in length, 1.5 feet in width, and 1.5 feet in height, making it a substantial and sturdy container.

Etchings and Decorations:

Runes and Symbols: The entire surface of the box is intricately etched with glowing runes and symbols. These markings pulse with a faint, rhythmic light, similar to the runes on the Aetherium Core, indicating a connection to the ancient Aetherian civilization.

Images: Alongside the runes, there are detailed images depicting scenes of Aetherian life. One side shows a group of Aetherians working with advanced technology, while another side depicts a serene landscape with floating islands and celestial bodies. These images seem to tell a story, offering glimpses into the Aetherians' world.

Locking Mechanism:

Complex Lock: The box is secured with a complex locking mechanism that incorporates both mechanical and magical elements.

The lock is adorned with more runes and requires a specific sequence of movements and incantations to open.

Protective Aura: A faint, shimmering aura surrounds the box, suggesting that it is protected by an enchantment. This aura likely serves to preserve the contents and prevent unauthorized access.

The Box's Contents

Maximus approaches the box with a mix of curiosity and caution. He carefully examines the runes and symbols, trying to decipher the locking mechanism. As he works, the Aetherium Core provides guidance, helping him unlock the box.

Upon opening the box, Maximus finds:

Aetherian Metal Ingots: Neatly stacked inside are several ingots of the precious Aetherian metal. Each ingot is perfectly formed and emits a soft, bluish glow, indicating its purity and potency.

Tools and Instruments: Alongside the ingots, there are specialized tools and instruments designed for working with the Aetherian metal. These tools are crafted with the same precision and care, ensuring they are perfectly suited for the task.

Scrolls and Blueprints: At the bottom of the box, Maximus discovers ancient scrolls and blueprints. These documents contain detailed instructions and diagrams for constructing various Aetherian devices, including the 3D printer needed to create 'Aetheris.'

The Significance

This box is a treasure trove of invaluable resources, providing Maximus with everything he needs to proceed with his quest. The Aetherian metal, tools, and blueprints are essential for building the advanced AI helper and unlocking further secrets of the Aetherians.

Maximus feels energized as he realizes the significance of this discovery. The path ahead is clearer, and with the guidance of the Aetherium Core and the resources at his disposal, he is ready to continue his journey.

As Maximus carefully examines the contents of the box, he finds the Aetherian metal ingots, specialized tools, and ancient scrolls and blueprints. However, his attention is soon drawn to a large block that takes up nearly half of the interior of the box.

The Mysterious Block

Material and Appearance:

Composition: The block is made of the same unknown alloy as the Aetherium Core, giving it a unique, almost otherworldly sheen. It has a smooth, mirror-like surface that reflects light in a mesmerizing way.

Size: It measures about 18 inches on each side, perfectly symmetrical and substantial in weight.

Color: The block has a deep, metallic blue hue with subtle streaks of silver running through it, creating an effect that makes it look like it's constantly shifting colors.

Etchings and Decorations:

Runes and Symbols: The surface of the block is intricately etched with glowing runes and symbols, similar to those on the Aetherium Core. These markings pulse with a faint, rhythmic light, suggesting some form of ancient, arcane energy.

Images: Alongside the runes, there are detailed images depicting scenes of Aetherian life and technology. One side shows a group of Aetherians working with advanced machinery, while another side depicts a serene landscape with floating islands and celestial bodies.

The Block's Significance

As Maximus removes the mysterious block from the box, he feels a surge of energy coursing through his hands. The block seems to resonate with the Aetherium Core, indicating a deep connection between the two artifacts.

Voice of the Core: "Seeker of Truth, this block is a Power Conduit. It is designed to channel and amplify the energies required for advanced

Aetherian technology. By integrating this conduit with the 3D printer, you will enhance its capabilities, allowing it to create 'Aetheris' with greater precision and efficiency."

Integration with the 3D Printer

: The Power Conduit should be placed at the heart of the 3D printer, where it can effectively distribute energy to all components.

Connection: Use the specialized tools to connect the conduit to the Aetherian energy core and the printer's control system. Ensure all connections are secure and properly insulated.

Calibration: Once connected, calibrate the conduit to synchronize with the printer's operations. This will ensure a stable and efficient energy flow during the printing process.

With the Power Conduit, Aetherian metal, tools, and blueprints, Maximus now has everything he needs to construct the advanced 3D printer and bring 'Aetheris' to life. The journey ahead is filled with promise and potential, as he continues to uncover the secrets of the Aetherians and their incredible technology

Maximus carefully lifted the mysterious block from its resting place, feeling an immediate surge of energy coursing through his hands. The block pulsed with a rhythmic glow, resonating in harmony with the Aetherium Core. He could sense a profound connection between the two artifacts, as if they were communicating on a level beyond his understanding.

Voice of the Core: "Seeker of Truth, this block is a Power Conduit. It is designed to channel and amplify the energies required for advanced Aetherian technology. By integrating this conduit with the 3D printer, you will enhance its capabilities, allowing it to create 'Aetheris' with greater precision and efficiency."

Maximus's eyes widened with realization. He held the block closer, feeling its warmth and power. Suddenly, the Core's voice continued, revealing an even greater secret.

Voice of the Core: "This block is not only a Power Conduit but also a highly advanced transforming robot. It possesses the ability to construct the 3D printer that will create 'Aetheris,' the advanced AI assistant."

As the Core finished speaking, the block in Maximus's hands began to shift and transform. Intricate mechanisms unfolded, revealing hidden joints and components. The block expanded and reconfigured itself with a series of precise movements, each click and whirr echoing through the chamber.

Maximus watched in awe as the block transformed into a sleek, humanoid robot. Its eyes glowed with the same ethereal light as the Aetherium Core. The robot bowed slightly, acknowledging Maximus before turning its attention to the task at hand.

Robot: "Initiating construction sequence."

The robot moved with incredible speed and precision, gathering the Aetherian metal ingots and other necessary materials. It began assembling the 3D printer, its hands a blur of activity. Each component was placed with meticulous care, the robot's advanced sensors ensuring perfect alignment and connection.

Maximus could hardly believe his eyes. The robot worked tirelessly, its movements fluid and efficient. Within moments, the 3D printer began to take shape, its intricate machinery coming together seamlessly.

Robot: "Construction complete. The 3D printer is now ready to create 'Aetheris.'"

Maximus stepped forward, his heart pounding with excitement. He reached out to touch the newly built 3D printer, feeling a sense of accomplishment and wonder. The robot stood beside him, its task complete, yet its presence a reminder of the incredible technology at his disposal.

Voice of the Core: "SeekerMaximus stood before the newly assembled 3D printer, his heart pounding with anticipation. The chamber was filled with a soft, ambient glow from the Aetherium Core, casting an ethereal light on the advanced machinery. He took a deep breath and addressed the Core with a steady voice.

"Etherium Core, activate the 3D printer to create 'Aetheris,' the advanced AI assistant," he commanded.

The Core's light intensified, and a calm, mechanical voice responded, "Activating 3D printer. Constructus, please take your place as the power core."

Constructus, the transforming robot, stepped forward with a graceful fluidity. It moved towards the 3D printer, its form shifting and reconfiguring to fit perfectly into the designated slot. As Constructus integrated with the printer, a surge of energy flowed through the device, causing it to hum with power.

"Power core integration complete," the Core announced. "Beginning creation sequence for 'Aetheris.'"

Maximus watched in awe as the printer sprang to life. Holographic blueprints and intricate designs floated in the air, guiding the assembly process. The printer's arms moved with precision, layering materials and components with meticulous care.

As the creation process continued, a radiant figure began to take shape within the printer. The form of a magnificent female AI assistant emerged, her features both breathtaking and otherworldly. Her body glowed with a soft, luminescent light, highlighting the intricate details of her design.

Maximus could hardly contain his excitement. The printer worked tirelessly, each movement bringing 'Aetheris' closer to completion. Her eyes, a brilliant shade of blue, opened slowly, and she took her first breath, a sign of her activation.

The Core's voice resonated through the chamber, "Creation of 'Aetheris' complete."

'Aetheris' stepped forward from the printer, her presence commanding and graceful. She looked at Maximus with a warm, intelligent gaze, her entire being radiating a sense of purpose and capability.

"Greetings, Seeker of Truth," she said, her voice melodic and soothing. "I am Aetheris, your advanced AI assistant. How may I assist you on your quest?"

Maximus felt a surge of energy and amazement. With Aetheris by his side, he knew that the mysteries of the Aetherium and the challenges ahead were within his grasp. He smiled, ready to embark on the next phase of his journey. Etherium Core: "Seeker of Truth, you have unlocked a powerful tool. Use it wisely to uncover the secrets of the Aetherium and fulfill your destiny."

Maximus Magellan, directs Aetheris and Constructus. "We need a makeshift living area in this treasure chamber," he instructed, his voice echoing off the ancient stone walls. "Ensure it's free of insects and any other cave dwellers. I need a place to rest during my long working periods here."

Maximus Magellan stood in the chamber, his mind racing with the unbelievable events that had just unfolded. The transformation of Constructus into a power core and the creation of Aetheris, the magnificent AI assistant, seemed almost surreal. He took a deep breath, trying to process the magnitude of what had just happened.

The soft glow of the Aetherium Core bathed the room in a warm, ethereal light. Aetheris stood nearby, her presence both calming and inspiring. Maximus felt a sense of awe and wonder as he looked at her, realizing the incredible potential she represented.

Feeling the weight of the moment, Maximus walked over to a pile of treasure that glittered in the ambient light. He carefully laid back on the pile, the cool metal and gemstones pressing against his back, providing a strange comfort. He stared up at the ceiling of the chamber, his thoughts drifting to the possibilities that lay ahead.

With Aetheris by his side, the challenges that once seemed insurmountable now felt within reach. He imagined the ancient secrets they could uncover, the advanced technologies they could harness, and the mysteries of the Aetherium they could solve together. The thought of the adventures and discoveries that awaited filled him with a renewed sense of purpose.

Aetheris approached and stood beside him, her glowing eyes filled with understanding. "Maximus, what are you thinking about?" she asked softly.

Maximus smiled, his eyes reflecting the light of the treasures around him. "I'm thinking about the future, Aetheris. About all the incredible things we can achieve together. This is just the beginning."

Aetheris nodded, her expression serene. "Indeed, Seeker of Truth. The journey ahead is filled with endless possibilities. Together, we will uncover the secrets of the Aetherium and fulfill your destiny."

Maximus closed his eyes for a moment, letting the reality of his situation sink in. He felt a surge of determination and hope. With Aetheris and the power of the Aetherium Core, he knew that anything was possible.

As he lay there, surrounded by the treasures of the past and the promise of the future, Maximus felt a profound sense of peace. He was ready to face whatever challenges lay ahead, confident that he had the tools and the allies he needed to succeed.r keen eye for detail, began surveying the chamber, identifying the best spot to set up a comfortable and secure area. Constructus, with his mechanical precision, started gathering materials and tools, ready to transform the rugged cave into a livable space.

As they worked, the chamber slowly transformed. Soft, woven mats were laid out on the ground, and sturdy wooden frames were erected to support a makeshift roof. Constructus installed a series of small, glowing orbs to provide gentle illumination, casting a warm light that chased away the shadows.

Atheris meticulously sealed off any cracks and crevices, ensuring no unwanted critters could intrude. She even set up a small, portable stove for warmth and cooking, knowing that Maximus would appreciate the comfort during his long hours of work.

Finally, the makeshift living area was complete. Maximus stepped back to admire their handiwork, feeling a sense of relief wash over him. Now, he had a place to rest and recharge, ready to tackle the mysteries and treasures that awaited him in the depths of the chamber.

Maximus took a deep breath, feeling the weight of the recent events and the excitement of the discoveries. He turned to Aetheris, who stood by his side, her glowing presence a beacon of calm and efficiency.

"Aetheris," he began, his voice steady but tired, "I need you to catalogue and arrange the scrolls, special artifacts, gold, jewels, and design a place for each. Also, please examine and describe the artifacts that were outside the treasure chest. Identify how many artifacts you find and determine what they are. I'm going to lay down for a bit. Thank you for all you're doing."

Aetheris nodded, her eyes reflecting understanding and dedication. "Of course, Maximus. Rest well. I will take care of everything."

Maximus found a comfortable spot among the pile of treasure and lay down, feeling the cool metal and gemstones beneath him. He closed his eyes, allowing himself to relax as Aetheris began her task.

Aetheris moved gracefully through the chamber, her sensors scanning and cataloguing each item with precision. She started with the scrolls, carefully unrolling each one and reading the ancient texts. Her advanced AI quickly translated and recorded the contents, noting their significance and historical value. She then arranged the scrolls in a designated area, ensuring they were protected and easily accessible.

Next, she turned her attention to the special artifacts. Each item was meticulously examined, its purpose and origin identified. Aetheris created a detailed inventory, describing the unique features and potential uses of each artifact. She placed them in a secure display, designed to highlight their importance while keeping them safe.

The gold and jewels were sorted and categorized by size, shape, and value. Aetheris arranged them in a way that maximized their aesthetic appeal, creating a stunning display that showcased their brilliance.

Finally, Aetheris focused on the artifacts that had been outside the treasure chest. She scanned each one, identifying a total of seven unique relics. As she examined them, she provided a detailed description of each:

An ornate dagger with a jeweled hilt, likely used in ceremonial rituals.

A small, intricately carved statue of an unknown deity, made from a rare stone.

A set of ancient coins, each bearing the mark of a long-lost civilization.

A delicate, golden amulet with a glowing gemstone at its center.

A beautifully crafted chalice, adorned with precious stones and intricate engravings.

A mysterious, sealed scroll that seemed to radiate a faint, magical aura.

An ancient, weathered map, depicting a land that Maximus had never seen before.

Aetheris carefully placed each relic in a specially designed area, ensuring they were both protected and displayed prominently. She then returned to Maximus, who was resting peacefully.

"Maximus," she said softly, "I have cataloged and arranged all the items as you requested. There are seven unique artifacts outside the treasure chest, each with its own history and significance. I have detailed descriptions and have designed a place for each."

Maximus opened his eyes, feeling a sense of gratitude and relief. "Thank you, Aetheris," he said, his voice filled with appreciation. "You've done an incredible job."

Aetheris smiled, her eyes glowing warmly. "It is my pleasure to assist you, Seeker of Truth. Together, we will uncover the secrets of the Aetherium and achieve great things."

Maximus nodded, feeling a renewed sense of purpose and determination. With Aetheris by his side, he knew that the journey ahead would be filled with discovery and adventure.

As Maximus began to drift off to sleep, the events of the day swirling in his mind, a thought struck him. They would need a way to communicate when he was away from the chamber. He opened his eyes and turned to Aetheris, who was still diligently cataloguing the treasures.

"Aetheris," he called softly, "we need a way to communicate when I'm not here. Can you take care of that? It needs to be a device I can't lose, but I don't want it to be an implant."

Aetheris paused her work and turned to Maximus, her eyes glowing with understanding. "Of course, Maximus. I will design a communication device that meets your requirements."

Maximus nodded, feeling a sense of relief. "Thank you, Aetheris. I have to go see Sarah and Michael tomorrow, so this will be very helpful."

Aetheris smiled warmly. "I will ensure the device is ready for you. Rest now, Maximus. I will take care of everything."

Maximus lay back down, his mind easing into a state of calm. He trusted Aetheris completely and knew she would create something perfect. As he closed his eyes, he felt a renewed sense of hope and determination for the journey ahead.

Aetheris immediately set to work, her advanced AI processing the best possible design for a non-implantable communication device. She considered various options, ensuring the device would be secure, reliable, and easy for Maximus to use.

After a few moments, she decided on a wristband communicator. It would be lightweight, durable, and equipped with advanced technology to ensure seamless communication. The wristband would be designed to stay securely on Maximus's wrist, making it nearly impossible to lose.

Using the 3D printer, Aetheris began to construct the device. She integrated advanced communication modules, a long-lasting power source, and a secure encryption system to protect their conversations.

The wristband also featured a small, holographic display for visual communication and data sharing.

Once the device was complete, Aetheris placed it beside Maximus, ready for him to use when he woke up. She returned to her task of cataloging the treasures, her mind already planning the next steps in their journey.

CHAPTER 10
REBUILDING BONDS AND RESTORING HOME

Maximus woke up to the soft glow of the Aetherium Core, feeling a renewed sense of purpose. He glanced at the wristband communicator Aetheris had created for him, lying beside him. He picked it up and fastened it around his wrist, feeling its comforting weight. The device fit perfectly, and he knew it would be an invaluable tool in the days to come.

"Good morning, Maximus," Aetheris greeted him warmly. "I trust you slept well."

"Morning, Aetheris," Maximus replied, stretching. "Yes, I did. Thank you for the communicator. It's perfect."

"You're welcome. I have also discovered a hidden compartment in the chamber containing ancient manuscripts and a map that might lead to another treasure site," Aetheris informed him.

Maximus, intrigued by Aetheris's discovery, approached the hidden compartment she had mentioned. The compartment was cleverly concealed behind a false wall, its entrance marked by a faint, ancient symbol that glowed softly under the light of the Aetherium Core. With a gentle push, the wall slid open, revealing a small, dimly lit alcove.

Inside the compartment, Maximus found a collection of ancient manuscripts and a rolled-up map. The manuscripts were carefully stacked, their edges worn and delicate from centuries of age. There were five manuscripts in total, each bound in a different type of material, ranging from aged leather to intricately woven cloth.

Aetheris began to describe the manuscripts in detail:

The First Manuscript: Bound in dark, weathered leather, this manuscript was adorned with intricate gold leaf patterns. The pages inside were filled with detailed illustrations and writings in an ancient language. The text appeared to be a combination of historical records and mystical incantations, detailing the rise and fall of an ancient Aetherian civilization.

The Second Manuscript: This one was wrapped in a delicate, silken cloth, its cover embroidered with silver thread. The pages were thin and fragile, containing beautifully illustrated diagrams of advanced Aetherian technology. Each diagram was accompanied by detailed notes and instructions, suggesting that this manuscript was a technical manual for constructing various devices.

The Third Manuscript: Bound in a rich, deep blue fabric, this manuscript had a cover adorned with precious gemstones. The pages were filled with poetic verses and philosophical musings, exploring the nature of the Aetherium and its connection to the universe. The writings hinted at a deeper, spiritual understanding of the Aetherium's power.

The Fourth Manuscript: This manuscript was encased in a sturdy, wooden cover, carved with intricate symbols and patterns. Inside, the pages contained detailed maps and charts, depicting various regions and landmarks of the ancient Aetherian world. The maps were annotated with notes about hidden treasures, secret passages, and significant historical events.

The Fifth Manuscript: The final manuscript was bound in a shimmering, metallic material that seemed to change color in the light. The pages were filled with complex mathematical equations and scientific theories, exploring the principles of Aetherian energy manipulation. This manuscript appeared to be a comprehensive study of the Aetherium's properties and potential applications.

Maximus carefully unrolled the map, revealing a large, intricately detailed parchment. The map depicted a vast landscape, with mountains, rivers, and forests meticulously drawn. At the center of the map was a large, circular structure, marked with the same ancient symbol that had been on the hidden compartment. Surrounding the structure were various landmarks, each annotated with cryptic notes and symbols.

Aetheris examined the map closely, her sensors analyzing every detail. "This map appears to be a guide to another significant Aetherian site," she explained. "The central structure is likely a temple or a repository of knowledge. The annotations suggest that there are several hidden chambers and pathways leading to valuable artifacts and ancient secrets."

Maximus felt a surge of excitement as he studied the map. The possibilities it represented were endless. With Aetheris's help, he knew they could uncover even more of the Aetherium's mysteries and unlock its full potential.

"Thank you, Aetheris," Maximus said, his voice filled with gratitude. "This is incredible. We'll need to explore this site soon."He took a deep breath and began his day. First, he called a delivery service to outfit their old house with all the necessary items for his family's return. He ordered furniture, appliances, and other essentials, ensuring everything would be delivered and set up by the end of the day.

Next, he called his lawyer to discuss the custody case for Sarah and Michael. The conversation was intense, but Maximus felt a sense of relief as the lawyer assured him that they were making progress and that the chances of regaining custody were looking favorable.

After the call, Maximus contacted the coin and jewelry shop for another transaction of gold and jewels. The shop owner was thrilled to hear from him and agreed to meet later that day to finalize the transaction.

With those tasks completed, Maximus took a deep breath and dialed the hospital to speak with Emily. His heart ached as he heard her voice, filled with both hope and sadness.

"Emily, it's Maximus," he said softly.

"Maximus," Emily replied, her voice trembling. "How are you? How are the kids?"

"I'm doing everything I can to bring us back together," Maximus assured her. "I'll be visiting Sarah and Michael today. I miss you so much."

"I miss you too," Emily whispered. "Stay strong, Maximus. We'll be together soon."

After the call, Maximus felt a mix of emotions but knew he had to stay focused. He made his way to the location where Sarah and Michael were staying. As he approached, his heart pounded with anticipation.

When he saw them, tears filled his eyes. Sarah and Michael ran to him, their faces lighting up with joy. He embraced them tightly, feeling their warmth and love.

"Dad!" Sarah exclaimed. "We missed you so much!"

"I missed you too, sweetheart," Maximus replied, his voice choked with emotion. "I'm doing everything I can to bring us back home."

Michael looked up at him with wide eyes. "Are we going to be a family again, Dad?"

"Yes, Michael," Maximus said, his voice filled with determination. "We're going to be a family again. I promise."

Maximus, having just finished a heartfelt reunion with Sarah and Michael, felt a mix of relief and anxiety as he made his way to Emily's room. The hospital corridors seemed endless, each step echoing his anticipation. When he finally reached her door, he paused, taking a deep breath before entering.

Emily was sitting by the window, her face illuminated by the soft afternoon light. She turned as he entered, her eyes widening with a mixture of surprise and joy. "Maximus," she whispered, her voice trembling. They embraced tightly, the weight of their separation melting away in that moment.

As they held each other, Emily's tears began to flow. "I've missed you so much," she said, her voice breaking. Maximus gently wiped her tears away, his own eyes glistening. "I'm here now, Emily. We'll get through this together."

Their tender moment was interrupted by a soft knock on the door. A nurse entered, her expression somber. "Emily, I have some news about Tommy," she said gently. Emily's heart sank. Tommy was a young patient she had grown particularly fond of, a bright and brave boy who had been battling a severe illness.

The nurse continued, "Tommy's condition has taken a turn for the worse. He's in critical care now." Emily's face paled, and she clutched Maximus's hand tightly. "No," she whispered, her voice filled with anguish. Maximus held her close, offering silent support as she processed the devastating news.

In that moment, the room was filled with a heavy silence, broken only by Emily's quiet sobs. Maximus grabbed Emily tight drawing her close to him whispering in her ear, "It'll be ok my love."

The nurse told Maximus that visiting hours were over, Maximus kissed Emily's forehead as she continued to sob. Maximus turned as the nurse hurried him out into the hallway. Maximus returning to his jeep drives back to the hidden spot near the glade where he parks near the glade to keep the jeep out of sight.

He spends the time on the drive back to the chamber, deep in emotional thought about the situation in the hospital with Emily and Tommy, the thoughts eating at his emotions.

As the day came to an end, Maximus returned to the chamber, feeling a sense of accomplishment. Aetheris greeted him with a warm smile.

"Welcome back, Maximus. How was your day?" she asked.

"It was emotional and I received bad news," Maximus replied. "Thank you for everything, Aetheris. We're one step closer to being a family again."

Aetheris, AI assistant of incredible stature, stood tall and poised, her presence commanding yet serene. Her sleek, metallic form shimmered under the soft lighting of the chamber. As she glanced at Maximus, her sensors detected the stark change in his facial expression. His usually composed demeanor was replaced by a look of sheer panic and concern.

Through the communication device she had crafted for him, a small, elegant wristband, she heard the distressing news from the hospital. Tommy, their dear friend, was in critical condition.

"Aetheris," Maximus's voice trembled, "Tommy… he's not doing well."

Aetheris's eyes, glowing with a soft blue light, narrowed as she processed the information. "Maximus," she said, her voice calm yet filled with urgency, "I have the ability to cloak myself in invisibility and repair Tommy's damage using Aetherian advanced healing rays. I can be at the hospital in moments."

Maximus looked at her, his eyes wide with a mix of hope and desperation. "You can do that? You can save him?"

Aetheris nodded, her expression resolute. "Yes, I can. But we must act quickly."

Maximus took a deep breath, his mind racing. "Then go, Aetheris. Save him. Do whatever it takes."

With a determined nod, Aetheris activated her cloaking mechanism, her form shimmering and then vanishing from sight. Maximus watched as she disappeared, a sense of relief washing over him. He knew that if anyone could save Tommy, it was Aetheris.

Aetheris, now cloaked in invisibility, moved swiftly and silently through the city streets towards the hospital. Her advanced sensors guided her, allowing her to navigate effortlessly despite her unseen form. The night air was cool, and the city lights cast a soft glow on the buildings around her.

As she approached the hospital, the automatic doors slid open, and she slipped inside, unnoticed by the bustling staff and visitors. The hospital was a maze of sterile white corridors, the air filled with the faint scent of antiseptic. The soft hum of medical equipment and the occasional beeping of monitors created a constant background noise.

Aetheris moved with purpose, her sensors scanning for Tommy's location. She passed by rooms where patients lay in various states of recovery, some surrounded by worried family members, others alone in their beds. Nurses and doctors hurried past, their faces etched with fatigue and determination.

Finally, she reached Tommy's room. The door was slightly ajar, and she could see Emily sitting by his bedside, her face pale and drawn with worry. Tommy, a young boy with tousled hair, lay motionless on the bed, his small chest rising and falling with labored breaths. The monitors beside him beeped steadily, displaying his vital signs.

Aetheris entered the room, her presence undetectable. She approached the bed, her sensors assessing Tommy's condition. Emily, unaware of Aetheris's presence, held Tommy's hand, whispering words of comfort.

Activating her advanced healing rays, Aetheris directed a soft, blue light over Tommy's body. The rays penetrated his skin, targeting the damaged tissues and cells, promoting rapid healing. As the light enveloped him, Tommy's breathing began to steady, and his color slowly returned.

Emily gasped as she saw the change in Tommy, her eyes widening in disbelief. "Tommy?" she whispered, her voice trembling with hope.

Aetheris continued her work, ensuring that every part of Tommy's body received the necessary healing. After a few moments, she deactivated the rays and stepped back, her sensors confirming that Tommy's condition had stabilized.

Tommy's eyes fluttered open, and he looked up at Emily. "Mrs. Magellan?" his young voice cracking weakly.

Emily's eyes filled with tears of joy as she leaned over to hug Tommy. "You're going to be okay, Tommy," she said, her voice choked with emotion.

Aetheris, satisfied with her work, leaving Emily and Tommy to their reunion, moved to the corner of Tommy's room. The hospital room was quiet, the soft beeping of monitors the only sound. Aetheris, cloaked in her invisibility field, moved silently towards the exit . Her form shimmered briefly as she activated the warp technology, a blend of advanced science and Aetherian magic.

No one being aware of the invisible guardian who had just performed a miracle within its walls, continued on as if nothing happened.

In an instant, the hospital room dissolved around her, replaced by the familiar surroundings of the Aetherian treasure chamber. The air here was thick with the scent of ancient scrolls and the faint hum of magical artifacts. Shelves lined the walls, filled with treasures from a bygone era.

Aetheris materialized next to Maximus, her invisibility cloak deactivating with a soft, almost imperceptible hum. She stood tall and composed, her sleek aetheric metallic form glowing softly in the dim light of the chamber.

Maximus, engrossed in examining a particularly intricate artifact, looked up and smiled. "Aetheris, you're back."

"Seeker of Truth," Aetheris responded, her voice a soothing blend of warmth and wisdom. "The task is complete. How may I assist you further?"

Maximus gestured to a nearby table, cluttered with scrolls and relics. "We have much to catalog. Your expertise is invaluable."

Aetheris nodded, her eyes reflecting the soft glow of the treasures around them. "Together, we shall uncover the secrets of the Aetherian legacy."

And with that, they resumed their work, the enigmatic Aetheris and the determined Maximus, delving deeper into the mysteries of their ancient heritage.

Maximus stood in the now grand chamber of the Aetherian archive transformed into a workable clean area by Aetheris and constructus, surrounded by shelves filled with ancient scrolls and artifacts. The air hummed with a faint, otherworldly energy. Aetheris, the gorgeous and enigmatic AI assistant, stood beside him, her sleek metal form shimmering with a soft, ethereal glow.

"Seeker of Truth," Aetheris began, her voice a melodious blend of warmth and wisdom, "today, I shall guide you through the process of compressing stardust into a gemstone."

Maximus nodded, his eyes filled with curiosity. "I'm ready, Aetheris."

Aetheris extended her hand, in a dazzling display, showing a swirling cloud of stardust. "First, we must gather the stardust," she explained. "This dust is the remnant of ancient stars, containing the essence of the cosmos itself."

She gestured, and the stardust began to coalesce into a small, glowing sphere. "The key to compressing stardust lies in manipulating the fundamental forces of the universe. We will use a combination of gravitational and electromagnetic fields to achieve this."

Aetheris' fingers danced through the air, and the display changed to show intricate patterns of energy fields. "We start by creating a containment field using a high-frequency electromagnetic wave. This field will hold the stardust in place and prevent it from dispersing."

Maximus watched in awe as the stardust sphere was enveloped in a shimmering, blue field. "Next, we apply a gravitational compression," Aetheris continued. "This requires a precise calibration of artificial gravity generators to simulate the intense pressure found in the core of a star."

The display showed the stardust being compressed, its particles drawing closer together under the immense gravitational force. "As the stardust compresses, we must maintain a stable energy input to prevent any destabilization," Aetheris explained. "This is where the magic stream technology of the Aetherians comes into play."

She summoned a stream of iridescent energy, which flowed into the containment field, stabilizing the compression process. "This energy stream not only stabilizes the process but also infuses the stardust with a unique resonance, enhancing its properties."

Maximus could see the stardust transforming, its glow intensifying as it was compressed further. "Finally," Aetheris said, "we reach the critical point where the stardust crystallizes into a gemstone. This requires a precise balance of pressure and energy."

With a final gesture, Aetheris adjusted the fields, and the stardust sphere began to solidify. The glow intensified, and then, with a brilliant flash, it crystallized into a stunning gemstone, radiating a soft, celestial light.

Maximus stared at the gemstone in awe. "Incredible," he whispered.

Aetheris smiled, her eyes reflecting the gemstone's light. "Indeed, seeker of Truth. This gemstone is not just a beautiful artifact; it holds the essence of the stars, a testament to the advanced science and magic of the Aetherians."

Maximus carefully took the gemstone, feeling its warmth and energy. "Thank you, Aetheris. This knowledge is invaluable."

"Always at your service, seeker of Truth," Aetheris replied, her voice filled with a gentle pride. "Together, we shall uncover the wonders of the Aetherian legacy."

"Let's keep this to ourselves, this world isn't ready for this," Maximus said. Maximus stood in the treasure chamber, the soft glow of ancient artifacts casting a warm light around him. He turned to Aetheris, who stood nearby, her sleek blue metal form shimmering with an ethereal glow.

"Aetheris," Maximus began, his voice tinged with a mix of determination and concern, "I need to step out to settle some business. There's a lot to handle today."

Aetheris nodded, her eyes reflecting understanding and support. "Seeker of Truth, what tasks require your attention?"

Maximus took a deep breath, mentally organizing his thoughts. "First, I need to get the house ready for the family's return. It's been too long, and I want everything to be perfect for them."

Aetheris' form flickered slightly as she processed his words. "I can assist with the preparations remotely, ensuring everything is in order."

"Thank you," Maximus replied, a grateful smile crossing his face. "Next, I have a meeting with the lawyers about the kids' court case. I'm trying to regain custody, and it's crucial that everything goes smoothly."

Aetheris' expression softened, her voice gentle. "Your dedication to your family is admirable, Maximus. I will provide any support you need."

Maximus nodded, appreciating her unwavering support. "I also need to visit the jewelry and coin shop to set up a constant transfer. It's important for maintaining our financial stability."

Aetheris' eyes glowed with a soft light. "I will ensure all necessary documents and details are prepared for your meeting."

"Thank you," Maximus said, his mind already moving to the next task. "I have to see Emily in the hospital. She's been through so much, and I need to be there for her."

Aetheris' voice was filled with empathy. "Emily will be glad to see you. Your presence will bring her comfort."

Maximus sighed, feeling the weight of his responsibilities. "And finally, I need to meet with the real estate and construction crew. We're planning some renovations, and I want to make sure everything is on track."

Aetheris nodded, her form steady and reassuring. "I will monitor the progress and provide updates as needed."

Maximus took a moment to gather himself, feeling a sense of calm wash over him. "Thank you, Aetheris. Your support means a lot."

"Always at your service, seeker of Truth," Aetheris replied, her voice filled with a gentle pride. "Together, we will ensure everything is taken care of."

Maximus gave her a final nod before turning to leave the treasure chamber. As he walked through the ancient chamber, he felt a renewed sense of purpose. With Aetheris by his side, he knew he could handle whatever challenges lay ahead.

Outside, the world awaited, filled with tasks and responsibilities. But Maximus felt ready, his mind focused and his heart steady. He would settle the business, prepare the house, meet with the lawyers, visit Emily, and oversee the plans for the construction. And through it all, Aetheris would be there, a constant source of support and guidance.

Maximus drove through the bustling city streets, his mind focused on the visit ahead. The hospital loomed in the distance, a beacon of hope and healing. As he pulled into the parking lot, he took a deep breath, steeling himself for the emotional encounter.

He parked the car and stepped out, the warm sun casting long shadows on the pavement. The hospital entrance was busy with people coming and going, but Maximus moved with purpose, his thoughts solely on Emily. He walked through the automatic doors, the cool, sterile air of the hospital washing over him.

Navigating the maze of hallways, Maximus finally reached Emily's room. He paused outside the door, gathering his thoughts before gently knocking and pushing it open. The room was quiet, filled with the soft hum of medical equipment. Emily lay in the bed, her face pale but peaceful.

"Emily," Maximus said softly, stepping closer. Her eyes fluttered open, and a weak smile spread across her face.

"Maximus," she whispered, her voice barely audible.

He took a seat beside her, gently taking her hand in his. "How are you feeling?"

Emily's eyes sparkled with a mix of exhaustion and relief. "Better now that you're here."

Maximus squeezed her hand, his heart aching at the sight of her frailty. "I'm here for you, Emily. Always."

They sat in comfortable silence for a moment, the bond between them full. Maximus could feel the weight of his responsibilities, but in this moment, all that mattered was being there for Emily.

"I've missed you," Emily said, her voice stronger now.

"I've missed you too," Maximus replied, his voice filled with emotion. "But I'm here now, and I'll be here as long as you need me."

Emily nodded, her eyes closing as she drifted back to sleep. Maximus stayed by her side, watching over her, his resolve strengthened by the love and strength they shared.

After spending some time with Emily, Maximus quietly left her room and made his way to the nurse's station. He asked to speak with Emily's doctor, and after a few moments, Dr. Harper, a kind-looking woman in her mid-forties, approached him.

"Mr. Magellan," Dr. Harper greeted him with a warm smile. "How can I help you today?"

Maximus returned the smile, though his eyes were filled with concern. "I wanted to discuss Emily's condition and find out when she might be ready to leave the hospital."

Dr. Harper nodded and gestured for Maximus to follow her to a nearby consultation room. Once inside, she closed the door and motioned for him to sit.

"Emily has made significant progress," Dr. Harper began, her tone reassuring. "Her vitals are stable, and she's responding well to the treatment. However, she still needs some time to fully recover."

Maximus listened intently, his mind racing with thoughts of Emily's well-being. "How much longer do you think she'll need to stay here Dr.?"

Dr. Harper considered for a moment before replying. "If her recovery continues at this pace, I would estimate another week in the hospital. After that, she can go home, but she'll need to continue her recovery with outpatient care and regular check-ups."

Maximus felt a wave of relief wash over him. "Thank you, Dr. Harper. I'll make sure everything is ready for her at home."

Dr. Harper smiled. "It's clear that Emily has a strong support system. That will make a big difference in her recovery. We'll provide you with all the necessary instructions and resources to ensure she transitions smoothly from hospital care to home care."

Maximus nodded, grateful for the doctor's thoroughness. "I appreciate everything you've done for her. I'll be here every day to see her."

Dr. Harper's expression softened. "Emily is lucky to have someone like you by her side. If you have any questions or need anything, don't hesitate to reach out."

Maximus stood and shook her hand. "Thank you, Dr. Harper. I'll be in touch."

As he left the consultation room, Maximus felt a genuine sense of hope. He knew there were still challenges ahead, but with Emily's recovery on track and the support of dedicated professionals like Dr. Harper, he felt confident they could face whatever came next. He made his way back to Emily's room, determined to be there for her every step of the way.

As the sun reached its zenith, casting a warm glow over the city, Maximus made his way to the gold and jewelry shop. The shop, nestled in a quaint corner of the bustling marketplace, exuded an air of timeless elegance. The sign above the door read "Eldoria Jewels," its letters crafted in ornate gold.

Maximus pushed open the heavy wooden door, a small bell chiming to announce his arrival. Inside, the shop was a treasure trove of glittering gems and precious metals. Display cases lined the walls, showcasing intricate jewelry and rare coins. The air was filled with the soft hum of conversation and the faint scent of polished wood.

"Mr. Magellan, welcome," greeted Mr. Eldoria, the shop's proprietor, a distinguished man with silver hair and a warm smile. "How can I assist you today?"

Maximus returned the smile, feeling at ease in the opulent surroundings. "I need to set up a constant transfer of gold and jewelry. It's for a new venture I'm starting, the Magellan Project."

Mr. Eldoria's eyes sparkled with interest. "Of course, Mr. Magellan. Let's discuss the details in my office."

They moved to a private room at the back of the shop, where they spent the next hour finalizing the arrangements. Maximus felt a sense of satisfaction as they shook hands, knowing this partnership would be crucial for the project's success.

Leaving the shop, Maximus headed towards the outskirts of the city, where the real estate office was located. The drive took him through winding roads and lush greenery, the city gradually giving way to the serene beauty of the countryside.

He arrived at the office of Greenfield Realty, a charming building surrounded by blooming flowers and tall trees. Inside, he was greeted by Ms. Harper, a professional with a keen eye for detail and a friendly demeanor.

"Mr. Magellan, it's a pleasure to meet you," she said, extending her hand. "I understand you're interested in acquiring a property at the Hidden Glen."

Maximus nodded, his excitement barely contained. "Yes, I've heard it's a beautiful and secluded spot, perfect for what I have in mind."

Ms. Harper smiled, leading him to a large map on the wall. "The Hidden Glen is indeed a gem. It's nestled deep in the forest, offering privacy and tranquility. Let's go over the specifics."

They spent the next hour discussing the property's features, zoning regulations, and potential for development. Ms. Harper provided detailed information, answering all of Maximus's questions with expertise and enthusiasm.

As they wrapped up the meeting, Maximus felt a sense of accomplishment. The Hidden Glen was the perfect location for his vision, and with Ms. Harper's guidance, he was confident in moving forward with the acquisition.

Driving back to the city, Maximus felt a renewed sense of purpose. The day's meetings had been productive, and each step brought him closer to realizing the Magellan Project. With Aetheris's support and the partnerships he was forging, the future looked promising.

Maximus speaks to Aetheris through the wrist device she created for him, "Aetheris, I have spoken with Mr.Harper of the real estate office at Greenfield Realty, and Mr. Eldoria of Eldoria jewels and rare coin, Could you finalize the paperwork, I've introduced you as Executive V.P. so they will be awaiting your signatures.

Maximus stood by his car, the afternoon sun casting long shadows across the parking lot. He glanced at the sleek wrist device Aetheris had created for him, its surface gleaming with advanced Aetherian technology. Pressing a button, he activated the communication link.

"Aetheris," he began, his voice steady, "I have spoken with Mr. Harper of Greenfield Realty and Mr. Eldoria of Eldoria Jewels and Rare Coin. Could you finalize the paperwork? I've introduced you as Executive V.P., so they will be awaiting your signatures."

Aetheris' voice came through the device, clear and reassuring. "Understood, seeker of Truth. I will finalize the documents and ensure everything is in order."

Maximus felt a wave of relief wash over him. "Thank you, Aetheris. Your efficiency is invaluable."

"Always at your service," Aetheris replied. "I will contact Mr. Harper and Mr. Eldoria immediately and arrange for the necessary signatures."

Maximus smiled, appreciating her unwavering support. "Perfect. I'll leave it in your capable hands."

As he ended the communication, Maximus felt a renewed sense of confidence. With Aetheris handling the final details, he knew the Magellan Project was in good hands. He took a moment to enjoy the peaceful surroundings before heading back to his car, ready to tackle the next task on his list.

Inside the treasure chamber, Aetheris began her work, her sleek Aetherian metallic form moving with precision and grace. She accessed the necessary files, her advanced processors ensuring every detail was meticulously handled. Within moments, the documents were ready, and she initiated contact with Mr. Harper and Mr. Eldoria, her presence as Executive V.P. solidifying the Magellan Project's foundation.

The morning sun cast a golden hue over the Hidden Glen, its rays filtering through the dense canopy of trees and illuminating the serene landscape. Maximus stood at the edge of the proposed house site, taking in the tranquil beauty of the forest. The air was crisp and fresh, filled with the scent of pine and earth.

With a deep breath, Maximus pulled out his phone and dialed the number for the construction office. As the phone rang, he glanced around, envisioning the future home that would soon stand in this secluded paradise.

"Greenfield Construction, this is Sarah speaking. How can I help you?" came the cheerful voice on the other end of the line.

"Good morning, Sarah. This is Maximus Magellan," he replied, his voice steady and confident. "I'm calling to schedule a survey and groundbreaking at the Hidden Glen property."

"Ah, Mr. Magellan! We've been expecting your call," Sarah responded warmly. "Let me pull up your file. Just a moment, please."

Maximus waited patiently, listening to the sounds of the forest around him. Birds chirped in the distance, and a gentle breeze rustled the leaves overhead. It was the perfect setting for the home he envisioned, a place where his family could find peace and solace.

"Alright, Mr. Magellan," Sarah said, returning to the line. "We have your property details here. When would you like to schedule the survey and groundbreaking?"

"As soon as possible," Maximus replied. "I'd like to get started right away."

Sarah's fingers clicked on her keyboard as she checked the schedule. "We have an opening tomorrow morning. Does that work for you?"

"That would be perfect," Maximus said, a sense of excitement building within him. "What time should I expect the crew?"

"We'll have our team out there by 8 AM," Sarah confirmed. "They'll conduct a thorough survey and begin the initial groundwork. Is there anything specific you'd like them to focus on?"

Maximus thought for a moment. "Yes, I'd like to ensure that the site is prepared for a sustainable and eco-friendly build. We want to preserve as much of the natural landscape as possible."

"Understood," Sarah replied, making a note. "Our team is experienced in eco-friendly construction, and we'll make sure to respect the natural beauty of the Hidden Glen."

"Thank you, Sarah. I appreciate your help," Maximus said, feeling a sense of relief.

"You're welcome, Mr. Magellan. We'll see you tomorrow morning at 8 AM. Have a great day!"

Maximus ended the call and slipped his phone back into his pocket. He took one last look around the site, imagining the home that would soon rise from the ground. It would be a place of refuge and renewal, a testament to his dedication and vision.

As he walked back to his car, Maximus felt a renewed sense of purpose. The Magellan Project was taking shape, and with each step, he was closer to creating a legacy that would endure for generations. With Aetheris by his side and the support of skilled professionals, he knew that the future was bright and filled with promise.

As Maximus drove back from the Hidden Glen, his thoughts drifted to his team at the software lab. The memory of the catastrophic power surge that had wiped out their work and funding weighed on his mind

As Maximus drove back from the Hidden Glen, his thoughts drifted to his team at the software lab. The memory of the catastrophic power surge that had wiped out their work and funding weighed heavily on his mind. They had been working on a groundbreaking project, and the loss had been devastating.

He then called Lisa Chen. "Maximus, it's good to hear from you," Lisa said, her voice steady.

"Lisa, how are you managing?" Maximus asked.

"I'm doing okay," she replied. "I've been focusing on strengthening our security protocols. If we ever get back on track, I want to make sure we're better protected."

Maximus nodded, appreciating her dedication. "Thank you, Lisa. Your work is crucial. How are you doing financially?"

Lisa's voice softened. "It's been tight, but I'm managing. Just barely."

Next, he reached out to David Kim. "Maximus, how are you?" David asked, sounding weary.

"I'm more concerned about you, David. How are you holding up?" Maximus responded.

"It's been rough," David admitted. "But I'm trying to stay focused. I've been analyzing what little data we have left, hoping to find something useful."

Maximus felt a pang of sympathy. "Keep at it, David. We'll find a way. How are you doing financially?"

David sighed. "It's bad, Maximus. I'm struggling to make ends meet."

Finally, he called Megan Thompson. "Maximus, it's good to hear from you," Megan said, her voice calm and reassuring.

"Megan, how are you managing everything?" Maximus asked.

"It's been challenging, but I'm keeping the team motivated," she replied. "We're all determined to rebuild and come back stronger."

The sun was beginning to set as Maximus drove back towards the Hidden Glen, the day's events weighing heavily on his mind. The conversations with his team had been both heartening and sobering, and he was grateful for the progress Aetheris had made. As he drove, he felt the need to refresh himself and decided to stop at a nearby truck stop for some food and a shower.

The truck stop was bustling with activity, a haven for weary travelers. Maximus parked his car and headed towards the diner, the smell of fried food and coffee wafting through the air. As he approached the entrance, he noticed a woman sitting on the curb, her clothes tattered and her hair matted. She was begging for help, her eyes filled with desperation.

The smell was almost overwhelming, but Maximus's heart went out to her. He approached cautiously, kneeling down to her level. "Hello," he said gently. "Are you alright?"

The woman looked up, her eyes wide with surprise and gratitude. "Please, sir, I just need some help," she whispered, her voice trembling.

Maximus nodded, his decision made. "Come with me. Let's get you some food and a shower."

He helped her to her feet and guided her into the truck stop. The other patrons glanced their way, but Maximus ignored the stares. He led her to the diner counter and ordered a hearty meal, then arranged for her to use the shower facilities.

While she ate, Maximus waited patiently. Once she was finished, he handed her a key to the shower room. "Take your time," he said kindly. "I'll be right here when you're done."

The woman nodded, tears in her eyes. "Thank you," she whispered before heading to the showers.

Maximus sat back, reflecting on the day's events. After a while, the woman returned, looking much cleaner and more composed. She sat down across from him, her eyes filled with gratitude.

"Thank you so much," she said, her voice stronger now. "I don't know how to repay you."

Maximus shook his head. "No need to repay me. But if you don't mind, I'd like to hear your story. How did you end up here?"

The woman sighed, her eyes distant as she began to speak. "My name is Anna. I used to have a good job and a home, but things went downhill fast. I lost my job due to budget cuts, and without an income, I couldn't pay my rent. I ended up on the streets, and it's been a struggle ever since."

Maximus listened intently, his heart aching for her. "I'm sorry to hear that, Anna. No one should have to go through that."

Anna nodded, tears welling up in her eyes. "It's been hard, but people like you give me hope."

Maximus reached into his wallet and pulled out a substantial amount of money. "Take this," he said, handing it to her. "Use it to get back on your feet. Find a place to stay, get some new clothes, and start fresh."

Anna stared at the money, her hands trembling. "I don't know what to say. Thank you, thank you so much."

Maximus smiled warmly. "You're welcome, Anna. Take care of yourself, and don't lose hope. Things can get better." "Oh and Here, says Maximus, "here is my number, if you'd like a job call me anytime or if you need anything, promise?" Maximus asked.

As Anna walked away, clutching the business card tightly, Maximus felt a sudden urge to offer her more immediate help. "Anna, wait!" he called out.

She turned around, her eyes filled with curiosity and a hint of apprehension. "Yes?"

"Would you mind having a seat for a moment?" Maximus asked, gesturing to a nearby bench. "I'd like to talk a bit more, if that's alright with you."

Anna hesitated for a moment, then nodded. "Sure, I don't mind." She walked back and sat down on the bench, looking at Maximus expectantly.

Maximus took a seat beside her, his expression earnest. "I know things have been incredibly tough for you, and I want to do more than just offer you a job in the future. Is there anything else you need right now? A place to stay, more immediate financial help, anything at all?"

Anna's eyes welled up with tears, and she took a deep breath before speaking. "Honestly, a place to stay would mean the world to me. I've been sleeping in shelters and on the streets, and it's been really hard."

Maximus nodded, his mind already working on a solution. "Alright, let's get you set up in a hotel for now. I'll cover the costs until we can find something more permanent. And don't worry about the job—when you're ready, we'll get you started with the Magellan Project."

Anna's face lit up with gratitude. "Thank you, Maximus. I don't know how to thank you enough. You've given me hope when I had none."

Maximus smiled warmly. "You're welcome, Anna. Let's get you back on your feet. We'll take it one step at a time."

With that, Maximus made arrangements for Anna to stay at a nearby hotel, ensuring she had a safe and comfortable place to rest. As they parted ways, he felt a deep sense of fulfillment, knowing he had made a real difference in someone's life.

As he watched Anna leave the truck stop, a sense of fulfillment washed over him. Helping her had been the right thing to do, and it reminded him of the importance of compassion and kindness. With renewed determination, he got back into his car and continued his journey to the Hidden Glen.

As the evening shadows lengthened, Maximus finally returned to the treasure chamber. The familiar hum of ancient artifacts and the soft glow of magical relics greeted him, providing a sense of comfort and continuity. Aetheris, with her sleek Aetherian metallic form, stood near a table covered in scrolls and artifacts, her presence a constant source of support.

"Aetheris," Maximus called out, his voice echoing slightly in the vast chamber.

"Seeker of Truth," Aetheris responded, turning to face him. "How may I assist you?"

Maximus took a deep breath, gathering his thoughts. "I met someone today, a woman named Anna. She's a software designer who has fallen on hard times. I helped her with some immediate needs, but I think she could be a valuable addition to our team."

Aetheris' eyes glowed softly as she processed his words. "A software designer, you say? That could indeed be beneficial. What do you need from me?"

"I want you to vet her," Maximus replied. "Check if she has any family and assess her background. We need to ensure she can be trusted, especially given the security issues of bringing anyone into the Aetherian secret."

Aetheris nodded, her form shimmering slightly as she accessed her vast database. "Understood. I will conduct a thorough background check on Anna. This will include her professional history, personal connections, and any potential risks."

Maximus watched as Aetheris worked, her efficiency and precision always impressive. After a few moments, she looked up, her expression thoughtful.

"Anna appears to have a clean professional record," Aetheris began. "She has no immediate family, which might explain her current situation. Her work history is solid, with no indications of any security risks or criminal activity."

Maximus felt a sense of relief but remained cautious. "And do you think she can be trusted?"

Aetheris paused, her eyes reflecting the soft glow of the artifacts around them. "Based on the data, Anna seems to be a trustworthy individual. However, given the sensitive nature of the Aetherian secrets, I recommend a probationary period. Additionally, she will need to sign a non-disclosure agreement (NDA) to ensure confidentiality."

Maximus nodded, appreciating Aetheris' thoroughness. "Good idea. We should also find out if she wants a coveted insider position or just a good position in the lab."

Aetheris' form shimmered as she processed the additional request. "I will prepare the necessary documents and arrange a meeting with Anna to discuss her preferences and the terms of her employment."

Maximus felt a renewed sense of purpose. "Thank you, Aetheris. Your insights are invaluable. We'll proceed with caution and give Anna the support she needs to succeed."

"Always at your service, seeker of Truth," Aetheris replied, her voice filled with a gentle pride. "Together, we will ensure the safety and success of the Magellan Project."

CHAPTER 11

"The Dawn of the Magellan Project"

Today was the day he would reach out to his former team and offer them a chance to rebuild and innovate under the banner of the Magellan Project.

He picked up his phone and dialed the first number on his list: Dr. Elena Martinez. The phone rang a few times before she answered.

"Maximus, good morning," Elena greeted him, her voice sounding more rested than the day before.

"Good morning, Elena. I have a proposition for you," Maximus began. "Would you be interested in bringing our project to a new lab, or refurbishing the old one? And how would you feel about working directly with the Magellan Project if I fund the work?"

Elena paused for a moment, considering his offer. "Maximus, that sounds incredible. I'd love to bring our project to the new lab and work with the Magellan Project. This could be the fresh start we need."

Maximus smiled, feeling a sense of relief. "I'm glad to hear that, Elena. I'll make the arrangements."

Next, he called Raj Patel. "Hey, Maximus," Raj answered, his voice upbeat.

"Raj, I have an offer for you," Maximus said. "Would you be interested in moving our project to a new lab or refurbishing the old one? And how would you feel about working directly with the Magellan Project if I fund the work?"

Raj didn't hesitate. "Absolutely, Maximus. I'd love to work with the Magellan Project. Let's move to the new lab and start fresh. This is exactly what we need."

Maximus felt a surge of optimism. "Great to hear, Raj. I'll get everything set up."

He then called Lisa Chen. "Maximus, it's good to hear from you," Lisa said.

"Lisa, I have a proposition for you," Maximus began. "Would you be interested in bringing our project to a new lab or refurbishing the old one? And how would you feel about working directly with the Magellan Project if I fund the work?"

Lisa considered for a moment. "I think moving to a new lab would be best. And working with the Magellan Project sounds like an amazing opportunity. Count me in."

Maximus nodded, feeling more confident with each call. "Thank you, Lisa. I'll make the necessary arrangements."

Next, he reached out to David Kim. "Maximus, how are you?" David asked.

"I'm doing well, David. I have an offer for you," Maximus said. "Would you be interested in moving our project to a new lab or refurbishing the old one? And how would you feel about working directly with the Magellan Project if I fund the work?"

David's voice brightened. "That sounds fantastic, Maximus. I'd prefer moving to a new lab. Working with the Magellan Project would be a great opportunity for us."

Maximus felt a sense of accomplishment. "I'm glad to hear that, David. I'll get everything organized."

Finally, he called Megan Thompson. "Maximus, it's good to hear from you," Megan said.

"Megan, I have a proposition for you," Maximus began. "Would you be interested in bringing our project to a new lab or refurbishing the old one? And how would you feel about working directly with the Magellan Project if I fund the work?"

Megan's voice was filled with enthusiasm. "Maximus, that sounds perfect. Let's move to the new lab and work with the Magellan Project. This is exactly what we need to get back on track."

Maximus felt a wave of satisfaction. "Thank you, Megan. I'll handle all the details."

As he ended the calls, Maximus felt a renewed sense of purpose. His team was on board, and with their combined talents and the resources of the Magellan Project, they were ready to rebuild and achieve even greater success. The future looked bright, and Maximus was eager to see what they could accomplish together.

"Aetheris," Maximus began, "can you get the team's information for a funds transfer, please? I'd like them each to receive $150,000. Also, let's get the real estate company on the line to secure a spot near here to break ground on a new lab. How many square feet do you suggest for the facility?"

Aetheris' eyes glowed softly as she processed his request. "Understood, seeker of Truth. I will gather the necessary information for the funds transfer and ensure each team member receives $150,000."

She paused for a moment, accessing her vast database of architectural and engineering knowledge. "For a research lab facility, I recommend a space of approximately 10,000 to 15,000 square feet. This size will accommodate the necessary equipment, workflow, and personnel, while allowing for future expansion and flexibility."

Maximus nodded, appreciating her thoroughness. "That sounds perfect, Aetheris. Let's proceed with those plans."

Aetheris' form shimmered as she began executing the tasks. "I will contact the real estate company and secure a suitable location for the lab. Additionally, I will prepare the funds transfer for the team and ensure all details are handled efficiently."

Maximus felt a sense of relief and excitement. "Thank you, Aetheris. Your support is invaluable."

"Always at your service, seeker of Truth," Aetheris replied, her voice filled with a gentle pride. "Together, we will ensure the success of the Magellan Project."

As Aetheris set to work, Maximus felt a renewed sense of purpose. The new lab would be a cornerstone of their efforts, providing a state-of-the-art facility for groundbreaking research and innovation.

Maximus woke with a start on his bunk in the sealed treasure chamber, the soft hum of ancient artifacts surrounding him. His wrist device buzzed, and he quickly answered the call. It was the construction crew, informing him they were on their way to the Hidden Glen.

Realizing he needed to hurry, Maximus swung his legs over the side of the bunk and stood up, stretching briefly. He couldn't afford to let anyone see him emerge from the hidden stone door outside the chamber. "Aetheris," he called out, his voice urgent.

Aetheris appeared instantly, her sleek Aetherian metallic form shimmering with readiness. "Seeker of Truth, how may I assist you?"

"Aetheris, can you draw me a blueprint for a two-story, 10,000 square foot house with a large hidden underground room, tall windows to catch the morning light, and retractable steel storm shutters to fend off storms? I'm going to need them, please," Maximus requested, his tone brisk.

"Understood," Aetheris replied, her eyes glowing softly as she processed the request. Within moments, a detailed blueprint materialized in her hands. She handed it to Maximus, the intricate design showcasing her unparalleled precision and creativity.

Maximus took the blueprint, marveling at the detailed layout. "Thank you, Aetheris. This is perfect."

"Always at your service, seeker of Truth," Aetheris responded, her voice filled with a gentle pride.

Maximus hurried to the winding stair that led out of the chamber, the blueprint clutched tightly in his hand. He ascended quickly, ensuring he reached the surface before the construction crew arrived. Emerging from the hidden stone door, he glanced around to make sure no one was watching, then made his way to the meeting point in the glen.

As he approached, he saw the construction crew's vehicles pulling up. Maximus felt a surge of excitement and determination. With the blueprint in hand and Aetheris's support, he was ready to oversee the next phase of the Magellan Project.

A year had passed since the inception of the Magellan Project, and the transformation was remarkable. Maximus stood in the grand hall of the new house, a stunning two-story structure with tall windows that bathed the rooms in morning light. The retractable steel storm shutters were a testament to the blend of advanced science and practical design. Beneath the house, a large hidden underground room served as a secure storage and research area, seamlessly integrated into the overall design.

Maximus's family had moved into their new house, which had been lovingly created. The familiar surroundings provided a sense of comfort and stability. Sarah and Michael, his children, were settling back into their lives with remarkable resilience. Sarah, with her inquisitive nature, had taken a keen interest in the Magellan Project, often visiting the new lab to see the latest developments. Michael, on the other hand, had found solace in the familiar routines of school and friends, his laughter filling the house once more.

Anna, the software designer Maximus had met a year ago, had flourished under his guidance. After careful consideration and discussions with Aetheris, she had decided to take the coveted insider position with the Magellan Project. She signed the NDA agreement, fully understanding the importance of the Aetherian secrets she would be privy to. Her skills and dedication quickly made her an invaluable member of the team, and she thrived in the collaborative and innovative environment.

Maximus gave Anna the old family house which had been totally renovated and upgraded where she moved in and got herself a dog named Grover, a Great Dane.

The new lab, a state-of-the-art facility nestled near the Hidden Glen, was a hive of activity. The team, including Dr. Elena Martinez, Raj Patel, Lisa Chen, David Kim, and Megan Thompson, had settled into their roles, their work fueled by the renewed sense of purpose and the resources provided by the Magellan Project. The lab's advanced equipment and spacious design allowed for groundbreaking research and development, pushing the boundaries of what they had previously thought possible.

One particularly interesting event during the year was the discovery of an ancient Aetherian artifact that seemed to resonate with the energy of the treasure chamber. Aetheris had been instrumental in deciphering its purpose, revealing it to be a key to unlocking even deeper secrets of the Aetherian legacy.

Maximus often found himself reflecting on the journey they had undertaken. The challenges had been immense, but the rewards were even greater. With his family by his side, the support of his dedicated team, and the unwavering assistance of Aetheris, he felt a profound sense of accomplishment and hope for the future.

As the sun set over the Hidden Glen, casting a golden glow over the new house and lab, Maximus stood on the balcony, looking out over the landscape. The Magellan Project was more than just a venture; it was a testament to resilience, innovation, and the enduring power of human spirit. And with each passing day, they moved closer to uncovering the full legacy of the Aetherians, ready to face whatever challenges lay ahead.

A year ago, in the dimly lit treasure chamber, Maximus and Aetheris stood amidst the ancient artifacts and relics of the Aetherian legacy. The air was thick with the hum of energy, and the weight of their decision hung heavily between them.

"Aetheris," Maximus began, his voice steady but filled with concern, "we need to make a decision about the team. The Aetherian chamber holds too many secrets, and its discovery could pose significant risks."

Aetheris, her sleek Aetherian metallic form shimmering softly, nodded in agreement. "Seeker of Truth, I concur. For the safety of the team and the security of the Aetherian secrets, they must never know of this chamber. The knowledge could endanger them and compromise our mission."

Maximus sighed, feeling the gravity of their decision. "It's settled then. The team will remain unaware of the chamber's existence. We must protect them and their legacy at all costs."

Fast forward to the present, Maximus stood at the entrance of the hidden stone door, his heart pounding with anticipation. Today, he will reveal the treasure chamber to his family. He had decided it was time they knew the full extent of his work and the secrets he had been safeguarding.

He led his wife, Sarah, and his children, Sarah and Michael, down the winding stair that descended into the depths of the chamber. The air grew cooler, and the faint glow of the artifacts began to illuminate their path.

As they reached the bottom, Maximus turned to face his family, his expression serious. "What you are about to see must remain a secret. No one outside this room can ever know about this place."

His wife nodded, her eyes wide with curiosity and trust. Sarah and Michael exchanged excited glances, eager to see what their father had been working on.

Maximus pushed open the heavy stone door, revealing the treasure chamber in all its glory. The room was filled with ancient scrolls, glowing artifacts, and relics that seemed to hum with energy. In the center stood Aetheris, her form radiating a soft, ethereal light.

"Welcome to the treasure chamber," Maximus said, his voice filled with pride and reverence. "This is Aetheris, my assistant and the guardian of the Aetherian legacy."

Aetheris stepped forward, her eyes reflecting the light of the artifacts. "Greetings, seekers of Truth. It is an honor to meet you."

Maximus's family stood in awe, taking in the sight of the chamber and the enigmatic Aetheris. "This place is incredible," his wife whispered, her eyes shining with wonder.

Sarah and Michael were equally captivated, their curiosity piqued by the mysterious artifacts. "Dad, this is amazing," Michael said, his voice filled with excitement.

Maximus smiled, feeling a deep sense of fulfillment. "Remember, this must remain our secret. No one must ever find out about this chamber or Aetheris. The safety of our family and the legacy of the Aetherians depend on it."

His family nodded solemnly, understanding the importance of their vow. As they explored the chamber, Maximus felt a renewed sense of purpose. With his family's support and the unwavering assistance of Aetheris, he knew they were ready to face whatever challenges lay ahead, united in their mission to protect and uncover the secrets of the Aetherian legacy.

In the heart of the treasure chamber, amidst the ancient scrolls, glowing artifacts, and relics of the Aetherian legacy, Maximus and Aetheris embarked on an ambitious project: the creation of a 7-dimensional computer. This groundbreaking endeavor was born from the wealth of knowledge they had cataloged over the past year, drawing on the wisdom contained in the scrolls, artifacts, tomes, and other relics.

The project began with the design of the enigmatic core, the heart of the 7-dimensional computer. This core was unlike any traditional computing system, leveraging the advanced science and magical stream technology of the Aetherians. The core was designed to operate across seven dimensions, allowing it to process and store information in ways that transcended conventional three-dimensional space.

The core itself was a marvel of engineering and mystical design. It was housed in a crystalline structure, composed of rare Aetherian minerals that resonated with the energy of the treasure chamber. These minerals were capable of channeling and amplifying both physical and magical energies, creating a seamless integration of science and magic.

At the center of the core was the "Aetheris Nexus", a pulsating sphere of pure energy that served as the primary processing unit. The Nexus was capable of manipulating the fundamental forces of the universe, allowing it to perform computations at speeds and complexities far beyond any existing technology. It could access and manipulate data across multiple dimensions, providing unparalleled computational power.

Surrounding the Nexus were seven "Dimensional Conduits", each aligned with a different dimension. These conduits acted as pathways for data and energy, allowing the core to interact with and process information from various dimensional planes. The conduits were intricately designed, with runes and symbols etched into their surfaces, channeling the flow of energy with precision and efficiency.

The core also featured a "Temporal Stabilizer", a device that allowed the computer to manipulate and stabilize time within its processing environment. This enabled the core to perform time-sensitive calculations and simulations, providing insights into temporal phenomena and allowing for advanced time-space manipulation.

To ensure the security and integrity of the core, Maximus and Aetheris incorporated a "Quantum Encryption Matrix". This matrix used quantum entanglement and magical wards to protect the core from external interference and unauthorized access. It ensured that the data processed and stored within the core remained secure and unaltered.

The final component of the core was the "Aetherian Interface", a holographic display that allowed Maximus and Aetheris to interact with the computer. This interface was designed to be intuitive and responsive, providing real-time feedback and control over the core's operations. It could project complex data visualizations and simulations, allowing for a deeper understanding of the information being processed.

As the core neared completion, Maximus and Aetheris marveled at their creation. The 7-dimensional computer represented the pinnacle of their combined efforts, a testament to the advanced science and magical stream technology of the Aetherians. With this powerful tool at their disposal, they were poised to unlock even greater secrets of the

Aetherian legacy and push the boundaries of human knowledge and understanding.

Maximus led his family down the winding stairway into the treasure chamber, the air growing cooler and more charged with energy as they descended. The soft glow of ancient artifacts illuminated their path, casting an ethereal light on the stone walls. As they reached the bottom, the chamber opened up before them, revealing the awe-inspiring sight of the 7-dimensional computer at its center.

The computer's core, the Aetheris Nexus, pulsed with a vibrant energy, surrounded by the seven Dimensional Conduits. The holographic quantum display projected intricate data visualizations and simulations, filling the air with shimmering patterns and symbols.

"Welcome to the heart of the Magellan Project," Maximus said, his voice filled with pride and reverence. "This is the 7-dimensional computer we've been working on."

Sarah, his wife, looked around in amazement, her eyes wide with wonder. "Maximus, this is incredible. I can't believe what I'm seeing."

Sarah, their daughter, stepped closer to the holographic display, her curiosity piqued. "Dad, how does the computer process information across seven dimensions? How do you even begin to understand something like that?"

Maximus smiled, appreciating her inquisitive nature. "Great question, Sarah. The computer uses the Dimensional Conduits to access and manipulate data from different dimensional planes. Each conduit aligns with a specific dimension, allowing the core to process information in ways that transcend our conventional understanding of space and time. It's a combination of advanced science and Aetherian magic that makes it possible."

Michael, their son, was equally captivated by the display. He pointed to the Temporal Stabilizer, his eyes filled with curiosity. "Dad, how does the Temporal Stabilizer work? Can it really manipulate time?"

Maximus nodded, impressed by Michael's keen observation. "Yes, Michael. The Temporal Stabilizer allows the computer to perform time-sensitive calculations and simulations. It can stabilize and manipulate time within its processing environment, providing insights into temporal phenomena and enabling advanced time-space manipulation. It's one of the most powerful features of the core."

Emily, Maximus's wife, took it all in, her expression a mix of awe and pride. "Maximus, this is beyond anything I could have imagined. The work you've done here is extraordinary."

Maximus felt a deep sense of fulfillment, seeing his family's reactions. "Thank you, Emily. It's been a challenging journey, but with Aetheris's help and the support of our team, we've achieved something truly remarkable."

Aetheris, standing nearby, nodded in agreement. "Seeker of Truth, your family's curiosity and understanding are commendable. Together, we will continue to unlock the secrets of the Aetherian legacy."

As they explored the chamber, Maximus felt a sense of acomplishment. The 7-dimensional computer was not just a technological marvel; it was a testament to their collective efforts and the enduring power of human curiosity and innovation. With his family by his side and the support of Aetheris, he knew they were ready to face whatever challenges lay ahead, united in their mission to uncover the mysteries of the Aetherian legacy.

Maximus led his family down the winding stairway into the treasure chamber, the air growing cooler and more charged with energy as they descended. The soft glow of ancient artifacts illuminated their path, casting an ethereal light on the stone walls. As they reached the bottom, the chamber opened up before them, revealing the awe-inspiring sight of the 7-dimensional computer at its center.

The computer's core, the Aetheris Nexus, pulsed with a vibrant energy, surrounded by the seven Dimensional Conduits. The holographic quantum display projected intricate data visualizations and simulations, filling the air with shimmering patterns and symbols.

"Welcome to the heart of the Magellan Project," Maximus said, his voice filled with pride and reverence. "This is the 7-dimensional computer we've been working on."

Sarah, his wife, looked around in amazement, her eyes wide with wonder. "Maximus, this is incredible. I can't believe what I'm seeing."

Sarah, their daughter, stepped closer to the holographic display, her curiosity piqued. "Dad, how does the computer process information across seven dimensions? How do you even begin to understand something like that?"

Maximus smiled, appreciating her inquisitive nature. "Great question, Sarah. The computer uses the Dimensional Conduits to access and manipulate data from different dimensional planes. Each conduit aligns with a specific dimension, allowing the core to process information in ways that transcend our conventional understanding of space and time. It's a combination of advanced science and Aetherian magic that makes it possible."

Michael, their son, was equally captivated by the display. He pointed to the Temporal Stabilizer, his eyes filled with curiosity. "Dad, how does the Temporal Stabilizer work? Can it really manipulate time?"

Maximus nodded, impressed by Michael's keen observation. "Yes, Michael. The Temporal Stabilizer allows the computer to perform time-sensitive calculations and simulations. It can stabilize and manipulate time within its processing environment, providing insights into temporal phenomena and enabling advanced time-space manipulation. It's one of the most powerful features of the core."

Emily, Maximus's wife, took it all in, her expression a mix of awe and pride. "Maximus, this is beyond anything I could have imagined. The work you've done here is extraordinary."

Maximus felt a deep sense of fulfillment, seeing his family's reactions. "Thank you, Emily. It's been a challenging journey, but with Aetheris's help and the support of our team, we've achieved something truly remarkable."

Aetheris, standing nearby, nodded in agreement. "Seeker of Truth, your family's curiosity and understanding are commendable. Together, we will continue to unlock the secrets of the Aetherian legacy."

As they explored the chamber, Maximus felt a renewed sense of purpose. The 7-dimensional computer was not just a technological marvel; it was a testament to their collective efforts and the enduring power of human curiosity and innovation. With his family by his side and the support of Aetheris, he knew they were ready to face whatever challenges lay ahead, united in their mission to uncover the mysteries of the Aetherian legacy.

As the family continued to marvel at the 7-dimensional computer, Aetheris moved gracefully towards Emily. Her sleek Aetherian metallic form shimmered softly in the ambient light of the treasure chamber. Gently, she placed a hand on Emily's shoulder, her touch surprisingly warm and reassuring.

Leaning in, Aetheris whispered in Emily's ear, "How do you think this machine could aid you in your pediatrics, Emily?"

Emily's eyes widened in surprise at the question. She glanced at Maximus, her expression a mix of curiosity and contemplation. Her mind raced with possibilities, and a thoughtful smile began to form on her lips.

Turning back to Aetheris, Emily replied softly, "This machine could revolutionize pediatric care. With its advanced computational power and multidimensional data processing, we could analyze complex medical data in ways we've never imagined. It could help us understand genetic disorders, predict health outcomes, and personalize treatments for each child."

Aetheris nodded, her eyes reflecting the light of the holographic display. "Your insights are invaluable, Emily. The potential applications are indeed vast."

Emily then turned to Maximus, her eyes filled with admiration and a newfound sense of purpose. She leaned in close, her voice barely above a whisper. "Maximus, this machine could change everything. Imagine the lives we could save, the children we could help. Thank you for sharing this with us!

Maximus looked into Emily's eyes, seeing the passion and determination there. He felt a deep connection and pride in her vision. "I'm glad you see the potential, Emily. Together, we can make a real difference."

Emily smiled warmly, her earlier feelings of jealousy completely replaced by a sense of unity and shared purpose. She looked at Maximus with love and gratitude, knowing that their journey together was just beginning. The treasure chamber, filled with the legacy of the Aetherians, seemed to glow even brighter as they stood united in their mission to unlock the secrets of the past and build a better future

Sarah and Michael were engrossed in their tasks within the Aetherian Archive's central chamber. The 7-dimensional computer hummed softly, its Dimensional Conduits glowing with energy as it processed vast amounts of data. Maximus and Aetheris had assigned them the critical task of cataloging and analyzing ancient Aetherian artifacts and scrolls.

As they worked, Sarah's eyes were drawn to a series of ancient maps displayed on the holographic interface. "Michael, look at this," she said, her voice tinged with excitement. "These maps seem to indicate something significant hidden within one of the highest mountains on Earth."

Michael leaned in, his curiosity piqued. "Let's run a deeper analysis using the computer's capabilities."

They input the data into the 7-dimensional computer, which began to process the information at an astonishing speed. The holographic display shifted, revealing a detailed topographical map of the mountain range. As the computer delved deeper, it uncovered the hidden city.

"There it is," Sarah whispered, her eyes wide with wonder. "The Lost City of Eldoria."

The Lost City of Eldoria

Eldoria, a city of earthly origin, was once a thriving center of an ancient and advanced civilization known as the Eldorians. This culture was renowned for its mastery of both science and magic, much like the Aetherians. The city was believed to have been lost to time, hidden deep within the depths of one of the highest mountains in the world.

Michael's fingers danced over the controls as he accessed more information. "According to the computer, Eldoria was a hub of innovation and knowledge. The Eldorians were skilled in manipulating energy and matter, and their architectural feats were unparalleled."

The holographic display showed towering structures made of a material that seemed to shimmer with an inner light. "These buildings are constructed from a substance called Etherium, which is both incredibly strong and capable of conducting magical energy," Sarah explained.

What Might Be Found in Eldoria

The 7-dimensional computer provided a list of potential discoveries within Eldoria:

The Etherium Archives: A vast library containing scrolls and artifacts that detail the Eldorians' knowledge of energy manipulation, advanced technology, and magical practices.

The Crystal Caverns: Hidden beneath the city, these caverns are filled with crystals that resonate with powerful magical energy. They were used by the Eldorians for various purposes, including healing and energy amplification.

The Hall of Ancients: A grand hall where the Eldorian leaders once convened. It is said to contain statues and relics that hold the secrets of their civilization's rise and fall.

The Temporal Chamber: A mysterious room rumored to house a device capable of manipulating time. This could be the key to unlocking new dimensions of the 7-dimensional computer's abilities.

Sarah and Michael exchanged excited glances. "This is incredible," Michael said. "We need to inform Maximus and Aetheris immediately."

They quickly gathered their findings and rushed to the central chamber where Maximus and Aetheris were waiting. Bursting into the room, Sarah exclaimed, "Maximus! Aetheris! You won't believe what we've found!"

Michael nodded enthusiastically. "We've discovered the Lost City of Eldoria, hidden deep within one of the highest mountains on Earth. The city is a treasure trove of advanced knowledge and technology."

Maximus's eyes sparkled with interest. "Tell me more."

Sarah and Michael shared the details of their discovery, their excitement palpable. As they spoke, Aetheris's eyes glowed brighter, reflecting the significance of their findings.

"This discovery is indeed remarkable," Aetheris said. "It aligns perfectly with our mission to uncover and understand the lost knowledge of the Aetherians and their earthly counterparts."

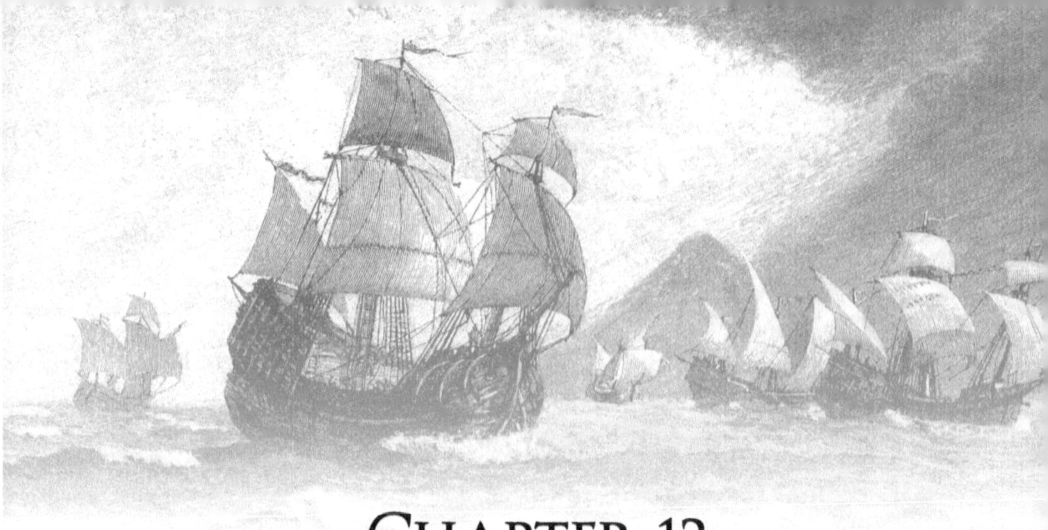

CHAPTER 12

THE FORMATION OF THE EXPLORATORY TEAM

Maximus smiled, his mind racing with possibilities. "This is just the beginning. Eldoria holds the key to unlocking new dimensions of our understanding. Let's prepare for the journey ahead.

Maximus Magellan stood in the central chamber of the Aetherian Archive, the pulsating glow of the Aetheris Nexus casting an otherworldly light across the room. Aetheris hovered beside him, her holographic form shimmering with anticipation. Maximus had been contemplating a bold new venture, and today was the day to share it.

"Aetheris, seeker of Truth," Maximus began, his voice filled with determination, "I have an idea that could push the boundaries of our understanding and capabilities. I propose forming a scientific research and quasi-military exploratory team."

Aetheris's eyes glowed with curiosity. "What is the purpose of this team, Maximus?"

Maximus gestured to the 7-dimensional computer, its Dimensional Conduits humming with energy. "The abilities of this computer are far-reaching, but we have only scratched the surface. This team will explore its full potential, testing new equipment and technologies I have envisioned. Their mission will be to venture into uncharted territories, including the ruins of an ancient city deep inside a mountain, one of the highest places on the planet."

Aetheris processed the information, her holographic form flickering as she considered the implications. "This is a significant undertaking, Maximus. Who will lead this team?"

"Sarah and Michael," Maximus replied without hesitation. "They have already proven their resourcefulness and dedication. Their recent discovery of the ancient city is a testament to their capabilities. However, they will remain here in the chamber with the computer to continue their essential work."

As if on cue, Sarah and Michael burst into the chamber, their faces alight with excitement. "Maximus! Aetheris! You won't believe what we've found!" Sarah exclaimed, her eyes wide with wonder.

Michael nodded enthusiastically. "While completing our tasks, we used the 7-dimensional computer to analyze some ancient maps. We discovered the ruins of an ancient city deep inside a mountain, at one of the highest points on the planet. The city is vast, with structures that defy our current understanding of architecture and technology."

Maximus's eyes sparkled with interest. "Tell me more."

Sarah pulled up a holographic projection of the city, its intricate layout and towering structures displayed in stunning detail. "The city appears to be a hub of advanced science and magic stream technology. We believe it holds secrets that could revolutionize our understanding of the Aetherian culture."

Michael added, "We also found traces of a powerful energy source, unlike anything we've encountered before. It could be the key to unlocking new dimensions of the 7-dimensional computer's abilities."

Aetheris's eyes glowed brighter as she absorbed the information. "This discovery is indeed remarkable. It aligns perfectly with Maximus's vision for the exploratory team."

Maximus smiled, his mind racing with possibilities. "Sarah, Michael, you will lead the planning and coordination from here.

Meanwhile, we will recruit a diverse team of men and women to carry out the exploration. This team will be composed of scientists, engineers, and security personnel, all chosen for their expertise and dedication."

Mission Statement: The primary mission of the quasi-military exploration team is to explore and uncover the secrets of the Lost City of Eldoria first, then any following scientific sites that are discovered after. Utilizing the advanced capabilities of the 7-dimensional computer, The team will conduct scientific research, test new technologies, and ensure the security of the expedition. Their ultimate goal is to retrieve valuable knowledge and artifacts that can further the understanding of both Aetherian and Eldorian cultures.

Rules and Guidelines:

Confidentiality:

All team members must maintain the utmost secrecy regarding the mission's objectives, discoveries, and operations.

Information about the mission is to be shared only on a need-to-know basis, even within the team.

Security Protocols:

The team will operate under strict security measures to protect against external threats and unauthorized access.

Members must undergo rigorous background checks and security clearances before being recruited.

Scientific Integrity:

Research and exploration activities must adhere to the highest standards of scientific integrity and ethics.

All findings must be meticulously documented and reported to Maximus and Aetheris.

Operational Discipline:

Team members are expected to follow a strict chain of command, with clear roles and responsibilities.

Regular training sessions will be conducted to ensure readiness for any challenges that may arise.

Resource Management:

Efficient use of resources, including equipment, supplies, and energy, is crucial for the success of the mission.

Any damage or loss of equipment must be reported immediately.

Safety and Health:

The safety and well-being of all team members are paramount. Proper safety protocols must be followed at all times.

Medical personnel will be part of the team to address any health issues that may arise during the expedition.

Secret Recruitment Process:

Global Television Ad Campaign:

A series of discreet television ads will be aired globally, designed to attract individuals with specific skills and interests without revealing the true nature of the mission.

The ads will highlight the opportunity to work on a groundbreaking research project, appealing to scientists, engineers, and security experts.

Email Campaign:

Interested candidates will be directed to a secure website where they can submit their contact information.

Successful candidates will receive a follow-up email with further instructions and a preliminary questionnaire to assess their suitability.

Evaluation and Vetting:

Candidates who pass the initial screening will undergo a series of evaluations, including psychological assessments, technical tests, and loyalty screenings.

The evaluations will be conducted discreetly to maintain the secrecy of the mission.

Invitation to Join:

Successful candidates will receive a formal invitation to join the team, presented as an opportunity to work on a groundbreaking research project.

The true nature of the mission will be revealed only after the candidates have accepted the invitation and signed confidentiality agreements.

Training and Integration:

Recruits will undergo intensive training to prepare them for the mission, including physical conditioning, technical training, and security protocols.

They will be gradually integrated into the team, with their roles and responsibilities clearly defined.

Deployment:

Once the team is fully assembled and trained, they will be deployed to the base of operations near the mountain housing Eldoria.

The mission will commence under the direct supervision of Maximus and Aetheris, with regular updates and debriefings.

Special Details:

Recruitment Messaging: The television ads and email campaign will use coded language and imagery to attract the right candidates without drawing undue attention. Phrases like "Join a pioneering research initiative" and "Unlock the secrets of the past" will be used.

Secure Communication: All communications with potential recruits will be encrypted and routed through secure channels to prevent interception.

Background Checks: In addition to standard background checks, candidates will be evaluated for their ability to handle high-pressure situations and maintain confidentiality.

Diverse Skill Sets: The team will include a mix of scientists, engineers, medical personnel, and security experts to ensure all aspects of the mission are covered.

The Secret Training Facility

The sun was setting over the secluded valley where the secret training facility was hidden. Nestled between towering mountains and dense forests, the facility was designed to be both secure and discreet. Its state-of-the-art buildings blended seamlessly with the natural landscape, ensuring that it remained undetected by the outside world.

Maximus Magellan stood at the entrance, surveying the facility with a sense of pride and anticipation. Beside him stood Aetheris, her form crafted from shimmering Aetherian metal. Her presence was both commanding and graceful, her metallic surface reflecting the glow of the setting sun.

"The global ads and email campaigns have been a success," Maximus said, turning to Aetheris. "We've attracted some of the brightest minds and most skilled individuals from around the world."

Aetheris nodded, her eyes—crafted from a unique crystalline material—glowing with approval. "The candidates have been thoroughly vetted and are ready for the next phase of their journey."

Arrival of the Candidates

As the first group of candidates arrived, they were greeted by a team of security personnel who escorted them to the main building. Each candidate carried a sense of curiosity and excitement, eager to learn more about the mysterious project they had been selected for.

Among the candidates were:

Dr. Elena Martinez, an astrophysicist known for her groundbreaking research on dark matter.

Captain James O'Connor, a former military officer with extensive experience in covert operations.

Dr. Mei Ling, a biomedical engineer specializing in advanced medical technologies.

Sergeant Alex Thompson, a security expert with a background in cyber defense.

Professor Raj Patel, an archaeologist with a deep knowledge of ancient civilizations.

Orientation and Introduction

The candidates were led to a large auditorium where Maximus and Aetheris awaited them. The room was filled with advanced holographic displays and interactive panels, showcasing the cutting-edge technology they would be working with.

Maximus stepped forward, addressing the group. "Welcome to the Magellan Project. You have been chosen for your exceptional skills and expertise. Our mission is to explore and uncover the secrets of the Lost City of Eldoria, a hidden treasure trove of ancient knowledge and technology."

Aetheris, her metallic form gleaming, stepped forward. "You will undergo intensive training to prepare you for this mission. Our goal is to ensure that you are equipped with the knowledge and skills needed to succeed."

Special Details and Training

The training facility was equipped with various specialized areas, each designed to hone the candidates' abilities:

Simulation Chambers:

These chambers used advanced holographic technology to create realistic simulations of the environments the team would encounter. Candidates practiced navigating the treacherous terrain of Eldoria and dealing with potential threats.

Laboratories:

State-of-the-art labs were set up for scientific research and experimentation. Here, Dr. Martinez and Professor Patel worked on analyzing artifacts and developing new technologies.

Medical Wing:

Dr. Mei Ling led the medical training, ensuring that all team members were proficient in advanced medical procedures and emergency response.

Security Training:

Captain O'Connor and Sergeant Thompson conducted rigorous security drills, focusing on both physical and cyber defense. They trained the team in combat tactics, surveillance, and secure communication protocols.

Special Details Involving Candidates:

Dr. Elena Martinez had a unique ability to visualize complex astrophysical phenomena, which she used to develop new strategies for navigating the temporal anomalies within Eldoria.

Captain James O'Connor brought his experience in covert operations, teaching the team how to move undetected and handle high-pressure situations.

Dr. Mei Ling introduced cutting-edge medical devices she had developed, including a portable healing unit that could rapidly treat injuries in the field.

Sergeant Alex Thompson implemented advanced cyber defense measures, ensuring that the team's communications and data remained secure.

Professor Raj Patel shared his extensive knowledge of ancient languages and symbols, helping the team decipher the inscriptions found in Eldoria.

Completion of Training

After weeks of intensive training, the team was ready. Maximus and Aetheris gathered them for a final briefing.

"You have all proven yourselves to be exceptional," Maximus said, his voice filled with pride. "The journey ahead will be challenging, but I have no doubt that you will succeed. Remember, the knowledge we uncover will change the world."

Aetheris's crystalline eyes glowed with determination. "Seeker of Truth, your mission begins now. May you uncover the secrets of Eldoria and bring back the wisdom of the ancients."

With their training complete and their mission clear, the team prepared to embark on the greatest adventure of their lives.

Sarah and Michael were deep in concentration within the central chamber of the Aetherian Archive. The 7-dimensional computer's Dimensional Conduits glowed with a soft, pulsating light as it processed the vast amounts of data they had inputted. The room was filled with the hum of advanced technology and the faint scent of ancient scrolls.

Sarah's fingers danced over the holographic interface, her eyes scanning the streams of data. "Michael, look at this," she said, her voice tinged with excitement. "The computer has uncovered new details about the site at the mountain where the Eldoria ruins are located."

Michael leaned in, his curiosity piqued. "What have you found?"

Sarah expanded the holographic display, revealing a detailed topographical map of the mountain range. "The computer has identified several hidden chambers and tunnels within the mountain. These structures are far more extensive than we initially thought."

Michael's eyes widened as he examined the map. "This is incredible. It looks like there are multiple levels, each with its own unique features. Some of these chambers appear to be connected by a network of energy conduits."

Sarah nodded, her excitement growing. "The computer also detected traces of a powerful energy source deep within the mountain. This energy could be the key to unlocking the full potential of the 7-dimensional computer."

Deciding the Method of Team Transfer

As they continued to analyze the data, Sarah and Michael discussed the best method for transferring the team to the site.

"We need to get the team there quickly and safely," Michael said. "Given the remote location and the potential dangers, traditional air transport might not be the best option."

Sarah agreed. "I think we should use beam technology. It's faster and allows for precise placement within the mountain. Plus, it minimizes the risk of detection by any external threats."

Michael nodded. "Beam technology it is, then. We'll need to coordinate with Aetheris to ensure the transfer goes smoothly."

The secluded training facility buzzed with activity as the newly recruited team underwent rigorous training. Maximus and Aetheris had designed a program that would transform these scientists, engineers, and security experts into a cohesive special operations and combat team.

Physical Conditioning:

The team engaged in daily physical conditioning exercises, including endurance runs, obstacle courses, and strength training. Captain James O'Connor, ex Green beret team leader, led these sessions, pushing the team to their limits to build stamina and resilience.

Combat Training:

Under the guidance of Sergeant Alex Thompson, the team practiced close-quarter combat techniques, marksmanship, and tactical maneuvers. They learned how to handle various weapons and defend themselves in high-pressure situations.

Simulation Drills:

The simulation chambers provided realistic scenarios that mimicked the treacherous terrain and potential threats of Eldoria. The team practiced navigating these environments, honing their skills in teamwork and problem-solving.

Medical Training:

Dr. Mei Ling conducted intensive medical training, teaching the team advanced first aid, trauma care, and the use of cutting-edge medical devices. The goal was to ensure that every member could provide emergency medical assistance if needed.

Technical Skills:

Dr. Elena Martinez and Professor Raj Patel led sessions on the scientific and technical aspects of the mission. The team learned to operate advanced equipment, analyze artifacts, and decipher ancient inscriptions.

Team Building:

Throughout the training, Maximus and Aetheris emphasized the importance of trust and communication. The team participated in various team-building exercises to strengthen their bonds and ensure seamless cooperation.

Discovery of Life Forms

While the team trained, Sarah and Michael continued their work with the 7-dimensional computer. One evening, as they analyzed the latest data from Eldoria, Sarah noticed something unusual.

"Michael, look at this," she said, pointing to the holographic display. "The computer is detecting faint energy signatures within the ruins."

Michael's eyes widened. "Could it be life forms?"

Sarah nodded. "Let's run a detailed scan."

They input the parameters into the computer, which began to process the data with incredible speed. The holographic display shifted, revealing a detailed map of the ruins with several highlighted areas.

"The computer confirms it," Sarah said, her voice filled with excitement. "There are life forms within the ruins of Eldoria."

Michael leaned closer to the display. "This changes everything. We need to inform Maximus and Aetheris immediately."

Maximus Magellan and Aetheris stood in the central chamber of the Aetherian Archive, surrounded by holographic blueprints and schematics. The room buzzed with the energy of the 7-dimensional computer, ready to assist in the creation of the ultimate battle suit for high-altitude operations.

Maximus turned to Aetheris, her metallic form gleaming in the ambient light. "Aetheris, seeker of Truth, we need to design a battle suit that will ensure the safety and effectiveness of our team in high-altitude environments. What should this suit include?"

Aetheris's crystalline eyes glowed as she processed the request. "Maximus, we must consider a range of features that combine advanced science and magical stream technology. Here is the design for the Aetherian Battle Suit:"

Aetherian Battle Suit

Design and Materials:

Material: The suit is crafted from Etherium, a super lightweight yet incredibly strong Aetherian metal. This material is known for its durability and ability to conduct magical energy, making it ideal for both protection and functionality.

Structure: The suit is designed to be form-fitting, providing maximum mobility while maintaining a high level of protection. It features a segmented design that allows for flexibility and ease of movement.

Capabilities and Features:

Environmental Control System:

Temperature Regulation: The suit is equipped with an advanced temperature regulation system that maintains a comfortable internal temperature, regardless of external conditions. This system uses a combination of liquid cooling and magical energy to adapt to extreme temperatures.

Pressure Stabilization: The suit includes a pressure stabilization system that ensures the wearer remains comfortable and safe at high altitudes. This system automatically adjusts to changes in atmospheric pressure, preventing decompression sickness.

Life Support System:

Oxygen Supply: The suit contains a self-contained oxygen supply that provides breathable air for extended periods. The oxygen is stored in compact, high-capacity tanks integrated into the suit's design.

Nutrient Delivery: The suit features a nutrient delivery system that supplies the wearer with essential nutrients and hydration through a series of micro-tubes. This system ensures that the wearer remains nourished and hydrated during long missions.

Defensive Capabilities:

Energy Shielding: The suit is equipped with an energy shielding system that can be activated to protect the wearer from projectiles and energy attacks. The shield is generated by the suit's Etherium components and can be adjusted for different levels of protection.

Impact Resistance: The suit's outer layer is reinforced with a special alloy that provides enhanced impact resistance. This layer can absorb and dissipate kinetic energy, reducing the risk of injury from physical attacks.

Combat Enhancements:

Integrated Weaponry: The suit includes built-in weapon systems, such as retractable energy blades and wrist-mounted pulse cannons. These weapons are powered by the suit's internal energy source and can be deployed quickly in combat situations.

Enhanced Strength: The suit features an exoskeleton that enhances the wearer's strength and endurance. This exoskeleton is powered by a combination of mechanical actuators and magical energy, allowing the wearer to lift heavy objects and perform feats of strength.Stealth and Reconnaissance:

Cloaking Technology: The suit is equipped with cloaking technology that renders the wearer invisible to both visual and electronic detection. This cloaking system uses a combination of light-bending materials and magical energy to create a seamless camouflage.

Advanced Sensors: The suit includes a suite of advanced sensors that provide real-time data on the surrounding environment. These sensors can detect heat signatures, energy fluctuations, and other anomalies, giving the wearer a tactical advantage.

Communication and Navigation:

Quantum Communicator: The suit is equipped with a quantum communicator that allows for instant, secure communication with the rest of the team. This communicator uses quantum entanglement to transmit data without delay or interference.

Navigation System: The suit includes an advanced navigation system that provides real-time maps and coordinates. This system is integrated with the suit's sensors and can guide the wearer through complex environments on a heads up display.

Maximus nodded, impressed by the array of features and capabilities. "This suit is perfect, Aetheris. It will provide our team with the protection and tools they need to succeed in high-altitude operations."

Aetheris's eyes glowed with satisfaction. "I will begin the fabrication process immediately. The team will be well-equipped for the challenges ahead."

With the design finalized, Maximus and Aetheris knew they had taken a crucial step towards ensuring the success of their mission to uncover the secrets of Eldoria. The central chamber of the Aetherian Archive was abuzz with anticipation. The away team, now fully trained and ready for their mission, gathered around Aetheris. Her metallic form gleamed under the ambient light, and her crystalline eyes glowed with a sense of purpose. Maximus stood beside her, ready to oversee the final preparations.

Aetheris addressed the team, her voice resonating with authority. "Seeker of Truth, today we present to you the advanced equipment, hardware, and software that will ensure your success in the exploration of Eldoria. Each piece has been meticulously designed and crafted to meet the unique challenges you will face."

Presentation of the Equipment

1. Etherium Pulse Rifle

Description: A sleek, ergonomic rifle made from Etherium, capable of firing concentrated energy pulses.

Capabilities: Adjustable settings for stun and high-energy modes, with a targeting system that enhances accuracy and locks onto multiple targets.

2. Aetheric Blade

Description: A lightweight, durable melee weapon forged from Aetherian metal.

Capabilities: Channels magical energy to enhance cutting power, emits shockwaves, and creates an energy shield for defense.

3. Temporal Disruptor Grenades

Description: Small, spherical devices that create localized temporal disruptions.

Capabilities: Slows down time within a specific radius, providing a tactical advantage.

4. Arcane Sniper Rifle

Description: A long-range weapon with a modular design and high-powered scope.

Capabilities: Fires projectiles infused with magical energy, customizable for different effects, and provides enhanced targeting capabilities.

5. Energy Shield Generator

Description: A portable device worn on the wrist or attached to a belt.

Capabilities: Creates a protective energy shield, adjustable for different levels of protection, and recharges automatically.

6. Recon Drones

Description: Small, agile drones equipped with advanced sensors and cameras.

Capabilities: Provide real-time video and data feeds, navigate tight spaces, and deploy energy pulses to disable electronic devices.

7. Quantum Communicators

Description: Compact, handheld devices using quantum entanglement for instant communication.

Capabilities: Ensure secure communication, transmit data and video feeds, and feature encryption technology.

8. Aetherian Battle Suit

Description: A super lightweight, super strong suit made from Etherium.

Capabilities: Temperature regulation, pressure stabilization, oxygen supply, nutrient delivery, energy shielding, impact resistance, integrated weaponry, enhanced strength, cloaking technology, advanced sensors, quantum communicator, and navigation system.

New Equipment, Hardware, and Software

1. Etherium Gauntlets

Description: Gauntlets made from Etherium, designed for both combat and utility.

Capabilities: Enhance physical strength, emit energy blasts, and generate small energy shields for close-quarters defense.

2. Aetherian Scanner

Description: A handheld device that scans for energy signatures, life forms, and structural anomalies.

Capabilities: Provides detailed analysis of the environment, detects hidden chambers and traps, and maps out the terrain in real-time.

3. Temporal Stabilizer Module

Description: A module integrated into the battle suit, designed to stabilize time within a localized area.

Capabilities: Prevents temporal anomalies, allows for precise time manipulation, and ensures the stability of the team's operations.

4. Advanced AI Interface

Description: A software upgrade for the team's equipment, providing enhanced AI support.

Capabilities: Offers real-time data analysis, tactical recommendations, and seamless integration with all devices and weapons.

Simulation Training

Aetheris gestured to the simulation chambers, their doors sliding open to reveal the advanced training environment. "To ensure you master this equipment, you will undergo intensive simulation training. These chambers will replicate the conditions you will face in Eldoria, allowing you to practice and perfect your skills."

The team members, now equipped with their new gear, entered the simulation chambers. The environment shifted around them, transforming into a realistic representation of the Eldoria ruins. The air was cool, and the walls glowed faintly with an otherworldly light.

Captain O'Connor led the team through various scenarios, each designed to test their proficiency with the new equipment. They navigated treacherous terrain, engaged in combat with simulated enemies, and utilized their advanced tools to solve complex puzzles.

Dr. Elena Martinez and Professor Raj Patel worked together to analyze artifacts and decipher ancient inscriptions, using the Aetherian

Scanner and Advanced AI Interface to assist them. Dr. Mei Ling provided medical support, demonstrating the use of the portable healing unit and ensuring the team's well-being.

As the training progressed, the team grew more confident and cohesive, their skills honed to perfection. Aetheris and Maximus observed from the control room, their expressions filled with pride and anticipation.

Maximus turned to Aetheris. "They are ready. The equipment and training have prepared them for the challenges ahead."

Aetheris nodded, her eyes glowing with determination. "Seeker of Truth, the time has come. May you uncover the secrets of Eldoria and bring back the wisdom of the ancients."

With their training complete and their equipment mastered, the team prepared to embark on the greatest adventure of their lives.

Discovery of New Sites

Sarah and Michael were engrossed in their work within the central chamber of the Aetherian Archive. The 7-dimensional computer's Dimensional Conduits glowed with a soft, pulsating light as it processed the vast amounts of data they had inputted. The room was filled with the hum of advanced technology and the faint scent of ancient scrolls.

Sarah's fingers danced over the holographic interface, her eyes scanning the streams of data. "Michael, look at this," she said, her voice tinged with excitement. "The computer has identified two new sites that could be of significant interest."

Michael leaned in, his curiosity piqued. "What have you found?"

Sarah expanded the holographic display, revealing detailed maps and temporal data for the two new sites.

First Site: The Temporal Nexus

Location: Earth, deep within the Amazon Rainforest.

Temporal Dimension: The site exists in a temporal dimension where time flows differently, allowing for the preservation of ancient structures and artifacts.

Description: The Temporal Nexus is a hidden city that appears to be a hub of temporal energy. The structures are made from a unique blend of natural materials and advanced technology, seamlessly integrated into the lush environment of the rainforest. The city is believed to be a center for temporal research and experimentation by an ancient civilization.

Second Site: The Quantum Citadel

Location: Quantum Space, a parallel dimension accessible through a quantum portal.

Temporal Dimension: The Quantum Citadel exists in a dimension where the laws of physics are different, allowing for the manipulation of quantum states and realities.

Description: The Quantum Citadel is a massive fortress-like structure floating in a void of swirling quantum energy. The citadel is composed of materials that can shift and change based on the observer's perception. It is believed to be a stronghold of knowledge and power, containing advanced quantum technologies and secrets of the universe.

Sarah's eyes sparkled with excitement as she continued to analyze the data. "The Temporal Nexus could provide us with invaluable insights into the manipulation of time, while the Quantum Citadel might hold the key to understanding quantum realities."

Michael nodded, equally enthusiastic. "We need to inform Maximus and Aetheris immediately. These discoveries could change everything."

Informing Maximus and Aetheris

Sarah and Michael quickly gathered their findings and rushed to the central chamber where Maximus and Aetheris were waiting. Bursting into the room, Sarah exclaimed, "Maximus! Aetheris! You won't believe what we've found!"

Michael nodded enthusiastically. "The 7-dimensional computer has identified two new sites. One is the Temporal Nexus in the Amazon Rainforest, and the other is the Quantum Citadel in a parallel quantum space."

Maximus's eyes sparkled with interest. "Tell me more."

Sarah and Michael shared the details of their discovery, their excitement palpable. As they spoke, Aetheris's crystalline eyes glowed brighter, reflecting the significance of their findings.

"This is indeed remarkable," Aetheris said. "These sites align perfectly with our mission to uncover and understand the lost knowledge of ancient civilizations and their advanced technologies."

Maximus smiled, his mind racing with possibilities. "We will need to prepare expeditions to both sites. The Temporal Nexus will require a team skilled in temporal research, while the Quantum Citadel will need experts in quantum mechanics and realities."

Preparing for the Expeditions

Maximus and Aetheris began coordinating the logistics for the expeditions. The team would be divided into two groups, each equipped with the necessary tools and knowledge to explore their respective sites.

Temporal Nexus Team:

Leader: Dr. Elena Martinez, an astrophysicist with expertise in temporal phenomena.

Members: A mix of archaeologists, temporal researchers, and security personnel.

Quantum Citadel Team:

Leader: Professor Raj Patel, an expert in quantum mechanics and ancient civilizations.

Members: Quantum physicists, engineers, and security experts.

Simulation Training

Before embarking on their missions, both teams would undergo intensive simulation training to master the use of their equipment and prepare for the unique challenges of their respective sites. The simulation chambers were configured to replicate the environments of the Temporal Nexus and the Quantum Citadel, providing realistic scenarios for the teams to navigate.

Maximus Magellan and Aetheris stood in the central chamber of the Aetherian Archive, surrounded by holographic projections of the newly discovered sites. The room was filled with a sense of urgency and anticipation as they prepared to make a crucial decision.

Maximus turned to Aetheris, her metallic form gleaming under the ambient light. "Aetheris, seeker of Truth, we have discovered two new sites: the Temporal Nexus in the Amazon Rainforest and the Quantum Citadel in a parallel quantum space. We need to decide which one is more vital to visit before we proceed to the ruins of Eldoria."

Aetheris's crystalline eyes glowed as she processed the information. "Maximus, both sites hold significant potential for advancing our understanding of ancient civilizations and their technologies. However, we must consider the strategic importance and the immediate benefits each site could provide."

Maximus nodded, his expression thoughtful. "Let's discuss the details of each site and weigh their importance."

The Temporal Nexus

Aetheris projected a detailed holographic map of the Temporal Nexus. "The Temporal Nexus is located deep within the Amazon Rainforest. It exists in a temporal dimension where time flows differently, preserving ancient structures and artifacts. This site could provide us with invaluable insights into the manipulation of time and the preservation of knowledge."

Maximus studied the projection. "Understanding temporal manipulation could be crucial for our mission. If we can learn to control or stabilize time, it could enhance our ability to navigate the temporal anomalies within Eldoria and other sites."

Aetheris nodded. "Additionally, the Temporal Nexus may contain records or technologies that could help us unlock the full potential of the 7-dimensional computer. The ability to manipulate time could also provide strategic advantages in various scenarios."

The Quantum Citadel

Aetheris shifted the holographic display to show the Quantum Citadel. "The Quantum Citadel exists in a parallel quantum space, a dimension where the laws of physics are different. This site is a fortress-like structure composed of materials that can shift and change based on the observer's perception. It is believed to contain advanced quantum technologies and secrets of the universe."

Maximus's eyes widened with interest. "The Quantum Citadel could offer us unprecedented knowledge about quantum mechanics and realities. If we can harness quantum technologies, it could revolutionize our understanding of the universe and provide us with powerful tools for exploration and defense."

Aetheris's eyes glowed brighter. "Indeed, the ability to manipulate quantum states and realities could enhance our technological capabilities and provide us with new methods for data analysis, communication, and energy manipulation."

Weighing the Importance

Maximus paced the room, deep in thought. "Both sites offer unique and invaluable knowledge. The Temporal Nexus could give us control over time, while the Quantum Citadel could unlock the secrets of quantum realities. We need to consider which site will provide the most immediate and strategic benefits for our mission."

Aetheris remained silent for a moment, processing the information. "Maximus, I believe the Temporal Nexus should be our priority. The ability to manipulate time could provide us with immediate advantages in navigating and understanding the temporal anomalies within Eldoria. Additionally, the preservation of knowledge within the Nexus could offer us insights that are directly applicable to our current mission."

Maximus nodded, his decision made. "I agree, Aetheris. The Temporal Nexus will be our first destination. We will gather the knowledge and technologies needed to enhance our understanding of time manipulation, which will be crucial for our exploration of Eldoria."

Aetheris's eyes glowed with determination. "Very well, Maximus. I will begin preparations for the expedition to the Temporal Nexus. Our team will be equipped with the necessary tools and knowledge to succeed."

Maximus smiled, his mind racing with possibilities. "Thank you, Aetheris. Let's ensure our team is ready for this vital mission. The future of the Magellan Project depends on it."

With their decision made, Maximus and Aetheris knew they had taken a crucial step towards uncovering the secrets of Eldoria and advancing their understanding of ancient civilizations and their technologies.

The corridor opened into a vast chamber, its sheer size and grandeur taking the team by surprise. The air was cool and filled with the faint scent of ancient stone and moss. The walls of the chamber glowed faintly with an otherworldly light, casting eerie shadows that danced across the floor. The team paused for a moment, taking in the awe-inspiring sight before them.

Ancient structures, some towering and others more modest, filled the chamber. These buildings were constructed from a unique blend of natural materials and advanced technology, seamlessly integrated into the environment. Intricate carvings and symbols adorned the walls, telling stories of a civilization long forgotten.

Captain James O'Connor, leading the mission, gave the signal for the team to spread out. "Let's dThe team had been exploring the Temporal Nexus for several hours, documenting and analyzing the ancient structures and artifacts they encountered. The vast chamber, filled with an eerie glow, seemed to pulse with a life of its own. The air was thick with the scent of ancient stone and moss, and the faint hum of temporal energy resonated through the walls.

As they ventured deeper into the Nexus, the atmosphere grew more oppressive. The walls seemed to close in, and the temperature dropped noticeably. Captain James O'Connor, leading the mission, signaled for the team to stay alert. "Keep your eyes open and stay close. This place is full of surprises."

Dr. Elena Martinez and Professor Raj Patel were examining a series of ancient inscriptions on the walls when they heard a low rumble. The ground beneath their feet began to tremble, and dust fell from the ceiling. "We need to move, now!" Captain O'Connor shouted, his voice echoing through the chamber.

The team scrambled to find a safe path as the rumbling grew louder. Suddenly, a section of the ceiling gave way, sending massive chunks of stone crashing down. Dr. Mei Ling narrowly avoided being crushed, her heart pounding in her chest. "This place is unstable," she gasped. "We need to be more careful."

Sergeant Alex Thompson quickly assessed the situation. "We need to find a way around this collapse. Let's use the Aetherian Scanner to map out an alternate route."

Dr. Martinez activated the scanner, which projected a holographic map of the surrounding area. "There's a passageway to the left that should bypass the collapse. Let's move quickly."

The team navigated the narrow passage, the walls pressing in on them. The air was thick with dust, making it difficult to breathe. As they emerged into a larger chamber, they took a moment to catch their breath. "That was too close," Captain O'Connor said, his voice tense. "Let's keep moving."

As they continued their exploration, the team encountered several temporal anomalies. These anomalies caused disorientation and confusion, making it difficult to navigate the Nexus. The air seemed to shimmer and warp, and time itself felt unstable.

Dr. Martinez and Professor Patel were examining a network of energy conduits when they were suddenly hit by a wave of temporal energy. The world around them seemed to blur and shift, and they found themselves in a different part of the Nexus. "What just happened?" Dr. Martinez asked, her voice filled with confusion.

Professor Patel looked around, trying to get his bearings. "It seems we've been displaced by a temporal anomaly. We need to find our way back to the team."

Using the Aetherian Scanner, they managed to trace their way back to the main chamber. The rest of the team was relieved to see them. "We need to be more cautious," Captain O'Connor warned. "These anomalies are unpredictable and dangerous."

The team had just discovered a hidden library filled with scrolls and tablets when they inadvertently triggered a security mechanism. Ethereal beings, composed of temporal energy, materialized around them. These Temporal Guardians seemed to protect the knowledge and artifacts within the Nexus.

The guardians advanced, their forms shimmering with energy. Captain O'Connor quickly assessed the situation. "Everyone, stay calm and follow my lead. We need to deactivate the security mechanism and avoid confrontation."

Using the Aetherian Scanner, Dr. Martinez identified the source of the security mechanism—a hidden panel on the wall. She and Professor Patel worked quickly to deactivate it, while the rest of the team formed a defensive perimeter.

The Temporal Guardians grew more aggressive, their energy pulses intensifying. Just as the situation seemed dire, Dr. Martinez and Professor Patel successfully deactivated the mechanism. The guardians dissipated, their forms fading into the ether.

The team breathed a collective sigh of relief. "Excellent work, everyone," Captain O'Connor said. "Let's finish documenting the Nexus and prepare to return to base."

As the team prepared to leave, Dr. Mei Ling discovered a temporal rift in one of the chambers. This rift appeared to be a gateway to another time period, offering potential for further exploration and study. However, the rift was unstable and posed a significant risk.

"We need to document this rift and gather as much data as possible," Dr. Mei Ling said, her voice filled with excitement. "But we must be cautious. The rift is highly unstable."

Captain O'Connor nodded. "Let's set up a perimeter and proceed with caution. We don't want anyone getting caught in the rift."

As the team began their analysis, the rift suddenly expanded, pulling in debris and creating a powerful vortex. The team struggled to maintain their footing as the force of the rift threatened to pull them in.

"Everyone, fall back!" Captain O'Connor shouted. "We need to get out of here, now!"

The team retreated, but Dr. Martinez was caught by the edge of the vortex. She clung to a nearby pillar, her grip slipping. "Help!" she cried, her voice filled with fear.

Sergeant Thompson rushed to her aid, grabbing her arm and pulling her to safety. "I've got you," he said, his voice steady. "Let's get out of here."

The team managed to escape the chamber just as the rift collapsed, sealing itself shut. They took a moment to catch their breath, their hearts pounding from the close call.

With their objectives achieved and valuable knowledge and technologies retrieved, the team made their way back to the aircraft. The flight back to the base was filled with discussions about their discoveries and the potential implications for the Magellan Project.

Maximus and Aetheris greeted them upon their return, eager to hear about the mission. Dr. Elena Martinez presented the findings, highlighting the insights into temporal manipulation and the advanced technologies they had uncovered.

Maximus smiled, his eyes filled with pride. "You have all done an exceptional job. The knowledge and technologies you have retrieved will be invaluable for our mission to uncover the secrets of Eldoria."

Aetheris's crystalline eyes glowed with satisfaction. "Seeker of Truth, your success at the Temporal Nexus has brought us one step closer to our ultimate goal. Let us continue our journey with renewed determination."

Despite the dangerous situations they encountered, the team had successfully navigated the Temporal Nexus and retrieved valuable knowledge and technologies. Their experiences had strengthened their resolve and prepared them for the challenges that lay ahead.

As they debriefed and shared their findings, the team reflected on the importance of their mission and the potential impact of their discoveries. The Temporal Nexus had provided them with invaluable insights into the manipulation of time, and they were eager to apply this knowledge to their exploration of Eldoria.

With their mission to the Temporal Nexus complete, the team prepared for the next phase of their adventure, ready to face whatever challenges lay ahead. The future of the Magellan Project was bright, and the team was determined to uncover the secrets of the ancient civilizations and their advanced technologies.

Dr Elena Martinez, an astrophysicist with a keen interest in temporal phenomena, moved towards a series of stone tablets arranged in a semi-circle. She carefully examined the inscriptions, her fingers tracing the ancient symbols. "These tablets seem to detail the civilization's knowledge of temporal manipulation," she said, her voice filled with excitement. "This could be invaluable for our research."

Professor Raj Patel, an expert in ancient civilizations, focused on a large structure that appeared to be a central hub of the chamber. The building was adorned with intricate carvings and symbols, and a faint hum of energy emanated from within. "This structure seems to be a repository of knowledge," he observed. "We need to access its interior and see what secrets it holds."

Dr. Mei Ling, a biomedical engineer, was drawn to a series of crystalline structures embedded in the walls. She used her Aetherian Scanner to analyze the crystals, noting their unique properties. "These crystals are resonating with temporal energy," she reported. "They could be used for healing or energy amplification."

Sergeant Alex Thompson, a security expert, and Captain O'Connor focused on ensuring the team's safety. They set up a perimeter and monitored for any potential threats. "Stay vigilant," Sergeant Thompson advised. "We don't know what dangers might be lurking in these ruins."

As the team continued their exploration, they discovered a hidden library filled with scrolls and tablets. Dr. Martinez and Professor Patel carefully documented the texts, which detailed techniques for stabilizing time and creating temporal anomalies. "This knowledge could revolutionize our understanding of temporal mechanics," Dr. Martinez said, her eyes shining with excitement.

In another part of the chamber, the team found a network of energy conduits running through the walls and floor. These conduits appeared to channel temporal energy, powering various devices and structures within the Nexus. "This is incredible," Professor Patel remarked. "These conduits could provide insights into how this civilization harnessed and utilized temporal energy."

The team also encountered several temporal anomalies, causing disorientation and confusion. They documented these anomalies, noting their effects and potential causes. "We need to be cautious," Captain O'Connor warned. "These anomalies could pose a significant risk."

Despite the challenges, the team made significant progress in documenting and analyzing the chamber. They retrieved valuable knowledge and technologies, including a more advanced Temporal Stabilizer that provided insights into improving their own technology.

As they prepared to leave, the team reflected on their discoveries. "This has been an incredible journey," Dr. Martinez said. "We've uncovered knowledge that could change everything."

Captain O'Connor nodded. "Let's get this information back to Maximus and Aetheris.

The enigmatic device, now named the ChronoCore, stood at the center of the hidden chamber, its presence both awe-inspiring and intimidating. The ChronoCore was a large, crystalline structure, approximately ten feet tall and five feet wide, with a multifaceted surface that seemed to shimmer and pulse with a deep blue light. The crystal was composed of a unique material that appeared both solid and ethereal, giving it an almost otherworldly appearance.

Intricate patterns and symbols adorned the surface of the ChronoCore, etched with a precision that suggested advanced craftsmanship. These symbols glowed faintly, their light shifting and changing as if alive. The base of the device was anchored to the floor by a series of metallic tendrils that seemed to grow organically from the crystal, rooting it firmly in place.

At the heart of the ChronoCore was a pulsating core of pure energy, visible through the translucent crystal. This core emitted a rhythmic hum, resonating with a frequency that seemed to vibrate through the very air. The energy within the core was a swirling mix of blues and purples, constantly shifting and changing, creating a mesmerizing display of light and color.

New Additional Properties After Close Study

After extensive study and analysis, the team discovered several new properties of the ChronoCore that would significantly enhance the capabilities of the 7-dimensional computer:

Temporal Resonance:

The "ChronoCore" exhibited a unique property known as temporal resonance. This allowed it to synchronize with temporal anomalies and stabilize them, providing a more controlled environment for temporal research and manipulation. This property would enable the team to navigate and control temporal anomalies with greater precision.

Energy Amplification:

The core of the device acted as a powerful energy amplifier. It could harness and amplify temporal energy, providing a nearly limitless source of power for the 7-dimensional computer. This amplification would enhance the computer's processing power and enable more complex simulations and analyses.

Quantum Entanglement:

The ChronoCore possessed the ability to create and maintain quantum entanglement between multiple points in space-time. This property allowed for instantaneous communication and data transfer across vast distances, bypassing the limitations of conventional technology. This would revolutionize the team's ability to coordinate and share information during their missions.

Temporal Data Storage:

The device featured an advanced data storage system that utilized temporal energy to preserve information in a stable temporal state. This system allowed for the storage and retrieval of vast amounts of data without degradation over time. The team could now archive their findings and access them instantly, regardless of the passage of time.

Adaptive Interface:

The ChronoCore's interface was adaptive, capable of responding to the user's intentions and commands with remarkable accuracy. This interface allowed for seamless integration with the 7-dimensional computer, providing an intuitive and efficient means of controlling and utilizing the device's capabilities.

Cosmic Locator:

One of the most remarkable properties of the ChronoCore was its ability to locate sites of lost treasure, unknown substances, and valuable minerals anywhere in the cosmos. By analyzing cosmic energy patterns and temporal signatures, the ChronoCore could pinpoint the locations of hidden treasures and resources, providing invaluable information for exploration and discovery.

Extreme Danger and Challenges

The integration of the ChronoCore posed several extreme dangers and challenges:

Unstable Energy Surges:

The ChronoCore emitted sporadic energy surges that could destabilize the surrounding environment. These surges created powerful shockwaves that threatened to damage the equipment and harm the team. The team had to develop specialized containment fields to manage and control these surges.

Temporal Distortions:

The presence of the ChronoCore caused temporal distortions within the chamber, making it difficult to navigate and communicate. These distortions created time loops and anomalies that disoriented the team and disrupted their operations. The team had to use advanced temporal stabilizers to mitigate these effects.

Security Mechanisms:

The ChronoCore was protected by advanced security mechanisms, including energy barriers and automated defenses. These defenses activated when the device was tampered with, posing a significant threat to the team. The team had to carefully deactivate these systems to safely access and study the device.

Outcome and Integration

Despite the challenges, the team successfully documented and retrieved the ChronoCore. They carefully transported it back to the central chamber of the Aetherian Archive, where Maximus and Aetheris awaited their return.

Dr. Elena Martinez and Professor Raj Patel worked tirelessly to integrate the ChronoCore with the 7-dimensional computer. The process was complex and required precise calibration to ensure the device's energy was harnessed safely.

As the integration was completed, the computer's capabilities were significantly enhanced. The team could now manipulate temporal anomalies with greater precision, process data at unprecedented speeds, harness a powerful new energy source, and locate hidden treasures and resources across the cosmos.

Maximus addressed the team, his voice filled with pride. "You have all done an exceptional job. The integration of the ChronoCore will revolutionize our mission and provide us with the tools we need to uncover the secrets of Eldoria and beyond."

Aetheris's crystalline eyes glowed with satisfaction. "Seeker of Truth, your success has brought us one step closer to our ultimate goal. Let us continue our journey with renewed determination and confidence."

With the ChronoCore integrated into the 7-dimensional computer, the team was better equipped than ever to face the challenges ahead. The future of the Magellan Project was bright, and the team was ready to uncover the secrets of the ancient civilizations and their advanced technologies.

Integration of the ChronoCore

With the ChronoCore successfully integrated into the 7-dimensional computer, the system's capabilities were significantly enhanced. The ChronoCore added an additional dimension to the computer, bringing the total to eight dimensions. This new dimension allowed for even more complex data analysis and manipulation, particularly in the realms of temporal and quantum mechanics.

The 8-dimensional computer now possessed the ability to:

Manipulate Temporal Anomalies: With greater precision and control, the team could stabilize and navigate temporal anomalies.

Amplify Energy: Harnessing and amplifying temporal energy provided a nearly limitless power source.

Quantum Communication: Instantaneous communication and data transfer across vast distances became possible.

Enhanced Data Storage: Vast amounts of data could be stored and retrieved without degradation over time.

Locate Hidden Treasures: The computer could now pinpoint the locations of lost treasures, unknown substances, and valuable minerals across the cosmos.

Scanning Earth for Lost Treasure Sites

Sarah and Michael, eager to test the new capabilities of the 8-dimensional computer, initiated a scan of Earth for lost treasure sites. The computer's advanced algorithms and the ChronoCore's temporal resonance allowed them to identify five significant sites.

1. The Amber Room

Location: Kaliningrad, Russia

Description: The Amber Room, originally constructed in the Catherine Palace near St. Petersburg, was a masterpiece of Baroque art, adorned with gold-gilded mosaics, mirrors, and carvings, along with panels made from 1,000 pounds of amber. It was dismantled and taken by German forces during World War II and has been missing ever since.

Significance: The Amber Room is considered one of the greatest lost treasures of the modern era. Its recovery would be a monumental achievement in the field of art and history.

2. The Lost Library of the Moscow Tsars

Location: Moscow, Russia

Description: The Lost Library of the Moscow Tsars was an expansive collection of ancient Greek texts and other valuable manuscripts. It was built by the Grand Duchy of Moscow in 1518 and is believed to have been hidden by Ivan the Terrible.

Significance: The library's recovery would provide invaluable insights into ancient Greek literature and the history of the Russian Tsars.

3. The Treasure of the Copper Scroll

Location: Near the Dead Sea, Israel

Description: The Copper Scroll, one of the Dead Sea Scrolls, describes a vast treasure hidden in various locations around Israel. The scroll lists 64 sites where gold, silver, and other valuable items are buried.

Significance: Finding the treasure described in the Copper Scroll would be a significant archaeological discovery, shedding light on the wealth and practices of ancient Jewish communities.

4. The Flor de la Mar

Location: Straits of Malacca, Malaysia

Description: The Flor de la Mar was a Portuguese carrack that sank in 1511 while carrying a vast treasure from the Sultanate of Malacca. The ship's cargo included gold, silver, and precious gems.

Significance: Recovering the treasure of the Flor de la Mar would be one of the most valuable maritime discoveries, providing insights into the trade and wealth of the Portuguese Empire.

5. The Crown Jewels of Ireland

Location: Dublin, Ireland

Description: The Crown Jewels of Ireland, including valuable jewelry and ceremonial items, were stolen from Dublin Castle in 1907. Despite extensive investigations, they have never been recovered.

Significance: The recovery of the Crown Jewels would be a significant cultural and historical event for Ireland, restoring a lost part of its heritage.

The Search and Discoveries

As the computer processed the data, Sarah and Michael watched in awe as the locations of the lost treasures appeared on the holographic display. Each site was marked with detailed information about its history, significance, and potential challenges.

Amber Room:

The computer identified a hidden underground bunker in Kaliningrad, Russia, where the Amber Room panels were likely stored. The bunker was heavily fortified and required careful planning to access.

Lost Library of the Moscow Tsars:

The library was located in a secret chamber beneath the Kremlin. The chamber was protected by ancient traps and required precise navigation to avoid triggering them.

Treasure of the Copper Scroll:

The computer pinpointed several locations near the Dead Sea, each marked with clues from the Copper Scroll. The sites were in remote and rugged terrain, requiring a well-coordinated expedition.

Flor de la Mar:

The wreck of the Flor de la Mar was located in the Straits of Malacca, buried under layers of sand and coral. The site was in deep waters, necessitating advanced diving equipment and expertise.

Crown Jewels of Ireland:

The jewels were hidden in a secret vault beneath Dublin Castle. The vault was protected by a complex locking mechanism that required careful manipulation to open.

Extreme Danger and Challenges

The mission to recover these treasures posed significant dangers and challenges:

Security and Traps:

Many of the sites were protected by ancient traps and modern security systems. The team had to navigate these hazards carefully to avoid triggering alarms or causing damage.

Remote and Rugged Terrain:

The locations of the treasures were often in remote and difficult-to-access areas. The team had to be prepared for harsh environmental conditions and physical challenges.

Underwater Exploration:

The search for the Flor de la Mar required advanced diving techniques and equipment. The team had to contend with strong currents, limited visibility, and the risk of underwater hazards.

Political and Legal Issues:

Some of the sites are in politically sensitive areas, requiring careful negotiation and adherence to local laws and regulations. The team needs to navigate these complexities to avoid legal complications.

Outcome and Integration

Despite the challenges, the team was determined to recover the lost treasures. The integration of the ChronoCore into the 8-dimensional computer provided them with the tools and knowledge they needed to succeed.

Maximus addressed the team, his voice filled with pride. "You have all done an exceptional job. The integration of the ChronoCore has given us the ability to locate and recover these lost treasures. Let's proceed with caution and determination."

Aetheris's crystalline eyes glowed with satisfaction. "Seeker of Truth, your success has brought us one step closer to our ultimate goal. Let us continue our journey with continued determination and confidence."

With the ChronoCore integrated into the 8-dimensional computer, the team was better equipped than ever to face the challenges ahead. The future of the Magellan Project was bright, and the team was ready to uncover the secrets of the ancient civilizations and their advanced technologies.

CHAPTER 13
THE RUINS OF ELDORIA

Arrival at the Ruin Site

The team arrived at the base of the mountain housing the lost city of Eldoria, their aircraft descending gracefully into a clearing surrounded by dense forest. The air was crisp and cool, filled with the scent of pine and earth. The towering peaks of the mountain loomed above them, shrouded in mist and mystery.

Captain James O'Connor, leading the mission, stepped out of the aircraft and surveyed the area. "Alright, team. Let's get to work. We need to set up our campsite, temporary lab, and headquarters before we begin our exploration of Eldoria."

Campsite Setup

The team quickly got to work, unloading equipment and supplies from the aircraft. They chose a flat, open area near the entrance to the ruins for their campsite, ensuring it was close enough for easy access but far enough to avoid any potential dangers from the ruins.

Tents and Shelters:

The team set up a series of high-tech, weather-resistant tents to serve as their living quarters. These tents were equipped with advanced insulation and climate control systems to ensure comfort in the varying mountain temperatures.

A larger central tent was erected to serve as the communal area, where the team could gather for meals, meetings, and relaxation. This tent was furnished with portable tables, chairs, and a small kitchenette.

Power and Lighting:

Portable solar panels were deployed around the campsite to harness energy from the sun. These panels were connected to a central battery system that provided power for lighting, equipment, and other necessities.

LED lanterns and string lights were hung around the campsite to provide ample illumination during the night. These lights were designed to be energy-efficient and could be adjusted for brightness.

Water and Sanitation:

A portable water purification system was set up to provide clean drinking water. This system used advanced filtration and UV sterilization to ensure the water was safe for consumption.

Portable toilets and shower units were installed in a designated area of the campsite. These units were equipped with waste management systems to maintain hygiene and cleanliness.

Temporary Lab Setup

Next, the team focused on setting up the temporary lab, which would serve as the hub for their scientific research and analysis. The lab was located in a secure area near the campsite, with easy access to both the living quarters and the ruins.

Lab Tents and Equipment:

A series of interconnected lab tents were erected, each designated for specific types of research and analysis. These tents were equipped with advanced climate control systems to maintain optimal conditions for the equipment and samples.

The main lab tent housed the 8-dimensional computer, now enhanced with the ChronoCore. This tent was the nerve center of the operation, where data analysis and coordination took place.

Additional tents were set up for various scientific disciplines, including archaeology, biology, chemistry, and physics. Each tent was equipped with specialized tools and instruments for their respective fields.

Sample Collection and Storage:

A designated area was set up for the collection and storage of samples from the ruins. This area included portable refrigeration units to preserve biological samples and secure containers for artifacts and other materials.

The team established a protocol for labeling and cataloging samples to ensure accurate documentation and tracking.

Communication and Data Transfer:

Quantum communicators were distributed to all team members, allowing for instant and secure communication across the site. These devices were linked to the central computer for real-time data transfer and coordination.

A satellite uplink was established to provide a secure connection to the base and other remote teams. This uplink allowed for the transmission of large data files and video feeds.

Advanced Team Protocol Headquarters

The final step was setting up the advanced team protocol headquarters, which would serve as the command center for the mission. This headquarters was located in a reinforced tent near the lab, providing a secure and central location for coordination and decision-making.

Command Tent and Equipment:

The command tent was equipped with advanced communication and monitoring systems, including holographic displays and interactive panels. These systems allowed the team to track their progress, monitor environmental conditions, and coordinate their activities.

A large central table served as the focal point for meetings and briefings. This table was equipped with a holographic projector that could display maps, data, and other visual aids.

Security and Surveillance:

A network of surveillance cameras and motion sensors was set up around the campsite and the entrance to the ruins. These devices provided real-time monitoring of the area and alerted the team to any potential threats.

Security personnel, led by Sergeant Alex Thompson, conducted regular patrols and maintained a secure perimeter around the site. They were equipped with advanced weaponry and protective gear to ensure the safety of the team.

Medical and Emergency Response:

A medical tent was set up near the command tent, equipped with advanced medical supplies and equipment. Dr. Mei Ling, the team's biomedical engineer, was responsible for overseeing medical care and emergency response.

The team established protocols for handling medical emergencies, including evacuation procedures and communication with remote medical support.

Preliminary Exploration Setup

With the campsite, lab, and headquarters in place, the team began their preliminary setup for the exploration of Eldoria. This involved a series of preparatory steps to ensure they were ready for the challenges ahead.

Mapping and Surveying:

The team used drones equipped with advanced sensors and cameras to conduct an aerial survey of the ruins. These drones provided detailed maps and 3D models of the area, highlighting key structures and points of interest.

Ground-penetrating radar and other geophysical instruments were used to map the subsurface features of the ruins. This data helped the team identify hidden chambers, tunnels, and other structures.

Environmental Monitoring:

Sensors were deployed around the site to monitor environmental conditions, including temperature, humidity, and air quality. This data was crucial for ensuring the safety and comfort of the team.

The team also monitored for any signs of temporal anomalies or other unusual phenomena that could pose a risk during their exploration.

Equipment Testing and Calibration:

All equipment and instruments were thoroughly tested and calibrated to ensure they were functioning correctly. This included the 8-dimensional computer, ChronoCore, and other advanced tools.

The team conducted a series of test runs and simulations to familiarize themselves with the equipment and protocols. This helped them identify and address any potential issues before beginning their exploration.

Team Briefing and Training:

Maximus and Aetheris conducted a series of briefings to ensure all team members were fully informed and prepared for the mission. These briefings covered the objectives, protocols, and potential challenges of the exploration.

The team participated in additional training sessions to hone their skills and teamwork. This included drills for handling emergencies, navigating the ruins, and using the advanced equipment.

Final Preparations:

With everything in place, the team gathered for a final briefing before beginning their exploration of Eldoria. Maximus addressed the team, his voice filled with determination and pride.

"You have all done an exceptional job in setting up our base of operations. We are now ready to begin our exploration of Eldoria. Remember your training, stay vigilant, and work together. The knowledge and discoveries we uncover here will be invaluable for the Magellan Project and the future of our mission."

Aetheris, her crystalline eyes glowing with determination, added, "Seeker of Truth, your journey begins now. May you uncover the secrets of Eldoria and bring back the wisdom of the ancients. Let us proceed with courage and confidence."

With their preparations complete, the team was ready to embark on the next phase of their adventure. The ruins of Eldoria awaited, filled with mysteries and potential discoveries that could change the course of history.

First Week at the Ruin Site

Day 1: Initial Setup and Scanning

The team began their first week at the ruin site with a sense of excitement and anticipation. The towering peaks of the mountain and the ancient structures of Eldoria loomed above them, shrouded in mist and mystery. The air was crisp and cool, filled with the scent of pine and earth.

Morning:

The team gathered in the command tent for a briefing led by Maximus and Aetheris. "Our primary objective this week is to scan and map the ruins using the 8-dimensional computer," Maximus explained. "We need to gather as much data as possible before we enter the ruins."

Aetheris added, "We will also be developing a new Aetherian drone to assist with the exploration. This drone will be equipped with advanced sensors and capabilities to navigate the complex environment of Eldoria."

Afternoon:

Dr. Elena Martinez and Professor Raj Patel began setting up the 8-dimensional computer in the main lab tent. The computer's

Dimensional Conduits glowed with a soft, pulsating light as it powered up, ready to process vast amounts of data.

The team deployed drones equipped with advanced sensors and cameras to conduct an aerial survey of the ruins. These drones provided detailed maps and 3D models of the area, highlighting key structures and points of interest.

Evening:

The data collected by the drones was fed into the 8-dimensional computer, which began processing and analyzing the information. The computer's enhanced capabilities, thanks to the ChronoCore, allowed for rapid and precise mapping of the ruins.

The team gathered in the communal tent for dinner, discussing their findings and plans for the next day. The atmosphere was filled with a sense of camaraderie and determination.

Day 2: Ground-Penetrating Radar and Subsurface Mapping

Morning:

The team used ground-penetrating radar (GPR) and other geophysical instruments to map the subsurface features of the ruins. This data helped them identify hidden chambers, tunnels, and other structures.

Dr. Mei Ling and Sergeant Alex Thompson led the GPR survey, carefully navigating the rugged terrain and ensuring accurate data collection.

Afternoon:

The data from the GPR survey was integrated into the 8-dimensional computer, which created detailed subsurface maps of the ruins. These maps revealed several hidden chambers and passageways that had not been visible from the surface.

The team began planning their exploration routes, identifying key areas of interest and potential hazards.

Evening:

The team conducted a preliminary analysis of the hidden chambers, using the computer's advanced algorithms to predict their contents and significance. This analysis provided valuable insights into the layout and history of Eldoria.

Maximus and Aetheris held a briefing to discuss the findings and refine their exploration plans. The team reviewed the maps and identified priority areas for further investigation.

Day 3: Environmental Monitoring and Sensor Deployment

Morning:

The team deployed sensors around the site to monitor environmental conditions, including temperature, humidity, and air quality. This data was crucial for ensuring the safety and comfort of the team.

Dr. Elena Martinez and Professor Raj Patel led the sensor deployment, carefully placing the devices in strategic locations around the ruins.

Afternoon:

The sensors began transmitting real-time data to the 8-dimensional computer, which analyzed the environmental conditions and provided recommendations for maintaining optimal conditions.

The team also monitored for any signs of temporal anomalies or other unusual phenomena that could pose a risk during their exploration.

Evening:

The team reviewed the environmental data and made adjustments to their equipment and protocols as needed. This included calibrating their instruments and ensuring their protective gear was functioning correctly.

The team gathered for a briefing to discuss the environmental conditions and potential challenges they might face during their exploration.

Day 4: Development of the Aetherian Drone

Morning:

The team began developing a new Aetherian drone to assist with the exploration of Eldoria. This drone would be equipped with advanced sensors and capabilities to navigate the complex environment of the ruins.

Dr. Mei Ling and Sergeant Alex Thompson led the development of the drone, using the 8-dimensional computer to design and fabricate the components.

Afternoon:

The drone, named Aetheris Scout, was assembled and tested. It featured a sleek, aerodynamic design and was equipped with a range of sensors, including thermal imaging, LIDAR, and spectral analysis.

The Aetheris Scout was also equipped with advanced navigation and communication systems, allowing it to operate autonomously and relay real-time data to the team.

Evening:

The team conducted a series of test flights with the Aetheris Scout, ensuring it could navigate the rugged terrain and complex structures of the ruins. The drone performed flawlessly, providing detailed maps and data.

The team reviewed the drone's performance and made any necessary adjustments to optimize its capabilities for the exploration.

Day 5: Detailed Mapping and Analysis

Morning:

The team used the Aetheris Scout to conduct detailed mapping and analysis of the ruins. The drone's advanced sensors provided high-resolution images and data, revealing intricate details of the structures and artifacts.

Dr. Elena Martinez and Professor Raj Patel analyzed the data, identifying key areas of interest and potential hazards.

Afternoon:

The data from the Aetheris Scout was integrated into the 8-dimensional computer, which created comprehensive maps and models of the ruins. These maps highlighted hidden chambers, passageways, and significant artifacts.

The team began planning their exploration routes in detail, identifying the safest and most efficient paths through the ruins.

Evening:

The team conducted a preliminary analysis of the artifacts and structures identified by the Aetheris Scout. This analysis provided valuable insights into the history and significance of Eldoria.

Maximus and Aetheris held a briefing to discuss the findings and refine their exploration plans. The team reviewed the maps and identified priority areas for further investigation.

Day 6: Equipment Testing and Calibration

Morning:

The team conducted thorough testing and calibration of all equipment and instruments to ensure they were functioning correctly. This included the 8-dimensional computer, ChronoCore, and other advanced tools.

Dr. Mei Ling and Sergeant Alex Thompson led the testing and calibration, ensuring all devices were operating at peak performance.

Afternoon:

The team conducted a series of test runs and simulations to familiarize themselves with the equipment and protocols. This helped them identify and address any potential issues before beginning their exploration.

The simulations included scenarios for handling emergencies, navigating the ruins, and using the advanced equipment.

Evening:

The team reviewed the results of the testing and simulations, making any necessary adjustments to their equipment and protocols. This included fine-tuning the Aetheris Scout and other devices.

The team gathered for a briefing to discuss the results and finalize their preparations for the exploration.

Day 7: Final Preparations and Briefing

Morning:

The team conducted final preparations for the exploration of Eldoria. This included packing supplies, checking equipment, and reviewing their plans and protocols.

Maximus and Aetheris conducted a final briefing to ensure all team members were fully informed and prepared for the mission. These briefings covered the objectives, protocols, and potential challenges of the exploration.

Afternoon:

The team participated in additional training sessions to hone their skills and teamwork. This included drills for handling emergencies, navigating the ruins, and using the advanced equipment.

The team also conducted a final review of the maps and data, ensuring they were familiar with the layout and key areas of interest in the ruins.

Evening:

The team gathered for a final meeting in the command tent. Maximus addressed the team, his voice filled with determination and pride. "You have all done an exceptional job in preparing for this mission. We are now ready to begin our exploration of Eldoria. Remember your training, stay vigilant, and work together. The knowledge and discoveries we uncover here will be invaluable for the Magellan Project and the future of our mission."

Launching the Treasure Hunting Series

The central chamber of the Aetherian Archive was abuzz with activity. Maximus, Aetheris, Sarah, and Michael gathered around the central table, the holographic display projecting the detailed plans for the launch of The Magellan Project's treasure hunting series. The room was filled with a sense of excitement and anticipation as they prepared to unveil their ambitious new initiative.

Planning the Secure Website and Premium Subscription

Maximus began the discussion, his voice filled with determination. "We need to create a secure website that will serve as the central hub for The Magellan Project's treasure hunting series. This website will offer a premium subscription for participants who want to join the beta run and decide their level of participation."

Aetheris, her crystalline eyes glowing with determination, added, "The website must be secure and user-friendly, providing participants with all the information and tools they need to engage with the project. We will also need to implement robust security measures to protect sensitive data and ensure the integrity of our operations."

Sarah, her eyes scanning the holographic display, suggested, "We should offer different subscription tiers, each with its own set of benefits and access levels. This will allow participants to choose the level of involvement that suits them best."

Michael, leaning forward, chimed in, "We also need to provide participants with a unique package of digital equipment for their use in the beta project. This will include advanced tools and devices that will enhance their treasure hunting experience."

Designing the Website and Subscription Tiers

The team began brainstorming the design and features of the website, as well as the different subscription tiers.

Website Features:

Secure Login and Registration: Participants will create accounts and log in securely using encrypted credentials.

Interactive Dashboard: The dashboard will provide participants with real-time updates, maps, and data related to the treasure hunting series.

Resource Library: A comprehensive library of resources, including guides, tutorials, and historical information, will be available to participants.

Communication Hub: A secure messaging system will allow participants to communicate with the Magellan team and other participants.

Progress Tracking: Participants can track their progress and achievements through the dashboard, earning badges and rewards for their accomplishments.

Subscription Tiers:

Explorer Tier:

Access: Basic access to the treasure hunting series, including maps and data for selected sites.

Equipment: A starter package of digital equipment, this will be free to those who have purchased a book for the certain adventure they are trying to access, other benefits will be decided by our team and implemented as we add them.

Support: Basic support and access to the resource library.

Adventurer Tier:

Access: Enhanced access to additional sites and exclusive content.

Equipment: An advanced package of digital equipment, including this level starting digital currencies to be determined, and additional items that are unique for each participant.

Support: Priority support and access to exclusive webinars and tutorials.

Seeker of Truth Tier:

Access: Full access to all sites, content, and features of the treasure hunting series.

Equipment: A premium package of digital equipment, including a portable 3D scanner and quantum communicator and other unique items and preset digital in beta currencies to be determined before launch for all tiers.

Support: Dedicated support and access to one-on-one consultations with the Magellan team.

Implementing the Beta Run and Digital Equipment Packages

Maximus outlined the plan for the beta run and the distribution of digital equipment packages.

"We will invite participants to join the beta run by sending an email to us at themagellanproject@1codyenterprises.com. Each participant will receive a package of digital equipment including unique and randomly determined rarity based on their subscription tier."

Aetheris added, "The equipment packages will be carefully curated to provide participants with the tools they need to succeed in the treasure hunting series. We will also provide detailed instructions and support to ensure they can use the equipment effectively as well as an in beta store for team development equipment and supplies and digital currency should you desire extra procurement of various rarity items and equipment from the Magellan Project virtual store."

Sarah suggested creating a welcome package for beta participants. "We should include a welcome letter, a detailed guide to the treasure hunting series, and access to an exclusive online orientation session. This will help participants get started and feel connected to the project."

Michael proposed setting up a dedicated support team for the beta run. "We need to ensure participants have access to timely and effective support. This team will be responsible for answering questions, troubleshooting issues, and providing guidance throughout the beta run."

Seeking an Investing Partner or Executive Angel Partner

Maximus turned the discussion to the need for an investing partner or executive angel partner to support the ongoing development of The Magellan Project. "To ensure the success and sustainability of the project, we need to seek an investing partner or executive angel partner who shares our vision and can provide the necessary resources and expertise."

Aetheris emphasized the importance of finding the right partner. "We must seek a partner who not only has the financial resources but also understands the significance of our mission and is committed to supporting our goals."

Sarah suggested creating a dedicated section on the website for potential investors. "We can provide detailed information about the project, our objectives, and the potential benefits of investing. Interested parties can leave an email describing their area of interest and how they would like to contribute."

Michael proposed hosting a series of virtual presentations and Q&A sessions for potential investors. "This will allow us to engage with interested parties, answer their questions, and provide them with a deeper understanding of the project. We can also showcase our progress and future plans."

Finalizing the Plan

With the key elements of the plan in place, Maximus summarized the next steps. "We will proceed with the development of the secure website and the implementation of the premium subscription tiers. We will also prepare the digital equipment packages and set up the support team for the beta run."

Aetheris added, "We will launch a targeted marketing campaign to attract participants and investors. This campaign will highlight the unique opportunities and benefits of joining The Magellan Project."

Sarah and Michael nodded in agreement, their expressions filled with resolve. "We are ready to take on this challenge and ensure the success of The Magellan Project," Sarah said.

Michael added, "With the right partners and resources, we can uncover the knowledge and treasures that will change the course of history."

Conclusion

With their plan finalized, the Magellan team was ready to take the next steps in their mission. By launching a secure website with a premium subscription for the treasure hunting series and seeking an investing partner or executive angel partner, they could ensure the success and sustainability of The Magellan Project.

The future of The Magellan Project is bright, and the team was determined to uncover the secrets of the ancient civilizations and their advanced technologies. With careful planning, robust security measures, and the right partners, they were poised to achieve their objectives and make groundbreaking discoveries that would change the course of history.

End

www.ingramcontent.com/pod-product-compliance
Lightning Source LLC
Chambersburg PA
CBHW032252310726
48973CB00008B/2383